WHITE LIES

Lynn Michell

Shattered: Life with ME

"This is a timely and powerfully written book and Lynn Michell is uniquely qualified to write it."
Bernard MacLaverty, Author of Cal, Lamb and Grace Notes.

"Inspiring stories, not simply of broken lives, but of survival and hope in the face of terrible adversity."
Dr Vance Spence, Chairman of MERGE

"Shattered is a powerfully written account of life with ME — an unpredictable and devastating illness. Definitely a 'There but for the grace of God go I' book, and one that should throw some much-needed light on this terrible condition."
Tuam Herald

"Puts into words the thoughts and serious issues of coping with this devastating chronic illness. Michell sincerely describes her own experiences and also includes the perspectives of many other patients, from young to old, male and female. The reader is kept on a steady and reassuring journey of validation and support. The stories by other ME patients work to solidify Michell's broad but well-rounded overview of a life made more difficult by an invisible chronic illness. Identifying with the ME stories in this book reminds us that we are not alone in this fight."
CF Alliance Newsletter

Published by:
Linen Press, Edinburgh, 2011
1 Newton Farm Cottages
Miller Hill
Dalkeith
Midlothian
EH22 1SA

Email: lynnmichell0@googlemail.com
Website: www.linenpressbooks.co.uk
Blog: linenpressbooks.wordpress.com

ISBN: 978-0-955 961830
Cover photographs: Corbis Images
Cover design: Submarine, Edinburgh

WHITE LIES

Lynn Michell

EDINBURGH
2005

Chapter 1

Edinburgh 2005
Ann

The plane hurtles along the runway and tilts into the sky. A middle-aged woman with her head twisted to the window, her invisible shield pulled up between herself and the passenger next to her, says a silent goodbye to the steel grey sea below. In minutes they are banking across the shoreline at Cramond, where the tide is out and the causeway to the small island, spiked on one side by concrete pylons, marches into the Forth. Often she has walked here and stopped to admire the old stone houses, whose roofs of clay pantiles can burn ochre and orange when light streams out from behind a cloud or in the evenings when the sun is sliding low. Sometimes she walked back along the River Almond, past the yacht club where modest sailing boats bobbed on their moorings, to the quietness and solitude of Dalmeny Woods. Edinburgh. Ironic that she should end up in the city where her mother... and here she bites her lip... her mother trained as a nurse during the war. It has been her home for many years.

Mother. Parents. Simple words which until a few weeks ago evoked a reaction no more complex than quiet loss, but now in unexpected moments they ambush her. Since the letter arrived, the edges of the pain have softened somewhat so that it's less of a knife stab and more of a soft punch in the stomach. Of course the letter is folded safely at the bottom of her rucksack; she carries it everywhere. Crumpled, cried-on pages which will be taken out, spread smoothly, and read again because she is still trying to squeeze another drop of meaning from words in blue biro, or from an image of four people in a hot, war-torn country, each of them ten years younger than she is now. Now, all she can see is a silence as big as the sky and a secret as deep as the ocean below. Metaphors are easier than facts because the truth is missing. So much is missing and missed out.

A seasoned traveller to conferences, she, like others, has developed a technique of tuning out the intrusive, nerve-jangling input of the journey from the moment the revolving doors spin her into the airport terminal, through the inevitable inch-by-inch sighing queues of holiday makers who remove their shoes and belts and pass through the security archway, to the final tedious wait in the departure lounge. Already invisible because she is middle-aged, she can make others invisible too so that she wastes no energy reacting to sun-bedded sixty year olds in white gypsy skirts or lardy blokes with tattoos or businessmen who shout their egos into mobile phones. She knows she is critical – at least as much of herself as of others – and a very private person who flinches if her personal space is invaded. And so she creates a protective glass bubble and doesn't break out until she is past the Exit sign of her destination. On her forehead, she writes Do Not Disturb so that the woman sitting beside her is frightened away from relating her life story, and the man will not begin his tedious chat-up line. She knows she looks passable – for a woman who is forty-something. The gym is her battleground against a body that is succumbing to gravity and she paints over the grey in her hair with a box of liquid amber. Childless, she only has herself to take care of. Now, for extra insulation against chit-chat, she puts on headphones – those huge Bose ones that make her look like an insect – and buries her face in a book.

Thus protected, she can turn her gaze inwards and push away instructions about life jackets and close her eyes to jangling images on tiny screens repeated a hundred times down the entire length of the plane. She rests her head against the window and drifts. It is a long flight. Seventeen hours. The white noise of the engines and the dull stomp stomp of feet up and down the aisle soon lull her to sleep but even here, thirty five thousand feet above the ground, the same recurring dream comes back to her. In a clearing in woodland, a woman hands a baby to another woman. One is black and one is white and they mischievously exchange roles each time she dreams so there is no knowing which one will carry away the child.

There is only one small photograph from that period and this too she carries with her. Four blurred figures standing in front of a white building almost burnt out in the photograph by the brightness of the light, maybe a club or an army mess. The first man, in his khaki uniform, is tanned a conker brown. Next to him, a woman, golden skinned, golden haired, has arranged herself self-consciously for the camera. She wears a poppy-strewn frock with a wide belt circling her small waist. Next to her, a tall, sandy-haired man in civvies smiles wryly. The other woman stares straight at the lens with indifference. One couple look like any army officer and his wife posing in some hot part of the world where colonial supremacy is taken for granted. The other two avoid easy classification.

About their time in Nairobi, Ann's parents told her little. When she asked them about their past, they said that Harry had been in the Intelligence Corps during the Mau Mau uprising and that they had left soon after things turned nasty. Harry always made an impassioned plea for the dispossessed Kikuyu people; much later she understood his viewpoint and agreed wholeheartedly with his opinions. She read the novels of Ngũgĩ wa Thiong'o, written in Kiswahili and only recently translated into English. She read the dark flipside of the official white version of that period in David Anderson's *Histories of the Hanged*. Ann knew where she stood: with Harry and Marjorie on the side of the tribes who had walked the red soil since the beginning of time. A few years ago, she had helped organise a retrospective exhibition of Marjorie's paintings of Masai warriors in a trendy London art gallery because, with the truth about that time in Kenya filtering into the British consciousness, East African art was coveted and interesting. The media discovered her and her hoard of inherited paintings. She found herself talking on the radio and on television about a woman from her past. At that point there was no emotional connection. She could talk about history and art and politics. Facts.

That African past had faded into an English present where she grew up in a pleasant and undisturbed suburb in the south of England and attended a single-sex grammar school in High Wycombe. After a year travelling – not to Africa but to France, to learn about the joys of food and to polish her accent – she took a degree in English at Sussex university. For her doctoral thesis she wrote about vanishing dialects and so set in motion a fascination and obsession with speech that has remained with her throughout her life. If she hears a voice with a strong accent, she can pinpoint its birthplace to within a radius of twenty miles. Like a magpie, she still darts across the country with her tape recorder to pick up a snippet of speech here and an anecdote there before the old and wonderful words and phrases disappear forever into the common denominator of media-washed Estuary English.

Yes, Africa faded into the background but it was never quite erased, so when the letter came all she had to do was blow on the embers to bring back the fire and light. There never was an if about making this journey. With her gift for language, she is already at an advantage because she knows not to say 'Jambo' to the people she will meet and pass on the streets of Nairobi, having read it's a crass tourist gaffe, like saying 'Top o' the morning' to someone who lives in Dublin. Apparently she must say 'Sasa?' and expect the reply 'Fit!'

If she manages this, along with the other phrases of Kiswahili she has been practicing before setting off, and asks for nyama choma and Tusker lagers in the cafes and restaurants frequented by the locals, she might not draw attention to herself. She might be mistaken for one of their own, which in a way she is. Not born and bred, but conceived in the Green City of the Sun. Something she hardly knows herself yet.

Her ears are popping. When she opens her eyes, sore and dirt dry, she sees a red half-disc of sun rising above a sugar almond horizon, and smiles. An African horizon, she says to herself, where tonight this same sun will skitter down the sky and vanish. Harry told her about the sunsets. There will be no lingering Scottish dusk nor the grey half-light that makes you miss, however hard you stare and stare, the exact second when day turns into night. Her heart is beating hard as the plane drops, circles, circles again and makes its final descent into Jomo Kenyatta Airport. Her eyes fill with tears and spill down her cheeks. As the plane hits the tarmac she is ice cold and shivering. While other passengers, as tired and crumpled and red-eyed as herself, jump up the moment the plane taxies to a halt to press open the lockers and heave down their hand luggage and poke urgent fingers into keyboards, and then stand for ten minutes, fifteen minutes, twenty minutes until the cabin doors are opened, Ann stays in her seat and keeps her wet face averted, pressed against the window. Here she stays until everyone else has left the plane. A steward touches her shoulder. Yes, she nods, I am fine. She wipes away the tears with the back of her hand, shrugs her rucksack on to one shoulder, and walks towards the exit.

Breaking the glass of her bubble, she emerges from the airport into an onslaught of heat and noise and chaos. It is exactly what she expected. A taxi driver is bribing a police officer after jumping the queue, and cars speed in and out of the airport breaking every rule in the book.

In the back seat of a cab, already so hot that the back of her legs stick to the plastic, she speeds towards the brutal, elemental, pulsing, contradictory heart of Nairobi. The drive from the airport takes her past her first acacias, a purple jacaranda, a red hibiscus smothering the building it decorates, bleached yellow grass. She acknowledges a landscape of extremes and violent colours. The muted palettes of England and Scotland fade into a fast-retreating background.

Her plan, if something as vague as a sense of longing and rootlessness can be called a plan, is to walk in the footsteps of ghosts who were here fifty years ago when blood was spilt across this savagely beautiful country. Two couples. One guerrilla war. A child who was christened Ann.

Chapter 2

EDINBURGH 2005
EVE

My father's story about his uncle's tragic death begins as we pull out of his driveway. Because I cannot simultaneously watch the traffic, find my way, and listen to how Uncle Edward hanged himself from the apple tree while his children played underneath, we have a few close encounters. My father raises an eyebrow at my driving without interrupting the flow of the plot or the drama of its telling. The story is well under way as I back the car into a tight parking space outside the Eye Hospital, continues through the revolving doors of the main entrance, and now, at the reception desk, is reaching its climax. My father's stories are part of his very fabric, as necessary to his existence as breathing. The more nervous he is, the more he talks. Low anxiety switches on stories about 'rich and famous people I once knew'. He had dinner with Churchill and played soccer with Billy Liddell. Whether they are true or not I do not know but reality and wish-fulfilment no doubt merge a bit when you are ninety and your life is a reel of memories. The stories are the scaffolding of his life and only in their retelling does he exist. He doesn't get out much these days so audiences are limited and more often than not he has to make do with me. A medium level of anxiety produces either family history, which bores me to tears, or war stories and tales from his life in the army which I find fascinating and informative. Perhaps I can arrange for a medium level of worry to dominate his life so that we can stick to these. High anxiety makes me anxious too because I know what's coming and feel an urgent need to hide. Today, as we pass a trolley bearing its victim to A&E, we enter high-anxiety territory, prompting him to switch mid-sentence from Uncle Edward to:

'Did you read that story in the *Mail* today?'

It's odd that my father, whom I see almost every day, cannot/will not remember that I never read/never have read the *Mail*, nor that I never get round to opening any newspaper before 8 p.m. if at all. The tabloid he reads would probably sum me up, disapprovingly, as a forty-five-year-old mother of two with a full-time job. While I juggle plates and rush about trying to fulfil my multiple duties, his days are increasingly void of events and episodes.

'And I thought he was a decent man,' he continues. 'A family man. And then you find out... this! You know how I feel about it. They should all be shot. That's what I would do. Line them up and shoot them. They're not real men. It's against nature. What is cottaging anyway?'

My father's style of speaking is to dispense with all preliminaries and get straight to the point. This I find endearing, like when I phone and he picks up the receiver and begins mid-sentence '...awful match! Owen was useless. Should have been a penalty when Scholes was fouled.' Missing out all the social niceties saves time and usually I know exactly what he is talking about without them. But right now, in the queue for reception, I am stuck for a reply. His homophobia is terrifying and if somebody politically correct and unrelated to him is listening, my father may end up in court with a prison sentence. A gay friend once told me that this kind of hatred is most often voiced by repressed homosexuals. I have sometimes wondered. My father's voice rises a notch.

'I'd castrate the lot of them. I don't understand the world we live in nowadays.'

'Dedd?' enquires the receptionist, looking at his card; distracted perhaps by this patient's thought for the day, she misreads it. She rescues me just in time – people are staring at us over the tops of their magazines.

'Not yet!' my father shouts, quick as a flash. He is still so sharp. 'Dell. Colonel Dell.'

He laughs, and when he laughs his eyes pop out and he looks like Yoda. And the rest of his noisy, fun-loving, working-class tribe. If we were in Crufts, we would be in the mongrel class, a mix of Irish, Liverpudlian, and Eastern European Jews. I find it sad that my parents, out of insecurity and low self-esteem, mistakenly spent a lifetime erasing their lovely sing-song accents, stretching their vowels in a failed attempt to blend into the public-schooled, moneyed classes. In the bathroom, my mother would say 'tarl' and 'shar' and I would shudder.

'Date of birth?'

'The tenth of May 1915,' my father growls.

Perhaps he expects a medal for being so old, or at least a smile, but the receptionist remains stony. In this context he is no exception. In the waiting room, falling forwards, sideways, and into their little plastic beakers of nasty beverages, are a whole generation of ancients. Some look like they've been sitting here all their lives, and many are a damn sight worse off than my upright father.

'Take a wee seat,' the receptionist says.

While we wait, my father plays the I Spy game, squinting, closing one eye then the other. He shuts his right eye and peers upwards.

'I can see the clock.'

Of course he can't see the clock: he is blind in one eye, and just now is squeezing his good eye shut. There has been no explanation for this sudden loss of sight, which is why we spend so much time sitting in the Eye Hospital.

'It happened soon after my dear wife died,' he told the consultant on our first visit here. 'Oh she did suffer and they would not give her morphine. I nursed her for three years before she died. Did everything for her.' There were tears in his failing eyes.

'I see. So when exactly did your sight deteriorate?' the consultant asked, clearly out of his comfort zone.

'Oh… one eye blew up in the middle of the night,' he said. 'I woke at three in the morning unable to see out of my right eye.'

And didn't tell me until two days afterwards, even though his flat is within walking distance of mine. Stiff upper lip, that's my father. Steady under fire.

'Do you know, when I was in the trenches,' he starts to tell me now, apropos of nothing, 'I was the only one who could sleep through anything. Rocket fire. Grenades. It didn't bother me like it bothered some of them. Once I woke up and the man beside me was dead. Both legs blown off. I didn't hear a thing,'

'You were very stoic,' I say.

'I suppose so,' he replies.

Are hospital waiting rooms so morgue-like because for some souls they are a halfway house between life and death, I wonder, scowling at the bilious pea-green paint lit by flickering neon tubes. Do others find this place as oppressive and as depressing as I do? Why not soft peach with some lamps? Even the chairs are green: a dirty, sticky green plastic. I exchange sympathetic glances with a woman of my age accompanying her own Aged P, a minute old woman in a wheelchair wearing bottle-thick spectacles who is slowly sinking into her layers of fluffy pink clothing. Already her collar is above her chin. Maybe she will have vanished, leaving only her clothes, by the time her name is called.

I am wearing my sensible-dutiful-daughter face and it's making me hungry. Surreptitiously, because my father does not approve of eating in public places, I tear off a hunk of the baguette poking out of my carrier bag and chew unobtrusively. He won't notice, not with one blind eye.

'What are you eating?'

'Bread.'

'Why?'

'It's my lunch.'

'Lunch! It's past two o'clock.'

'I know but I haven't had time to eat yet.'

'Why not?'

'I came straight from college to pick you up.'

This conversation, oft repeated, is not about lunch or food at all. It is about my strange refusal to stay at home and do the ironing. Or whatever. My work does not count as work. Despite an art degree and a few exhibitions under my belt, my father manages to demote my stained glass to 'Eve's hobby'. The teaching scores a few brownie points but the pay is laughable so that can be jettisoned too. My husband works. My son Alex works. Clara works. She has to because she is recently divorced and, thanks to the incompetence of the Child Support Agency, which has failed to extract money from her ex-husband, has to support herself and her two sons. My mother never worked, except part-time in Nairobi because there she had three servants and nothing to do all day. And that is how it should be!

'You don't need to work,' he tells me right on cue.

Here we go. He is nothing if not predictable. If he were anyone but my dear old father I would bite his bloody head off.

'I enjoy working,' I say.

'But you don't need to… I mean you don't need the money like Clara. You could stop any time, couldn't you?'

The subtext of this exchange, as he and I know full well, is that I should stay at home and clean the house and make sure there is a hot meal waiting for my husband's return. Like my mother did nearly all her married life.

'Mr Dell!' someone shouts.

'Colonel Dell!' my father shouts back, standing up and pulling back his shoulders.

And so, after an eternity, in we go.

'The trees all along the river wave their branches in the wind. The river banks are flooded and the water remains...'

For a moment the nurse looks confused and turns back to my father's notes while he carries on reading. She has covered his good eye but he is reading fluently. Now – how do I phrase this without putting him, or her, down?

'He's read that passage so many times he knows it by heart. He has an excellent memory.'

Fortunately the nurse is amused. She smiles, pats him as if he were a child, and finds another card.

'Can't even see the card,' my father says crossly. 'I can't read a word. I'm blind in this eye. It happened when my dear wife died. Married sixty-five years. Overnight. Bang! It blew up!' He is getting tearful.

'Cover your other eye please. Can you read now?'

Reading distracts him from his burden of sorrow. Like the soldier he was, he carries his backpack of tears courageously and uncomplaining through all his days. He tackles the new passage in a rich, deep-brown voice as if he were giving a speech to a crowded auditorium.

'Very good,' the nurse says; whether in response to his sight or his performance I am not sure. 'Now can you close your good eye and look over there at the board?'

'I can see L. That's all.' Suddenly his loss of vision is just too upsetting so he removes himself from the immediate to a better time and place. 'When we were in Nairobi I used to do the sports broadcast every week.' He turns to me. 'Do you remember? Every Friday night. No, you won't remember.'

Oh but I do, and I remember how proud I was that it was my father's voice that came from the radio when we were in Africa or Portsmouth or Cyprus. His deep voice. Of course we always listened, my mother, Clara and I, even if we were doing something else at the same time: a jigsaw or playing cards when we were small, homework or hemming miniskirts on the Singer sewing machine when we were older. We always had the radio on when my father was up there in the Forces broadcasting hut. Clara and I knew nothing about cricket or football then, not like now after bringing up two sons each, but the fact that he was there, in the radio, made him special.

And in Nairobi, during the Mau Mau troubles, not just special but comforting and reassuring when the three of us were huddled together in one bedroom with the night an unseen threat outside the window. It gave the evenings a thin veneer of normality. We weren't supposed to know about it, but Clara and I had discovered a revolver underneath my mother's pillow. Would she have used it if we were attacked? Even though I was so young, I imagined her nerves like tightly-pulled elastic bands that might snap at any minute and leave her all undone. Like a parcel without the string which holds it together. And so we tuned in one evening a week to hear our father's voice talking about cricket or rugby and for an hour or so forgot about the Mau Mau. It makes no sense, I know.

'I used to work for the BBC you know,' he is telling the nurse now. 'Sports broadcasting. I have shared a studio with Kenny Dalglish, and Bobby Robson, and Barnes who played for Liverpool, went to Rangers, got the sack and now works for Channel 5. And Ian Botham. And Geoffrey Boycott. He got cancer. He's a weirdo. He's been broadcasting from the West Indies. Of course, he's gone over to Sky. Jonathan Agnew, who has been broadcasting on Radio 5 for at least ten years…'

The nurse gives me a look which says, 'It's OK. I'm used to this,' but I am not attending because a plan is taking shape and I am excited that I may have solved something here in this over-bright cubicle where my father is having his eyes tested.

'Try and read the letters with the other eye now for me, Mr Dell,' the nurse says.

'Colonel Dell,' my father snaps.

On the way home I say, 'You do have a remarkable memory, you know.'

He shrugs. 'It's the one thing I do have. Not very clever but a sharp memory. Especially for the past. I can still recite the first book of *Paradise Lost*, learnt it after reading it through just twice…'

'I know,' I interrupt, not wanting a recitation of Milton just now as I drive through the tea-time traffic. 'I do think you should write some of your stories down. Write a memoir about your time in the army, in the desert…'

'No one would be interested,' he replies, but I catch a twinkle in his poor old eyes.

I decide to say no more for now but to let the idea settle and take hold of him, which I think it will.

Chapter 3

Edinburgh 2005
Eve

The phone makes me jump. The answer machine is on downstairs so I choose to ignore it.

Spread out before me are sharp-edged pieces of stained glass: a streak of dragonfly green, a copper orange as dark as treacle, and shards of sea blue. I am lovesick with the colours of glass and infatuated by the infinite possibilities of shade and shape. This is my time, away from teaching and daughterly duties. My time to create and dream. Yes, my creative spirit is complaining about being squashed into smaller and smaller segments. Be quiet, I say. No good fretting. This is how it is and this is how it must be.

Two days each week are taken up with teaching, which would be fine if my father were not gradually encroaching on the rest of my time. I enjoy teaching; I learn from my students as much as they learn from me. In my class are middle-aged women, young women, and Eddie. My mature women, let's call them Dorothies, wear sensible shoes and aprons, work hard, chat about their grown-up children and the war in Iraq, and produce traditional leaded panels of fishes and flowers. The Dorothies go away at the end of the term with their work wrapped in bubblewrap and a feeling that they have accomplished something. The young women, having signed away eight years of their lives for a part-time degree, surprise and delight me. Ruth is sticking bits of mirror into a weathered lump of driftwood which she found on a beach, the mirror edges nibbled away with pliers as though she has bitten round them with sharp teeth. Silvie is combining slate, transparent glass and some kind of dried weed she found in Greece.

Then there is Eddie. He whistles as he works, smells of stale sweat and makes truly horrible panels of orange, blue, red, yellow and green. Last term he made a lumpen, sweetie-coloured butterfly.

I say, 'Eddie, you should be chuffed with that.'

He says, 'Oh I am.'

I am at ease in the glass room. Behind even the most delicate piece is the cutting and hammering and nailing and fingers in plasters. Before my students arrive I put out the cutters, pliers, meths, putty, black paint for lead. For those who are so inclined there is silver stain and etching powder and acrylic paint. I open up the huge plastic bins of glass, sorted into whole sheets, large broken pieces, little pieces, and the fragments and dust to be recycled. I plug in the two electric grinders so beloved of beginners, supposedly for fine-tuning or squaring a corner but used by them to correct gross mistakes.

Here they come. Good morning, Dorothy! Classic FM is playing the same hundred best tunes, the grinders are whizzing, glass is being secured on a board with horseshoe nails, someone's hands are black as she mixes putty and black paint, and for half an hour the atmosphere is heavy with pooled concentration. Put goggles on, Eddie! I don't want to take you to the eye hospital! Put gloves on, Dorothy, if you're using silver stain. It's toxic!

Then someone drops a piece of glass. Someone cracks a joke. I call a break for chocolate biscuits and coffee, which I brew at the sink against all the safety rules, but they just carry on. Noses to the grindstone. No one needs me for a few minutes so I retreat inside my head, shutting out the class and drifting...

...drifting back to an image of a glass panel which I have begun sketching at home and which calls to me, whatever I am doing, and makes me see it and work on it in my mind's eye. It will be a requiem for my mother. It has taken me all this time to let go of guilt and loss and to find a way to say goodbye to her. As I make it I will think of her when she was younger, standing at the sea's edge in Tripoli or Cyprus, waiting to swim away in the element she embraces. She has strong swimmer's shoulders. She swims with her head down and arms bent at the elbows, achieving a slow rhythmic crawl, left, right, breathe, left, right, breathe, which barely disturbs the surface of the ocean. The glass will be light and shade, sea and wind, wave and dune. It will feel like salt and tough grass and seaweed. In one corner a female form will stand poised. About to swim away.

Quick. I dry my tears before anyone notices.

*

The phone rings again. This time I run downstairs and answer it.

'Hello. So you are there.' It's Clara.

'Sorry. I was in the middle of cutting glass.' Not that this counts as work, I know.

'I'm at home. Taking half a day off to sort out papers before going to see my lawyer. Again. Eve, I've spent an absolute fortune but no progress. Neil just refuses to hand over his financial documents and says all his money is tied up in property. And university fees to be paid. Anyway, you know all this. I thought I'd give you a quick call before I go out. How's Father?'

'You're getting as bad as the boys,' I say. 'Is this our only topic of conversation these days?'

Clara laughs. 'I know. Just getting it over with.'

'He's fine. He walks to the end of the road every morning to get his paper. Shoulders back. I was chatting to a neighbour the other morning who was out gardening and she said, "Your father walks like a soldier. He marches." It's true. Slower… but still a soldier's stride.'

'He's doing incredibly well,' Clara says. 'Thanks to you.'

I silently thank her for the acknowledgment and store it away for when I next feel cross and rushed and resentful that all this care in the community has landed on my shoulders.

'Remember when he came up and I said I was worried about being his carer for the next ten years and you said, "Oh, it won't be longer than a year or two at most"? Well, it's over two years now and he is still going strong. He'll live to be a hundred,' I sigh.

'We just don't know, do we? I know it's all fallen on you. Do you feel resentful?'

'I did. Now, well... I've found out it hurts me, not him, when I feel cross and resentful, so I try to do things willingly. It's easier that way and I suppose I am glad of the chance to get to know him, at the eleventh hour so to speak. After all, he has hardly spoken to me for thirty-five years. I was about thirteen when he washed his hands of me...'

'And me,' Clara adds. 'He stopped speaking to both of us. Oh God, those duty visits twice a year all the way down to Folkestone... can you imagine being a daughter who actually wants to go home, I mean looks forward to it? Some of my friends do. And the weekly phone calls! "I'm not speaking to you!" I got so weary of hearing that. Why couldn't they ever be supportive...'

'Yes, well, we've said all this before...'

These are ruts we have walked in together for most of our lives, searching for answers, but, finding none, we now voice the refrains. Our father loved us when we were small, and I, his firstborn, his Blondie as he called me, was his favourite, but he turned away from me. For good. My sister lasted a bit longer, until she was about fifteen, but she lost him too. Since then there has been no relationship. We have done our duty.

'You have always been better with him than me,' I start up again. Why do we pick at this childhood scab rather than leave it to heal? 'You played Scrabble with him, and his bloody card games. I don't think he ever disliked you the way he disliked me.'

'I like Scrabble! And you're just more bossy! And strong. He doesn't like strong women.'

'Doesn't like women.'

'He doesn't, does he?'

'His only friends were men. His men in the army.'

'He liked Mother... but then she never stood up to him. She was always so submissive...'

'Oh, please don't start up again!'

We laugh because we have done this repartee a thousand times. We know our lines by heart.

'Are you still typing his memoir?' Clara asks.

'Yes.'

'Because that's why I'm ringing,'

Typical Clara! This is how we operate. So little time and so much to say. We forget the new while we deal again with the old. Sometimes one of us will phone back after a long call and say, I forgot to tell you what I called about.

'You know that box of stuff I took back with me when Mother died?' Clara continues. 'Well, I've finally gone through it. I know, years late. Most of it is rubbish, as I expected – hospital appointment cards and notes to the cleaner and birthday cards from long long ago – but I've found a diary, pages and pages of tiny writing in an old army exercise book with a buff cover. Do you remember those notebooks with the crown on? So... I started reading it. It's surprisingly detailed, especially about her time in Nairobi. Anyway, I thought, since you're writing up Father's stories, you might like to look at this as well. I don't have time.'

Clara has to compare her full, work-packed life with mine.

'Do you want it? Shall I post it up?'

'Not really, thank you!' I laugh, although it's not funny. I too have enough to do. I'd rather finish one single glass panel than plough through my mother's notes on the heat and the housekeeping and the servants. But, 'All right. I'll read it,' I hear myself say. 'While I'm typing up one story, I might as well include a few lines from the female perspective. Father's well into the handed-down history about how the Colonials stood firm against the butchery of the Kikuyu tribes. Maybe Mother has something different to say. OK, send it up.'

'That's great. Thanks. You never know…'

'Clara, do you remember much about our time in Nairobi?' I interrupt.

'No, I don't. I was so young. Except being terrified at night.'

'But did anything awful happen?'

'The whole thing was awful.'

'No, I mean did anything happen to us? Our family?'

'I think we might have heard about it by now!'

'But Father is telling his story about Nairobi as if there is something unsaid. You know how he always rambles on about the war and makes things up as he goes along, but this is different. There's an urgency in the telling of it. And it's very coherent.'

'I remember us leaving, you, me and Mother standing in a line outside the bungalow in the early hours of the morning, before it was light, with suitcases at our feet, waiting for the army car to take us to the airport. I suppose Father was there too. Mother was weeping. I remember Malinge came out to say goodbye and that made me cry too. You know how fond I was of Malinge. I suppose we were frightened a lot of the time, Mother and you and me. I'm still frightened of the dark and I'm in my forties!' she laughs. 'And I still sleep on my left side, you know.'

'So do I!'

'So that the knife won't enter the heart!' we chime in unison. Our nursery rhyme. Our shared legacy of Nairobi.

'I'd better go,' Clara says. 'Things to do. Talk to you again soon.'

My sister is gone and an unwanted diary in an army notebook is on its way. Damn, I say out loud as I climb the stairs back to my studio. Here comes another story. My father's story and now my mother's. Dutifully I will type one and read the other. I might even write them up together. Do I do this to heal a painful childhood? No, I don't need therapy. I accept my mother's story because my father's account is the male version. One-sided. Black and white. I'm just curious about the female version.

I am just back at my bench, exactly where I was before Clara interrupted me, the first piece of jade-green glass marked ready for cutting, when the doorbell rings. I look at my watch and sigh in exasperation. 'Shit!' I say. 'Shit, damn and blast!'

'I've been lying awake half the night going over and over the past. You shouldn't have started me on this writing...' my father chides when I've raced down the three flights of stairs, and opened the front door. So it's my fault. Nothing new about that.

He is an hour early, which is completely out of character, but I don't want to upset him by pointing out his error. Punctuality is still everything. Maybe he is keen to continue. 'Up you come. Take your time.' He's puffing a bit. 'Here, let me take your jacket. Heavens, it weighs a ton. You can't buy anything of this quality nowadays. You go on into the study and sit down and I'll be with you in two minutes.'

I often say that. I'll just do x and y and then I'll be right there. Be with you in a minute. I won't be a second. Why does my life have to take place on the fast track? I had hoped by the time I reached my late forties that I might have slowed down a bit.

So now I have my teaching, my desperate wish to get on with my own glass designs, my father's multiplying hospital appointments, the occasional SOS from one son or the other, my father turning up at all hours to dictate his memoir at breakneck speed – and my mother's diary in the post.

LIVERPOOL AND PRESTATYN
1937–1940

Chapter 4

When I think of Nairobi, I think of two places as far apart as two planets in space. Time too is split into halves – before and after. While my own disjoint phases coincided with public events either side of the first Mau Mau uprisings and the brutalities which finally shook a colonial community out of its complacency, they were unrelated to them except in the sense that I took advantage of what was happening on the world stage to enable my own subterfuge. When everyone else was tuned in to the Mau Mau terrorism I used it to my advantage because the political and military drama offered me a perfect screen behind which to hide my duplicity. While the Mau Mau lay in wait, dangerous and undetected amongst the dark, dripping forests of the most inaccessible regions of the Aberdare Mountains, so I came and went, invisible, because we were living with a siege mentality and fear was blown in the red dust to blind almost every white man and woman.

The Mau Mau uprising was reported in the world media as a coup that came out of the blue – a series of shockingly bestial and barbaric maimings and killings of innocent white families. The reality was that the Kikuyus' desperate rebellion against white rule resulted in thirty-two white deaths. In retaliation, and in an attempt to restore the established and comfortable hierarchy of white above black, twelve thousand Kikuyu rebels were killed by the police and army, and a further seventy thousand Africans were detained in camps without trial. We cover our tracks to suit our desires. History's victors write the past. After the first Mau Mau attacks, the colonials and the military spun round and turned their backs on the truth and repainted the history of Africa with white lies.

And yet... if my life were ever made into a film, the backdrop would not be a blood-drenched field where hamstrung cattle and disembowelled men lie moaning and dying. Nor would it be a detention camp where thousands of Kikuyu stand at the miles of barbed-wire fences. You see, the huge significance of these events did not, at the time, touch me, and so it would be dishonest to use it for dramatic effect.

No, the backcloth would be a cricket pitch – an incongruity because I am not interested in the game, but that's where I will begin.

*

The first cricket pitch I wandered across one fateful Saturday afternoon in July was in Liverpool, where I was still living with my parents and working as a shorthand typist in the Alfred Holt shipping company down by the Docks. The reason for straying on to the pitch, or at least its surrounds, was nothing more exciting than a maternal asthma attack. I had planned, once we had pegged the week's washing on the line, to get the Number 7 bus into the city centre and take the ferry across the Mersey just to smell the sea and listen to the cries of the gulls and feel the wind in my hair. To be alone. To dream. But my mother had an asthma attack, brought on perhaps by the stirring and slapping down of the sheets and towels with a wooden spoon as they bubbled up in the soapy water, and then from the effort of turning the handle of the mangle to squeeze the water from heavy cotton folded lengthways twice, with me holding one end off the floor. So I stayed with her until she was able to breathe more easily.

It often happened – mother trying to suck air through bronchial tubes as useless as squashed paper straws. She would sit on the edge of her bed, her hand working away at the black-rubber bulb of the inhaler that forced her liquid medication through a transparent tube, into a rubber face mask, and down into her lungs. The need to attend to her took a chunk out of my day and forced a change of plan. With only the afternoon left, I went for a walk. As simple as that. I walked along Aigburth Hall Road, down Riversdale Road past the Liverpool Rugby Ground, to the Odyssey Cricket Ground. In those days it was almost rural, with splashes of pink Ragged Robin in the hedges.

A high wooden fence around the perimeter of the cricket club led to gates which were open wide. I stood still and listened to the other world inside. The papery rustle of leaves and bird song, the thwack of wooden bats, the cheers of the men. All of this, and the raw green smell of newly cut grass, drew me inside.

From one of the men came a whistle, followed by quiet laughter. I blushed. But they were just men in pressed white flannels with their sleeves rolled up, doing what men do. Some were dotted about the field. One wearing stiff leg pads stood motionless in front of the wicket as the bowler started his run, and then the batsman tap-tapped a patch of ground in front of him with his bat until the ball came spinning towards him. The game proceeded. Stately and ordinary. Spirited and lethargic. Predictable and unpredictable. I suppose that was the pleasure of it for them. Occasionally, as I trod round its edges, the game broke into a frenzy of running and roaring as one of the men did something wonderful, or walked off.

The air was sweet with the smell of meadow flowers that had escaped the mower in the long grass around the far reaches of the pitch. A few women in summer frocks, sandals kicked off, sat in deck chairs, either watching the game or pretending to watch it. Men leant on the railings around the pavilion in flannels and cream sweaters waiting their turn, already bowled out, or just taking part vicariously. What struck me most about the game that day was its utter Englishness. In years to come, during the war and afterwards, I would watch cricket matches in India and Africa and Australia, but without the luminous green of rain-soaked grass, without the call of thrushes and blackbirds in the oak trees, without the summer gentleness which makes tea a refreshing drink, it always seemed misplaced.

That afternoon I was wearing a pale-blue cotton dress with a print of large flowers. I remember buying it, standing in the shop thinking, 'Well, it's nothing special but it could be cheered up with a lace collar and lace edging around the cap sleeves.' I'm good with a needle and a sewing machine, so that's what I did, and now it is the frock I reach for most frequently when I stand in front of my wardrobe and look at its sorry contents. We were not well off, and my salary as a secretary was not enough to keep me in silk stockings. As usual I had used neither foundation nor face powder because my complexion was good, but I had smudged my lips with Max Factor Strawberry Fair. My hair was loose but pinned up at the sides with tortoiseshell combs. This was 1937, before the fashion for sausage rolls, when we rolled strands of hair round our fingers and held the loops in place on top and at the sides of the head with kirby grips which were not supposed to show.

Women started doing their hair like that as the war broke out, when they were working in the factories and in hospitals where long, free hair was unhygienic and dangerous, and we all became fond of that style because if you needed to wear a headscarf, the curls sat nicely underneath. A lot of women just kept their curlers in all day so that when the scarf came off their hair was perfectly curly for a night out.

That day in Liverpool the breeze was almost warm and teased wisps of my wavy brown hair free of the combs that held it up at the sides. I liked to be neat but the smell of hair lacquer, which other girls used to keep their hair in place, was too nauseating, and of course it would have finished Mother off.

The fielder who had whistled was a chap with ginger hair, stocky legs and a face that was fiery red and dripping with perspiration. Best not even to look his way. Some of the others who were near the edge of the pitch took their eyes off the ball for a second or two to glance at me as I made that circumnavigation of the field, not because I was particularly beautiful but because I was a woman walking on her own round a cricket pitch. I suppose they didn't see that many – loose, I mean. Women sat in deck-chairs. Women busied themselves in the pavilion with cakes and tea. Another roar went up and I turned my head in time to see one man walking off and the next batsman making his way to the stump, pulling on his gloves, his bat tucked under his arm, to the accompaniment of loud cheers and clapping.

Funny how the future is sealed in one moment, in one glance. Afterwards you go back over the past and retrace your footsteps, literally in my case, wondering how my whole life would have taken a different course if my mother had not had an asthma attack, if I had not chosen to go in that gate, if I had not walked around that pitch, if that batsman had not been bowled out as I reached the corner of the field and turned my face to the pavilion. What passed between myself and the new batsman in that single second sealed my fate and changed my life. He always said afterwards that it was love at first sight, but he could not possibly have seen me properly from that distance. I think of it as recognition. I don't know how else to describe it. His stride faltered, noticeable to me if not to the others, when he looked up and his eyes met mine.

I sat down on the grass then for quite some time because he was an excellent batsman and neither the first bowler, nor the tall gangly one who took his place soon afterwards, could bowl him out. If the look that passed between us had diminished his ability to concentrate on the game, I might have got up and walked away. Instead I liked his commitment as he hit ball after ball, sometimes as far as the boundaries, where the red-faced man failed to catch it. Nor was he playing to impress me; there was no bravado, no eye on the audience. No. This man played with every cell in his body. And I admired that.

Daisies had popped up everywhere in the summer grass. Between glances at the batsman I picked them compulsively, because I needed to keep my hands occupied the way his were. With my thumb nail I split the stalk of one, noting the drop of clear blood which seeped out of the cut, and pushed another through the gash. I threaded stalk into stalk until my chain was a long string of flower pearls. When the batsman was finally bowled out, to howls from the crowd, I slipped the last stalk into the first and wound the necklace of flowers several times around my neck while he strode back to the pavilion in the fading light.

Only at the very last minute did he glance my way again. I knew that when the game was over and the pavilion was shuttered up, he would come over to sit beside me.

Chapter 5

LIVERPOOL 1937
MARY

Late into the afternoon and early evening, long after the game was over, we sat as the light faded and the sun slowly dropped behind the trees, and talked about cricket and everything else that mattered to us. I was twenty. He was a year older. Only when I realised that my skirt was damp with dew and my stockings soaked did I jump up, saying I had to get home to change before I caught a chill. The time had slipped by and we had not thought of moving. He walked beside me, accompanying me as far as the end of my road, as he would accompany me for much of my life.

We talked about tennis and football and cricket. No, that's not exactly correct. He talked about his passion for sport and I nodded in the right places and made appropriate noises of approval. When a man is totally engrossed in a subject dear to his heart, it really doesn't matter what the listener says provided that she listens willingly, and I did. I was content with the imbalance of the conversation because listening gave me the chance to observe his face and his body, and to watch the little gestures and mannerisms that tell you as much about a person as the words they speak. I noticed that his eyes were blue like mine and I read in them sincerity and shyness, stubbornness and insecurity. There was an understated defiance, as if he were always ready to put up his fists to defend himself. From the way he dropped his eyes whenever I looked up, from the slight colour which remained in his cheeks long after the air had cooled, and from his still hands which never once strayed unasked over my body, I assumed, correctly as it turned out, that he was sexually inexperienced, and I was glad. He told me, laughing, that he was much too busy playing cricket and football and coaching the lads after school to chase after girls. He gave the impression of a man with limitless physical energy. But what I liked most, as he told me about his bowling style and the position he played on the football pitch, was his total lack of ego. This man was modest about his sporting prowess, despite his passionate commitment to the games he played, and I guessed he was also modest about himself. He was an unusual man.

'Sorry,' he said at last. 'I've been droning on about sport. Forgive me. I get carried away because it's my passion.'

'It's fine,' I said, smiling inwardly because he looked quite abject for a moment, probably thinking he had bored me so much that I would never want to see him again. He could not have been more mistaken. 'I have enjoyed listening to you.'

'And you? Tell me about yourself,' he said quickly, glancing at me.

'There's not much to tell,' I replied, and paused because I was thinking about what to reveal and what to hold back.

'Don't be modest,' he said.

I was pleased that he did not seize, in my hesitation, the opportunity to talk more about himself. 'It's true,' I said. 'I work as a secretary in the typing pool at the Alfred Holt shipping company. It's an enjoyable job and I am good at it; in fact I've just been told I'm going to be promoted to personal secretary to one of the managers, so that's an improvement. I live at home with my parents in Allerton. I have an older brother in Peru whom I rarely see. And my life is really very ordinary.'

'What else do you do? Sorry, that sounds rude – as if you don't have plenty to do already – I mean, what do you do when you are not working?' he pursued, not aggressively, but kindly.

'Well… I walk and cycle. I play tennis at the Allerton Club. I go swimming at the baths. I love music and play the piano a bit, and when it rains and I can't get out, I sew. Will that do?'

'Perfectly. You should have said you were a sporty young woman yourself when I was boring you with my cricket.'

'I love being outdoors. I love fresh air,' I replied. 'And I adore the water. I go with my friend Nora to Garston Baths every week, and occasionally I get the bus to town, to the Adelphi Hotel, and treat myself to twenty lengths in the biggest swimming pool in Liverpool. I think I was a fish in a previous life.'

'I'm afraid this cricketer dislikes swimming…'

'And to be honest, this swimmer is not all that keen on cricket.'

We both laughed. 'But I'll be happy to give you a game of tennis any time and to go cycling with you,' he said with tremendous enthusiasm. Then he pulled himself up short.

'Sorry. I'm jumping the gun in thinking you would be free or would want… May I ask…,' and here he really blushed, 'do you have a boyfriend?'

'I do,' I replied. 'I am walking out with someone from the office.'

His face dropped. He really was so transparent in those days. I could see he was thinking it was all over, that I had led him on a wild goose chase, and his disappointment was apparent in his eyes and his beautiful drooping mouth. So, not wanting to hurt him further, I quickly added, 'But I don't think I want to see him anymore. The relationship isn't going anywhere.'

He walked beside me as the sky darkened and at the end of my road we said a quiet goodbye after making a date to meet for lunch during the coming week, and to play a game of tennis the following weekend. There was no silly leering expression on his face, no clumsy kiss, no fumbling attempt to unbutton my clothing.

Like him, I was shy and sexually unawakened. I was no more

than a girl, unaware that a woman lay coiled inside me like a foetus, undeveloped, dreaming and dormant.

Chapter 6

LIVERPOOL 1937
MARY

Our courtship was played out against a backdrop of green pitches, cries of 'out', the clink of square metal numbers hung and re-hung on scoreboards, and thinly cut sandwiches with fillings of egg and salad cream or fish-paste laid out by willing wives in wooden cricket pavilions. Through that long, peaceful summer in the year when war was nothing more than a whisper, I was willingly drawn into an English oasis of men in cream cable-knit sweaters who walked in creaking knee pads to bat. I sleepwalked round the edges of pitches and sat dreaming in deckchairs. What was expected of me, I could give – and I gave it willingly. Thoughts of war receded. I was at peace.

I told my parents all manner of white lies to cover my tracks while David and I spent our Saturdays together – white not for innocence, nor to cover any guilt, because we really were totally innocent, but because white will always burn brightly as cricket's primary colour. David can recall, even today, every one of those matches, including the names of every player and how many runs he scored.

'Do you remember,' he would begin, always ready to replay matches that took place the previous week or month or year, 'the day we took the tram to the Pier Head and got the ferry for the match against Camel Laird, and I took three good catches? Though I say it myself, I do have a good eye for a ball.'

'Yes,' I would say. Another white lie, because for me the matches quickly blurred into a single composite game as I had eyes only for the man who walked beside me, the man who strode out on to the pitch, the man who sat down on the grass at the end of the game content and fulfilled.

Yes, I remember that day. I recall the ferry ride with a man whose arm was slipped firmly through mine. I remember the taste of salt and seaweed in the wind and the grey-blue scarf I had twisted round my head to keep the cold from my ears and because it matched the colour of my eyes. I remember I sat on the dry grass, on a tartan rug we had brought with us, ostensibly to watch, but surreptitiously reaching for the novel in my handbag, and when that ceased to hold my attention, getting up and wandering around the grounds and beyond. David told me afterwards he had looked up and noticed that I was gone.

It sounds like a threesome – David, me and cricket – but it was not all sport. I remember us walking hand in hand for miles round and round Sefton Park and through the hidden back streets of Allerton; it didn't matter where. Sometimes we cycled out to Halewood, where we followed the tracks through the wood beside the village. There were plenty of ancient trees to act as props for bikes, and lots of long, sweet-smelling grass where we could lie flat to catch our breath. There were wild raspberries – if you knew where to look – and in the village shop we were told a story about Squire Billy Grace, who owned a farm down Court Avenue and was known as the man who played music to his cows to encourage them to give more milk. There, we bought vanilla wafers before setting off for home, and David challenged me to race him. He was competitive even on a Saturday afternoon's outing. So away I'd pedal, half-killing myself to keep up with him on the uphill stretches and free-wheeling down with the wind hard in my face and my hair streaming out behind. Of course he always arrived first.

Our first lunch date was in Coopers. Other men had taken me out to dine at the best hotels and restaurants in Liverpool, flashing their wallets like marriage calling cards after they had ordered chicken in cream and a glass of white wine to pleasure me. Look at me, rich and successful and generous, more than able to support a wife in the style she longs for. Afterwards, they wanted their reward in a car or on a park bench, but I turned away from their damp fish mouths and slapped their spider hands crawling under my blouse. They called me frigid and did not ask me out again.

'Mary, Mary Quite Contrary!' one of these initially so-eager men spat out after I had clenched my teeth together and refused to part my lips for the thick wet tongue lapping against my face, trying to find my mouth. He had his hands clamped around my head, hurting. When I did open my mouth, it was to bite as hard as I could. I drew blood.

I suppose word got around that I was not going to lift my skirts to say thank you for my dinner, no matter how expensive, and after a while the queue of admirers dwindled to a couple of faithful but dull souls with whom I very occasionally sat through a film or went for a near-silent walk in Sefton Park.

In Coopers, a shilling bought each of us a bowl of tomato soup, fish and chips, and a small ice cream in a paper wrapper. It was clearly a lot of money for David, and I guessed that in any future life with him my purse strings would be tightly drawn. It did not worry me. I had always lived simply. Over that first lunch together, he told me his family story, deliberately and pointedly, so that I could never accuse him of misleading me. He recounted flatly that his father was a gambler and an alcoholic who eventually drank away the family fortune. They lost everything – their heirlooms handed down through the generations, the dinner services, the linen, his mother's jewellery.

One day, his mother had walked into the dining room to find that the polished walnut table and six chairs had gone − taken away by creditors. From a large handsome home, the family, now destitute, moved into a council house with an outside privy and a drafty black wind tunnel dividing it from its neighbour. Yet still his mother, Kitty, adored his handsome, straying, scoundrel of a father and when he died soon afterwards of liver failure, she seemed to die too.

'All she had left was her piano, which was much too big for our cramped front parlour, but I hadn't the heart to sell it. She could pick up a tune after hearing it once. It was a gift which not one of us inherited. I think when she sits on the stool she is back in the big house, young and beautiful, her dashing husband at her side. My mother plays the piano to blot out the present and to remember the past.'

At the age of fifteen, David, the eldest, took on the care of his mother and his younger siblings.

'There was no option. I had no choice,' he said, shrugging his shoulders. 'Before my father died, the plan had been that I would go to university, not because I was particularly bright but as the normal route into Sandhurst. I was good at sport and that too would go in my favour. I had always wanted to join the army, from when I was a small kid. I used to march up and down our garden with a stick over my shoulder shouting left, right, left, right.'

I put my hand on his arm. I felt so sorry for him. 'I can just imagine it. Though I can't imagine you swotting for three years at university. You'd never keep still long enough.'

'I would have done it if it took me into a career I wanted with all my heart.'

'So why didn't you go?'

'I had to support my family. I took the first job that came along or we would have had nothing to eat.' He sighed. 'Yes, I had once dared to imagine a glorious future for myself, fighting for my country, maybe working my way up to be a respected commanding officer. I wanted so very badly to be a professional soldier. It would have been a privilege to lead a battalion of men into action.' His face glowed.

'I'm sorry. I didn't know you'd suffered such disappointment. Is there no other way into the army? Surely you don't have to stay in an office job in Holts?'

'This may sound selfish, but I'm just waiting to see what happens across the water. My hunch is that England is in a very precarious and dangerous position. I just hope the politicians can sort it out, but if the worst happens – and we do go to war – I will be called up to active service and that will solve that.'

I remember I let out a gasp when he said 'war'. 'I didn't know the situation was that bad. I must have been burying my head in the sand.'

'I don't know either, Mary. No one knows. There are whispers and counter-whispers. Who can guess what is going on in the corridors of power?'

'So you would be called up?'

'I would sign up.'

'Are you not afraid?'

'No. Not to serve my country. It would be an honour.'

'And so we…'

Stupid of me. Stupid. I had been thinking of the two of us, of love, of romance, perhaps even of an engagement, even while he had been talking of regiments and military action and the army. I'd got it wrong. I was utterly mistaken. David, in his persistence and sweet kindness, had made me believe that we had a future together and now he was preparing me, gently, to break off our friendship because our country might go to war. This lunch was the end, not the beginning. I was on the verge of tears when he said, 'So given that we don't know what the future holds, I was wondering… if you would consider marrying me?'

I hadn't got it wrong. This was what he had been leading up to.

I was engaged to David. Somehow he had slipped it under the table while my hand was resting there, open, and now I held his commitment in my palm.

Chapter 7

LIVERPOOL 1937
MARY

Coincidence? Fate? Family history? What shapes our lives? I met David because my mother had an asthma attack. I married him because he, not she, was the first person to love me. One child will try until she bursts and still not please. That was me. Another child will be indifferent, cold and selfish, spending the minimum effort for the love that washes over him no matter what he does. That was him. Sam. In my mother's eyes he could do no wrong. She worshipped my elder brother.

I thought it was my fault that I was not loved. By the time I met David I was gutted and scraped bare, a glassy-eyed fish after a sharp knife had torn out its insides. The empty space was so huge it hurt – in the frequent stomach cramps that had me doubled over in pain, and in feelings of homesickness when I was already at home. I walked and swam and cycled as fast as I could with the wind in my face to try to blow off the labels of unworthiness which were stuck all over me.

OK. I have to stop here. Until now, I have not fully admitted even to myself how tangled up in the past I still am. I trail raw endings like seaweed stuck under stones on a beach waiting for the tide to release it back to the sea. I need to write about the years that have gone – washed away down life's slipstream – before I can continue, otherwise the future makes no sense.

My family was one big mess of skewed relationships. When Sam was born, my mother transferred all the love she had felt for the father to the son. While my father's tall, gaunt frame grew ever more thin and stooped, as he recognised himself as one of the objects of her rejection, my mother grew plump and buxom with maternal love. Her eyes followed Sam like a lover watching her beloved. He, in return, dropped crumbs of deceitful affection and cheap trinkets. A peck on the cheek. A bunch of flowers, not wrapped. A box of Black Magic left on the kitchen table on a Friday night. Otherwise, he avoided her. As soon as he was old enough he retreated every evening to the local pub, to return late, befuddled and swaying, needing her helping hand to guide him up the stairs to bed. Sometimes he couldn't manage a step further than the settee, where he crashed on to his back, his open mouth stinking of cigarettes and beer, while my mother untied his laces and peeled off his socks. As soon as he could, he got a job that took him to the other side of the world. He went to Peru and my mother waited for his postcard sent once a month from Lima.

My father's response to all of this was to absent himself from the family scene. After work, and after a meal round the kitchen table eaten more or less in silence, he would push his plate away, always leaving 'something for the fairies', and retreat to the garage, where his sawing and planing and hammering produced table after table after table as he banged out his frustration into darkly varnished wood. When he died in his early seventies, my mother and I were bequeathed nineteen coffee tables of almost black oak, polished to an angry gleam.

Meanwhile I, the ugly duckling, tried to please both of them by being a diligent scholar, a good girl guide, a strong swimmer, an accomplished pianist, an industrious and inventive seamstress; but the cups and medals I brought home as offerings were put away behind the closed doors of the sideboard. I made sure I was always well turned out, a credit to them, neat and tidy in starched white collars, lace trimmings, high-necked dresses. I wonder now why my father and I didn't turn to each other for solace, both unloved by her. She had tired of him and had never wanted me. When I came along four years after Sam, she had already cast my father adrift.

I remember she always wore a heart-shaped gold locket which she never removed from her neck, even when she went to bed. If I reached out to touch it, a little girl attracted to its sparkle, she slapped my hand away. But one day – I must have been about ten – she unfastened it and laid it on some newspaper beside the Brasso and a soft yellow cloth, ready to be polished along with the cutlery, when she was distracted by the doorbell and fell deep in conversation with a friend, leaving it unguarded on the kitchen table. I seized my chance. It was fiddly but I managed to get the two hinged halves apart, using my thumb nail. Inside were two tiny heart-shaped photos of my brother, one on each side.

I don't know if my mother loved me once but withdrew from me when I failed to please her, or whether from the start I was the surplus child, the female whom she could not love. Perhaps it was a fight I had lost before I ever entered the ring. Either way, my growing up was a slow drowning in the shallows of her indifference, and when I searched the horizon for the welcoming beam of a lighthouse, there was none. I was a snow-child, cold through and through from a lifetime of rejection, and I grew into a snow-woman. Until David came along and wrapped a soft, warm scarf around my throat.

David and I were a pair of orphans, he with a mother who could show no affection, I with one who felt none, and, falling into each other's arms, we found a safe haven.

Chapter 8

LIVERPOOL 1938
MARY

While David and I are smashing tennis balls across and into the net at the Odyssey Tennis Club, me nimble and quick with a good backhand, him more erratic but stronger, Neville Chamberlain is keeping a date of a rather different kind with Adolf Hitler in Munich.

It is September 30th, 1938. While David and I stroll arm in arm through Sefton Park, kicking up the crispy brown leaves, Chamberlain is on his way back from Germany clutching a useless scrap of paper bearing Hitler's signature. The crowds that have gathered in Downing Street hear his hollow promise that he has secured 'peace in our time'.

That year we all live in a fool's paradise of false security while war waits in the wings for the stage to be made ready. David and I walk out together, through the winter of 1937 and into the spring and summer of 1938, but while we are courting, workmen are digging trenches for air-raid shelters in Liverpool's parks and public gardens. Gas masks arrive in crates and are distributed by volunteers. We try on the black monkey faces and gag because they smell of rubber and disinfectant, but we have heard about the gassing of the men in the First World War and so we keep them ready. My mother and I cut out window-shaped squares of black cloth and small blackout shields lie on the back seat of Father's car because if there is a war, we must place them over the headlamps to change a full round beam into a tiny cross of light. All this time, David and I are waiting to be married. I think I knew it the day I threaded daisies into a chain and waited for him to join me after his cricket match. Because we are so sure of each other, there is no rush. We are content as we are.

It is 9 p.m. on September 2nd, 1939. David and I are sitting close together on the settee in my parent's front parlour, our fingers touching. Apart from the lamp on the table where my father is busy, the room is in darkness because light bulbs of more than 40 watts are considered a waste of energy and money. My mother knits. If she were transmogrified she would be a fast train swaying clackety clackety clack over the rails with an unstoppable regularity. Clickety clickety click. She needs no light because she knits by touch and instinct, her needles shedding of their own accord row after row of tweedy sock as she stares straight ahead, rocking gently to accommodate the movement of her rhythmic jerking elbows. Under the only beam of light, Father is staring at the insides of a fob watch. With his jeweller's glass embedded in the deep, boney socket of his right eye and his face muscles scrunched up tight to hold it there, he operates on the watch's guts. He picks out body parts with tiny gold tweezers and places them, according to size or function, in saucers. My father mends watches and clocks when he is not making tables. The wireless is on, tuned to the Home Service. We are waiting to hear if the German troops have moved into Poland.

It is 11 a.m. on September 3rd, 1939. A sunny, warm, still Sunday, the kind of day when you listen to bees humming. I am leaning over the garden fence at David's house, watching him sweat over the digging of the hole for the Anderson air-raid shelter in the small back green. His instructions dictate he must dig down to a depth of four feet before piecing together the fourteen sheets of corrugated iron. We have the wireless on, well within earshot, at the open kitchen window. I have fled my own home because my father is doing exactly the same thing, only our air-raid shelter is being built in a stony silence broken by curses when the spade strikes brick or concrete, or a rock too large to be kicked aside by his size-eleven hob-nailed boots. All over Liverpool, men are digging and women are watching, or helping, or bringing out cups of tea and trays of biscuits and sandwiches.

David tackles the digging of the air-raid shelter with the physical ease and quiet concentration with which I am now familiar. Forgetting for a few moments the gruesome reasons for his labours, I sit on the wall and watch the slow dance as he raises his pickaxe and brings it down in a rhythmic thud thud thud as if in accompaniment to music only he can hear. His olive skin is still tanned from the summer sun and the hairs on his forearms are golden. He is beautiful, heavy-thighed, broad-shouldered. He carries not an ounce of excess fat on his compact body. I want to stroke those sun-kissed arms and press my lips to his, but he is wholly and appropriately absorbed in his task.

That morning, as David digs and we both wait, tuned to the radio, we know we are part of an audience that stretches from one end of the country to the other. Some of those who hold their breath, waiting for the news as we do, are young and in love like ourselves. When the words do come, they are brief. They fall out of the wireless into the air, hanging for a long moment while their meaning catches up with them. The voice of Chamberlain is sombre: 'We are now at war with Germany.' David leans on his spade. My eyes fill with tears.

It is May 2nd, 1940. David's birthday. I am on my way from work to his house carrying a brown-paper-wrapped package of white cotton handkerchiefs, each of which I have embroidered with his initials in fine satin stitch – red for Liverpool Football Club, of course – and am playing a game, trying to think of my own associations with red, a colour I heartily dislike, and deep in thought about Moira Shearer and The Red Shoes and amputated feet, when the door opens before

I have a chance to raise my hand to knock, and David races out with one arm in his jacket, spins me round and leads me away down the garden path and back into the road.

'Where are we off to…?' I laugh.

'I've had some news. Need to talk,' he interrupts. He is both serious and smiling, and bursting with something that makes him unable to keep still. Off we go at a cracking pace, with him hopping from side to side each time we cross the road so that he is always walking on the outside, protecting me from the splash of oncoming cars, down Mather Avenue until we reach the gates of what now seems our very own Sefton Park. Once inside and halfway down the path, on either side of which bloom red tulips and yellow primulas which so far have escaped the air-raid shovel, he plumps down on a bench and pats the seat for me to sit beside him. He pulls a buff envelope out of his pocket.

'My papers,' he says.

Why is he excited when my own heart sinks? Why is he spilling energy like a boat with too much sail when I am shocked into silence? I put David's birthday present on the ground, irrelevant now, pull out my own unadorned handkerchief, and burst into tears. For a while we sit in silence, David's arm around my shaking shoulders. He tries to comfort me not with words but with his physical presence, his warmth, his steadiness.

'Have you kept this from me?' I ask, ashamed of my feeble female tears.

'My dear, of course not. They only came this morning. On my birthday, of all days.' He pulls my head on to his shoulder and I sob silently into his tweed jacket until there is a damp patch under my ear. He tells me that he ran down the stairs, hungry for breakfast, and there was the brown envelope on the mat. 'I knew it wasn't a birthday card. I'd been expecting my papers for months, ever since my medical – in fact I'm surprised it's taken them this long to get round to me. They told me I was the fittest man they had ever seen.'

'They would!' I sniff.

'Just fortunate to be so fit.'

'Have you never been ill?' I ask.

'Don't know the meaning of the word.'

It takes a while to pluck up the courage to voice the next questions. I've rehearsed them twenty times to myself before I finally manage to get them out without more tears.

'Where are you being sent?'

'I've been conscripted into the Royal Signals, Second Battalion. They are based at Prestatyn.' He shrugs his shoulders. 'I was really hoping for a fighting unit, the Kings Liverpool Regiment, that would have been a feather in my cap...'

'When?'

'Two weeks,' he replies.

I know that I am one of many young women who in the early blush of love are already fearful of their lover's death. You have to be afraid. You have to. By imagining it, perhaps you can prevent it because you have already lived it in your imagination. Fate would not put you through it all a second time, would it?

Chapter 9

Prestatyn 1940
Mary

The wheels of war kept turning while my weeks were measured in five- and two-day blocks, week days and weekends, split between the city and sea.

Every Friday after work I walked to Lime Street Station carrying the small leather suitcase I had packed the night before and had kept stowed under my desk while I took dictation, typed letters and watched the clock. On Fridays the hands moved slowly.

Other girls boarded that train, clutching overnight bags like mine and pretending to read or staring out of the window. We were all bundles of nervous excitement. We could not keep still; we fidgetted, crossed and uncrossed our legs, opened and shut handbags, patted our hair. When the train slowed down on the final stretch of track before Prestatyn, one girl with red curls was straightening the seams of her stockings; another in a green felt hat which tilted over her pretty face opened her powder compact and painted a dark-red Cupid's bow that would leave an imprint with her first kiss. At last the train ground and screeched its way along the platform where the khaki-clad men waited, their faces vanishing and reappearing in the breathed-out clouds of white steam. We jumped up. We peered out. Is he there? Will he meet me? These questions were for others, not me. I knew David was waiting. He always was.

The girls on that train had come, like me, to snatch their last days with sweethearts who, like mine, would soon be departing for the war. Like us, they walked and talked and held hands. Like me, they turned out from an inhospitable guest house after a dismal breakfast and despite the cold, the rain, the wind, headed for the beach. We spread rugs to protect our delicate derrieres from the spiky pampas grass which sprouted from the sand dunes and put up our umbrellas as wind-breaks. If there was a downpour we rushed for shelter in one of the cafes along the promenade, steaming up the windows with cups of tea and making a fug with our cigarettes. If it wasn't raining, we settled like an audience before a film or a crowd in an amphitheatre to watch our men on the stage below. Our morning's entertainment was numbingly monotonous but we stuck it out, each pair of blue or brown or hazel eyes concentrating, some of the time, on her own hero among the many who dug trenches in the sand to guard the shoreline should Hitler, as rumour had it, decide to attack our less-defended north coast instead of the south.

I found myself mesmerised by the repetitive movements of the men, so much so that hours slipped by in a half-dream. Sometimes I woke from my reveries to find I had lost track of David's whereabouts, and I had to scan the ranks to find him again in case he looked up and gave me a cheerful wave. Like the other men, he was stripped to the waist, for it was hot work even in October. My eyes lingered on his shoulder muscles and sweat-soaked chest and back. All the men worked hard but I knew David well enough to see that he was enjoying himself down there and probably putting more energy into his digging than most of the others. How he relished physical work. How he loves being part of a team of men, pulling together.

I sat alone, always, while other young women formed pairs or little groups, and occasionally I was close enough to catch their words as they commented on the men's bodies, sometimes running a Mr

Universe competition, giving marks out of ten, and crowning the handsomest chap of the day. As the women stared at the good-looking lads, I felt their disloyalty. When they laughed at a man whose legs were too short or whose chest was too skinny, I felt offended for him, and wounded. Although I tried to block out their chatter, I couldn't help but overhear.

'Hey, don't you fancy that one, the one with the good legs over there?'

'Will you look at them shoulders and arms on that one with the glossy dark hair? Wouldn't mind those around me on a cold night.'

'Wouldn't mind seeing that one starkers!'

I knew without looking up that they had spotted David.

At noon, after four hours of digging, spades thrown down into the sand, some of the men scrambled up the sand dunes to press a hot, sweat-soaked body against the pretty ironed dress of a girl and to hold her head in a long embrace. Sweet red lips and cheeks were smudged with sand. I turned away from these public intimacies, knowing David would not touch me in that state. We walked back to his barracks, where he took a shower before we met again for lunch in the corner cafe, and only then, settled on our red banquette, did I rest my head on his shoulder and let my hand find his under the table. We grabbed a cheddar sandwich and a cup of tea, or eggs on toast. We didn't notice what we ate because we had too much to tell each other. Then we walked along the beach, hand in hand like other couples, and talked while time was jinxed, because before we knew it the sun was low in the sky and David had to return to his barracks. Other couples disappeared into the sand dunes at that hour when the light plays tricks and suddenly it's dark and you've missed the transition from day to night. In those moments, reckless lovers took advantage of the eye's confusion to hide themselves in one last lingering embrace. Once or twice David and I stumbled over entwined bodies, clothes cast off, half-buried in sand. We saw heaving buttocks, a quivering breast, white legs. We looked the other way.

Late at night a soldier outside a guesthouse stared up, threw pebbles against glass, shinnied up a drainpipe to reach a bedroom window. Another crushed underfoot the velvet petals of late summer flowers with his great army boots as he levered open a window with his penknife to climb in or to help his lover out. One lad risked detention and the clink simply by staying in the sand dunes with his girl because he couldn't let her go. We were on the brink of a war and emotions were at fever pitch.

I snuggled down in a single bed in threadbare cotton sheets and a slippery nylon bedspread, reading in a small pool of lamplight until I fell asleep. Tomorrow was the same. Every tomorrow was the same, every weekend tomorrow for five long months.

Chapter 10

PRESTATYN 1940
MARY

It was my idea to go away together, and it was my crazy idea to go skinny-dipping. With only two weeks left before our wedding, I had to hush the Prenuptial Gremlin that chattered away on my shoulder and asked teasing questions about love and marriage.

'Why hasn't that beautiful David of yours had lots of girls before you?' it questioned.

'Because he wasn't interested. He was too involved with his sport. Oh, do shut up.'

'He doesn't really notice other women, does he?'

'He told me he's never been very interested. Go away.'

'So why did he notice you? Bet you can't answer that.'

'Chance. Fate. I walked round a cricket pitch when for one moment he took his eye off the ball. Does that answer your question?'

'No.'

'I was the first woman he was attracted to.'

'Why you?'

'Oh for heaven's sake! Why do we fall for one person and not another?'

'Yes. Why?'

'He told me he likes slim, fair women and I fitted the bill. Maybe it was my dress. Maybe it was the sun on my hair. Maybe Cupid shot him with his arrow. Now leave me alone.'

'Better find out if he's a red-blooded lover before you marry him.'

'That's it. I'm not listening to you. Get off my shoulder and leave me alone.'

But the Gremlin clung on, and from time to time dropped words in my ear that upset and worried me. From the beginning of our courtship, there had been an unspoken agreement that David and I would not go to bed together until we were married. See how I write 'go to bed' because the word 'sex' was taboo. Too threatening. Sex was for prostitutes. Nice young women lay on their backs and thought of England, or so my elderly aunts had told me. In those days we used euphemisms for all bodily functions – spending a penny and tuppence and front bottoms and going to bed together. Remember this was still 1940; the dark ages. The fact that we had never talked about the physical side of our relationship troubled me slightly as our wedding day approached. If you had challenged me, if you had suggested that there was something lacking between David and me, I would have jumped to his defence. He was one of the few men I had ever known who did not put his own animal needs before a woman's more delicate wishes. I would have said that I respected and loved him all the more for his firm principles.

'Aren't you curious about sex?' the Gremlin asked.

'Making love is for after the wedding. Soon enough. It's the final act of marriage.'

'It's an important part of any relationship. What if you don't hit it off?'

'It won't matter that much, surely. I expect it's over-rated. The only reason everyone is talking about it now is because of the war and the counting of days and the possibility of losing someone very dear to you.'

'Be honest. You've never felt any physical passion. Has he?'

'I love David very much.'

'In a brotherly-friend kind of way.'

'Oh, nonsense. We are very much in love.'

'Then why no sex?'

'I've answered that.'

'Rubbish!' said the Gremlin, and laughed dryly.

Then an excuse for going away – right away from the routine and the barracks and the dozens of soldier-sweetheart pairs who walked up and down the beach at Prestatyn – was handed to us on a plate. Perhaps the Gremlin had arranged it. The Liverpool Collegiate old boys' football team was having a week away in the Isle of Man. Among their number was Jack Palmer, who played for Liverpool and England, but he was suffering from a minor hamstring injury and needed to rest up before the big match against Douglas on the Sunday. They knew David, knew his reputation as an all-rounder, and contacted him. He told them to clear it with his CO for the Friday and Saturday matches, but the colonel magnanimously told David to take the Sunday off as well.

'Stay on, old chap, and watch the big match. Give me a report afterwards.'

'Sir.' David was beaming.

'And do us proud. It's an honour to have been picked.'

'I know that.'

'We'll pay your fare and accommodation. Wish I could step in for Jack Palmer. Off you go then, and score a few goals.'

'Sir.'

So that was when I seized my chance.

'I'm coming with you to the Isle of Man.'

He said, 'You're coming… what for?'

'To be with you. To watch you play.'

'Oh… but it's only a football match, Mary. We won't get much time together; I mean, I'll be training and playing most of the time.

I'll be with the lads.'

Perhaps he wanted his sport without female company but I wasn't going to let him get away with that. So it had to be emotional blackmail.

'How many more days do we have together? Let me be with you while I can.'

He relented, somewhat grudgingly. I was allowed to go on the understanding that I did not distract him from his important mission.

'See,' said the Gremlin, 'Chooses a game of football any day over a chance to bed you.'

'Not you again. It's a once-in-a-lifetime opportunity. Of course his mind is on the game.'

'The game finishes on Saturday afternoon.'

'And he'll be celebrating with the others, I hope, and reliving every moment of the match.'

'You have an answer for everything,' the Gremlin said.

'I am happy to be on the sidelines. There's no need to complicate everything.'

'Sex isn't complicated.'

I didn't bother to answer.

*

Sunday morning. My husband-to-be was all puffed up with pride and trying not to show it. He had scored one of two goals and his side had won. Since he had no further involvement in the game, he had agreed to spend the morning with me before the big match against Douglas, which of course we were going to watch. Stupid. Stupid of me to choose this occasion when he was completely distracted, when his mind was running on someone's foul and someone's trick footwork and someone's heroic defending, to try to pull him into another ball game altogether.

I suppose the damn Gremlin had finally got to me and I wanted to know what was beyond our gentle kisses and holding hands and

David's arm around my shoulder. Or else, while sitting in the sand dunes for hour upon hour while the men laboured, I had read too many novels in which the heroine swoons for her Heathcliff, her Rochester, her Mr Darcy, and I wanted to swoon too. Maybe it was just the hysteria of war which made me decide, like so many other young women who stood poised on a cliff to watch their lovers sail to the horizon, to throw caution and morals to the wind. It was our last chance.

It was a cruelly cold October day, the sky heavily overcast with an unpleasant, stinging rain. The wind snatched at the hem of my coat and did its best to blow away my scarf. It was a brisk downhill walk from the guesthouse to the flat sands of Douglas beach, where we jumped on one of the trams that ran the length of the promenade to Onchen village. There we alighted, walked through the small estate, newly built, and on past the five-star Majestic Hotel.

'Where on earth are you taking me?' David shouted across the wind.

'Nearly there. We're going to a small cove I found yesterday.'

'In this weather!'

I was following in my own footsteps of the previous day, when I had caught the same tram and found this quiet stretch of coastline while David was training on the football pitch. I knew exactly where I wanted to go. Past the hotel, and after another few hundred yards we rounded the corner and there was my cove below. I took David's hand and half pulled him down the crumbling cliff-side. We grabbed bending branches to stop our feet sliding where the path was precarious, and stones dislodged from the soil rolled with us down the hill. Our shoes filled with sand as we slithered and slipped to the small sandy beach. A secret place. A lovers' secret.

I was shaking, but not with cold. 'Dare you!' I said. 'Let's go for a swim.'

'You're joking!' he replied, giving me a playful punch on the arm.

'I'm not. Are you coming in, or are you going to stand here and watch while I do?'

'We didn't bring our things...'

'Skinny-dipping.'

'It's freezing! The rain is turning to sleet. Mary, you'll catch your death of cold. You're mad.'

'It's not like you to be worried about the cold,' I teased. 'I'm game. Are you?' Did he see that my display of bravado was false?

'OK,' he said in a tone that told me (a) I had taken leave of my senses and (b) he was only doing this to humour me. Nor could he refuse a dare. Especially one offered by a woman.

Usually I don't feel the cold because I am fit and take enough exercise to keep the blood pumping round, but as I tried to take off my coat my clumsy fingers struggled to push the buttons through the button-holes. As the layers came off, the fastenings got more fiddly, and I despaired of ever getting the hook and eye of my skirt apart. David was peeling off his jumper and shirt, chucking them on the sand, then his vest. Don't look. We undressed with our backs to each other. I struggled with my lacy petticoat when he streaked away, a brown athletic body with a ridiculous white bottom. Don't look. I tried to fold my clothes as I took them off, creating a neat stack, but of course they blew about and I had to stop undressing to search, in bra and panties, for a rock big enough to hold them down. By the time I finally stood there stripped and shivering and as crushingly, hopelessly embarrassed as I have ever been in my entire life, regretting the whole absurd idiotic idea, I noticed that David was in the water, struggling to keep his head above the choppy grey waves. Thankfully he wouldn't see much of me with his eyes so full of sea water, and if he stopped to stare he would drown because he was not a strong swimmer. I dashed to the water's edge, one arm crossed over my breasts, one hand dangling over my groin, and plunged in. My heart was beating too hard as I struck out, lifting my arms over my head in a fierce crawl. By the time I had calmed myself somewhat with the rhythm of my swimming and stopped to tread water, I saw that David had turned round and was already heading back. He had lasted all of two minutes and managed about ten yards out from the shore. He waved at me and yelled, but the wind carried his voice far away. He got a hand above the sea to jab at the shore and beckoned for me to follow. The effort pushed his head under the next wave and he emerged with a roar. I pretended I hadn't seen. I swam further and further out until I was numb with cold and shame. Soon I couldn't feel my legs, and when the first signs of cramp pinched my calves, I knew I had to turn back.

Getting out of the sea is not easy when your body is anaesthetised. When I finally stumbled over the pebbles and stones at the water's edge, stubbing a toe and hurting the sole of one foot, I saw that David was dressed and seemed occupied with some object of great importance buried in the sand. Only when I reached him, and turned my back, did he straighten up, pull out his handkerchief and pat dry my neck, back and shoulders. I dried my breasts with my own handkerchief, flicking the useless square of damp fabric over the rest of my body. I balanced like a flamingo to push legs into panties, trying not to add a lining of sand, and fastened my brassiere while David busied himself once again with the mysterious object in the sand.

'I think you girls must have a different metabolism or something,' he said as I fastened my skirt and tried to push my arms, sticky with salt water, through the sleeves of my jumper. 'It was damn cold in there. Dangerously cold. I don't know how you stayed in as long as you did!'

'I'm all right. Not warm exactly.'

'I need a coffee. How about you?'

'A coffee,' I repeated. 'I'm sorry. It was a stupid thing to do.'

'Normally I enjoy a challenge,' he said, looking at me long and hard for the first time since we set foot on the beach. 'But you didn't pick the right day. I need to be back for the match and the weather is foul. I'm worried you'll be ill. That's sleet coming down. I reckon it's nearly freezing out there.'

'We'll soon warm up,' I replied, lips refusing to make word shapes because they too were swollen with cold. 'Come on. Walk fast and we'll soon reach the cafe next to the hotel.'

We sat at a corner table, biting rock cakes, sipping Camp coffee, shivering, thawing our hands on our cups. Fortunately he couldn't tell the difference between cheeks fired up from the wind and a face burning with shame. He teased me and laughed. I knew that there was unfinished business between us now. Did he? I felt an utter fool. What was I thinking of? The passionate loss of my virginity on an October beach in Onchen?

My Gremlin grinned and chattered.

Chapter 11

PRESTATYN 1940
MARY

We were married, David in his Signals uniform and fuzzy paper-boat hat, me in a suit of quiet pale grey trimmed with fur, a matching hat, and three pale pink roses in silver paper on my breast. In wartime, white weddings were considered frivolous, and anyway there were no wedding dresses to be had for love or money. Afterwards, we caught the train to Blackpool, where the November weather held freakishly clear and cold and bright while we walked briskly, arm in arm, along the coastal paths, and played golf.

For our wedding night, as a surprise, David had booked seats in the front row of the Odeon for the late showing of *Rebecca* starring Laurence Olivier and Joan Fontaine and I wept throughout the film, and wept again as we walked home, hand in hand, because I felt so sorry for the young unnamed heroine who, with such naivety, had married the widower Max de Winter. Or was I weeping for myself?

Back at the guest house we sipped Ovaltine until our conversation grew stiff and artificial. How to negotiate the move to the marriage bed? After a fake yawn or two and a 'time for sleep' from one of us, or some such euphemism, we undressed in front of the single-bar electric fire, which burned red patches on one side of your body while not warming the other, and slid like flat fish into the pale mauve nylon sheets. I was split into two people, one who felt the terrifying novelty of a male body stretched out against my own – hard shoulders, chest and legs, and parts that I was too shy to name – and one who watched the proceedings, noting that the woman has closed her eyes and is lying as rigid as death when the man turns on his side to face her and kisses her cheek. The woman opens her eyes and sees plain blue pajamas with red piping on the breast pocket, each button fastened, and is glad that she has brought a modest apricot satin nightdress with thin straps.

She is as wooden as a puppet and he does not know how to pull her strings. Feeling only embarrassment, she returns his smile and strokes his glossy dark hair. A holding operation. She strokes his arms, pushing her hand up into his sleeves and reaching up towards his powerful shoulders. He kisses her. She returns his kiss. He presses his body against hers and she is horrified to feel that part of him down there, hard and sort of swaying. Oh heavens. They go through the motions, copying the love scenes they have watched at the cinema, and try to get it right. Knees and feet and elbows bump and collide. The borrowed bed wheezes like an asthmatic. They manage to do what married couples do on their first night together and fortunately he does not see that when he penetrates her, her face is all screwed up and tight, and her hands are clenched.

'Ow,' she says.

'Am I hurting you?'

'No. Hardly at all.'

'Do you want me to stop?'

'No,' she says. Please get it over with. Be quick. I don't like this hard thing inserted in me.

It's not something they will discuss, now or in the future. Afterwards the man, who can sleep through anything, is soon dead to the world, but the woman lies awake for a very long time, staring up into the dark.

*

Train stations. Soot in my nostrils and on my white handkerchief. The screaming squelch of brakes piercing my ears. The great snorts of steam the train-animal breaths when it emerges from its tunnel. The landscape of my early years with David had shifted from a cricket pitch to a railway station. David had been at Colwyn Bay training camp for six weeks, complaining and fretting about wasting his time peeling tons of filthy, pock-marked, soil-smirched potatoes while he waited for his war posting to come through. All the young soldiers were marching on the spot – literally and metaphorically – impatient to be off and to get on with the job. They were waiting to go to war. On Fridays he met me off the train from Lime Street and on Sundays waved me off to Liverpool again, but he was not really with me. He had already left.

And now I was doing the waving. From his carriage window I imagined him watching me as I got smaller and smaller like Alice, until I disappeared altogether, but I was still standing there waving long after the train had gone. I was waiting for a rush of anguish but there was none. I read the timetable pasted on the wall then slowly made my way home.

It would be six years before we met again. He wrote when he could. From the cruise liner *Andes* on its maiden voyage to Libya. From somewhere undisclosed in the desert. From Suez. From a Greek island called Chios.

David did not know that a month after I stood at the station waving, the Germans turned north to drop their bombs on Liverpool's Gladstone Docks, hitting Edgehill Station and the India Buildings where I worked. This was one of the most prolonged and terrifying raids that we had yet witnessed. Afterwards, I learnt that 681 bombers dropped 870 tonnes of high-explosive bombs and over 112,000 incendiaries. I was told it was the major air assault on Merseyside and had put half of the Liverpool docks out of action.

The fires burned all night all over the docks and spread into the city itself. Over 1450 people were killed and many more were seriously injured, but casualties would have been far worse if most of us had not left the city and dock areas that evening after work. The bombs fell at night. If they had fallen during the day, I would probably not have survived.

That attack on Liverpool gave me the incentive to get out. The next morning, as I stumbled across the rubble, my handkerchief to my mouth because I was breathing dust and my eyes were stinging and my throat was as dry as rice paper, I tried to take in a scene of devastation which was impossible to comprehend. Soon I turned away, walking away not just from the bombs that fell on India Buildings but from a life which was lie-strewn and dishonest. I knew I had to get out of there, and 'there' meant Liverpool, all its deceptively benign parks and cricket pitches, places where I strolled in a pretence of peace.

Go, I told myself, and leave this dishonest woman in the rubble. Start again. Find yourself. There is nothing to hold you here.

EDINBURGH
1941–1945

Chapter 12

Edinburgh 1941
Mary

I never went back to Alfred Holt, not even to hand in my notice. Instead, I telephoned an old school friend, Vera, who had moved up to Edinburgh to be with her fiancé and had hastily married when war was declared. Now, like other women, she waited, not knowing whether, when it was all over, she would be a wife or a widow. But being Vera – flame-haired and not one to hang around feeling sorry for herself – she had quickly signed up as a nurse with the Red Cross and was now working in one of the casualty units at the Royal Edinburgh Hospital. We had kept in touch and more than once she had suggested I join her. 'I'm coming,' I shouted down the telephone the day after the bombs fell on Liverpool. 'I'll be on the train tomorrow.'

Not that her warm delight and encouragement prevented me from tossing and turning all night. So there I was, not quite sure if this was real or a dream, dressing by the grey half-light seeping through the bedroom curtains in my plain wool suit, my lyle stockings and flat brown shoes. I had packed my small leather suitcase with a change of clothes, underwear, cold cream, my hairbrush, my toothbrush. When I walked into the kitchen to tell my mother the night before, she barely paused from the rhythmic rubbing of fat into flour as she made shortcrust pastry, as she did every other day because Father would eat nothing but apple pie for his pudding. Perhaps she pursed her lips more tightly. The last thing I remembered were her plump, busy fingers sweeping around the cream porcelain bowl, pulling the crumbs and fat together into a soft ball.

On the train I thought of nothing. Vera couldn't come to meet me because she was on duty but this was for the good because I wanted to start as I meant to continue, alone and leaning on no one. I climbed the steps from the sunken station to Princes Street Gardens and as I walked the streets I was aware only of the weight of the suitcase and the pain from its hard metal handle pressing into the palm of my hand.

The receptionist didn't look surprised when I said that I wanted to report for training, and while I sat and waited and stared at the buff painted walls where posters told me that my country needed me, I batted back her predictable forays into small talk because I had nothing to say in return. I was blank.

And when Miss Wallis bustled in to greet me, a woman of indeterminate age with a shelf of a bosom and legs that didn't taper, I remained calm because I seemed to have left myself behind somewhere, possibly on a station platform – whether the one from which I waved David off or the one where no one waved me off I had no idea. When she asked me whether I had any training as a nurse, the sense that I was not really there served me well because I could reply calmly, 'No, none at all. I trained as a shorthand typist,' without feeling a hint of panic.

'No, don't worry, that's fine,' she replied. 'I need to get a bit of a picture, that's all. Now, why do you want to work for the Red Cross?'

'To help my country. My husband is fighting in the army and I feel useless,' the robot-me replied, when the real answer may have been to kill time, or to get away from home, or to grow up or to find out who I was. I didn't know why I was there.

She cast her expert eye up and down my body as if I were a tomato or a marrow on a market stall and I half expected her to press my flesh to see if I as ripe. 'You are not qualified to work in the hospitals as a nurse, but we are very short of nursing assistants to help on the wards alongside the qualified nursing teams. You will be given a day of lectures and ninety hours of basic training, and after that you go straight on the wards. You will work hard and be on your feet for long hours. You will do whatever you are asked to do; you will accept without complaint the dirty jobs and the boring ones. At first you will be shocked and tired and saddened by what you see but you will get used to it, and you will find the work fulfilling. If you do well, you will gain your qualifications as a Red Cross nurse and work your way up the ranks. Do you think you can cope?'

'I believe I will manage,' I heard myself reply. 'I suppose I have no way of knowing until I try.'

'Good answer,' she replied. 'Now, young woman, you strike me as the sensible sort who has thought this through. I would like to place you on the wards at the Princess Royal where they are desperate for help.'

I nodded, not knowing one hospital from another, but felt gratitude that she was not sending me away or to the same hospital as Vera, because I wanted to carve out my own space and do this my own way.

'I have to tell you, before you finally agree,' Miss Wallis continued, 'that this hospital takes men straight from the front. Some of them are very badly injured. Some have severe shell shock. Once you have settled in, one of your duties will be to meet the trains arriving direct from France. Now, how does that sound?'

'I hope I will manage,' I replied lamely.

'Good answer,' she said again, and for a second or two the old, insecure me snapped back into place and I wanted to give Miss Wallis a hug because she had shown faith in me and trusted me to cope, no matter how bad it got.

And it did get bad. When people ask me now, How did you

manage, a young slip of a thing like you? I reply, as others do, You just got on with it. You did not think about it. There was work to do, a ton of it, and you did it. You were on your feet from morning until night and still you did not get through all the jobs nor did you give enough attention to each of the sick and wounded men on your ward. At night in the dormitory sometimes you cried, but mostly you were so exhausted that you fell into a deep and dreamless sleep as soon as your head touched the pillow, until the alarm went off and you started all over again.

It was as bad as they said, and worse, but I settled in and was glad of the routine and the never-ending list of duties. I had a friend and ally in a young woman called Moira who arrived at the hospital on the same day as myself, and we learnt the ropes together. We whispered together, we rolled our eyes at each other as we dashed up and down the lines of beds carrying a bedpan or fresh bandages, and we wept together whenever one of the young men asked us tearfully, or worse, bravely, how he could possibly carry on living now that his body was useless.

Sooner than expected, because they were so short-staffed, the two of us were told that we were to meet the hospital trains which had started arriving in Haymarket Station straight from Dunkirk. The patients would tell us later how the quay was on fire and too broken up for the hospital ships to dock alongside it and so, because there was no gangway, the wounded men were dragged roughly over the ships' sides, while others were taken ashore by ships' officers and crews and stewards on stretchers, carried the length of the quay under steady, ceaseless fire from the Luftwaffe, across long stretches of wasteland where bomb casings and debris fell from the sky, until finally those men who were still alive were roughly loaded on to the trains. There they lay on makeshift beds, on the floor, or simply leant against the side of the carriage. Some of the wounded were hit a second time while they were being evacuated. Some died before they made it to the train. Others died on the journey to Scotland.

*

Moira and I waited on the platform in the clear light from the Scottish sky. We felt a dreadful spine-tingling anticipation standing there before the first hospital train of the morning rolled in. The engine snorted and steamed its way to a halt on the platform and for a moment there was a pause, and you wanted time to stand still for ever so that the carriage doors were held shut. But they opened, and the walking wounded stumbled out, dazed and dirty and sweating and bloodied in tattered battle dress and tin hats, limping and blinking at the light and supporting one another's bodies. The men walked in twos and threes, many limping, like a three-legged race gone wrong. There are images which will haunt you all your life. This – the disgorging of the wounded and the dying – is one.

After we had separated and sorted those who could walk and who didn't need urgent attention from those who were critically and severely wounded, and had allocated them to one or other ward in one or other hospital, we boarded the train, shivering no matter how hot it was, no matter how many times we did it, because in those enclosed spaces lay men who were more dead than alive. We got down on our knees to administer chloroform and sedatives to those who still screamed and to those who moaned like wounded animals. Usually there was at least one man who silently reached up to touch my hem as I passed along the carriage. I stopped to lay my hand on his forehead or to touch his shoulder, seeing as I stooped down that his wounds were so severe that he stood no chance. When that man died I knew that he had been hanging on for one last touch of humanity.

Those of us who met the trains swallowed back the ever-present fear of recognising, in one of the filthy, unshaven, bruised and brutalised faces, a friend, a cousin, a brother, a lover.

Each hospital could take only so many men, and so Moira and

I travelled on with the wounded, comforting them and staunching their bleeding as best we could, and as the train stopped at the next station and the next on its journey to Glasgow, we counted out nine or ten more men who would be taken away on stretchers and in ambulances. On we went, until there were only two or three men left in the carriages when we arrived at the final stopping point in Glasgow.

Back on the ward the next day, we maintained a face of cheerful optimism as we settled the new men in. Of course those who could flirted outrageously with us and we expected to be grabbed around the waist and told 'Come into bed, darling' and 'Honest to God I thought you were an angel' because that was how they coped. If you have only one arm, you can still pinch a nurse's bottom and perhaps grab at what's left of your manly self-respect. In the evenings, the men who were sufficiently recovered were allowed out to the pub. 'You stay sober,' we would shout after the uniformed line of raggle-taggle men, wagging our fingers and stretching to our full five-foot-something heights, but of course they returned tipsy and daft, demanding 'Gi'us a kish, nursh,' as we pushed them back to their beds and got them undressed. The arms went round our waists and the hands went up our skirts, and we slapped them hard and tried to be strict.

When a man died, Moira and I pulled the curtains round him and, as gently as possible, got him ready for the mortuary. That part was sad and perhaps because of that sadness, which of course we bit back, we often became hysterical with laughter later when we carried the body on a stretcher across the campus. If you know Edinburgh at all, you will know it as a windy city, and in the grounds of Princess Margaret Rose the wind seemed to blow harder than anywhere. So there we were, Moira and I, neither of us particularly big or strong, in the darkness, because you waited until night to discretely take the body away, one at each end of the stretcher walking across the grounds in a roaring gale, laughing and trying to keep the body from falling off as we tripped and stumbled in the rough, bumpy grass. With each gust, our load slipped and tipped sideways.

'Hang on, will you!' Moira would yell over the wind. 'He's falling off again!'

And we would have to stop, partly to prevent the body from sliding all the way into the grass, and partly because we were doubled up with laughter, barely able to catch our breath. Then we'd pick up the stretcher and set off again. Two women and a dead man.

Chapter 13

Suez 1944
Mary

Once and once only did my path through the war actually cross David's, and still we managed to miss each other – two ships literally passing in the night.

I had left the Edinburgh wards after VE Day, summoned out to Singapore alongside other Red Cross workers with the remit of accompanying Australian POWs back to their home country on a hospital ship. I was by then quietly confident and proud of my skills. I knew I could cope. I suppose I was a different woman from the one who had nervously stepped off the train at Waverley Station three years earlier.

Just as Pearl Harbour had caught the allies by surprise, so the troops in the Far East had not been prepared for the sudden Japanese attack on Singapore, with the horrific result that thousands of our own men and our allies fell easily into cruel Japanese hands. David told me afterwards that he might have been one of them. When war was declared, fifty-six ships had set off from England sailing to Cape Town escorted by the naval fighting ships *Renown* and *Repulse*. The voyage out was appalling, the men traumatised by repeated submarine attacks and sea-sickness, but they arrived and were given three days' shore leave to recover. Then they were split up, half sent on to the Far East, half to the Libyan desert. If David had been sent to Burma or Singapore, I might have found him, or what was left of him, in a POW camp, but he was assigned to the Libya contingent and survived.

Incredibly, David and I were in Suez on the same day soon after the war in Europe was over. The fighting had stopped, the men were starting to return home, but still we had to deal with the devastation and detritus that war had left behind. He had left Libya, handing over to American and Australian troops after Pearl Harbour, and had travelled to Tripoli to clear a great blockage of ships from the harbour, our own and others belonging to the enemy. Then he went by ship to a small Greek island called Chios, where he remained for a couple of months, loving every moment of his role in the occupying forces, making sure people were fed and protected. Finally he was sent to Suez, where he was responsible for loading all the armoury and supplies left behind on to ships bound for the Far East.

His VE Day was spent in Port Said. He was sweating it out on the quayside, he said, supervising the loading of an unimaginable amount of stuff on to ships when he saw a convoy arriving from Bangalore. Some of the ships were empty hospital ships on their way to Singapore to pick up the wounded. From the shore David could see nurses in Red Cross uniforms moving about the decks and his heart began to pound. Was Mary there? So began his frantic search in a small unstable vessel (and David is no sailor, I can tell you), rowing like a mad man from one ship to another, clambering aboard, asking, searching, saying my name over and over again. Is Mary there? By nightfall, he had not found me, but I was there and soon our ship was preparing to set sail. Perhaps he had climbed aboard it. Perhaps I was looking the wrong way when he ran amongst the uniformed women searching for my face. I was there. On VE Day we were almost reunited.

When the war was finally over, David asked me a few times about my work in the hospitals and on the hospital ship and I was not able to answer, until, after a while, he understood that he had to leave that period of my life untranslated into words. In his imagination he would like to accumulate some images, perhaps the sergeant in bed 7 whose lungs are full of shrapnel or the young private in bed 18 who will regain consciousness to be told that he has lost part of his face and will never see again. David wants to walk the aisles between the beds as I did and know a little of what I knew, but all I give him are generalisations because it was a visceral experience, felt in my bones and flesh. It is part of me. Others have tried to commit their thoughts to paper but I do not because you cannot know what it is like to be a young man, someone's son, someone's lover, aged nineteen or twenty, who, for the first time, turns back the bed covers and sees that he is maimed forever. You cannot know that loss. You can only guess at how they cope with that finality. I watched them. I sat with them. I nodded and smiled when they hid their despair behind brave words. I held them when they wept. And sometimes when they died. But I was never one of them and I do not have the right to speak for them.

Those men, cruelly torn apart, showed us the raw stuff of their souls. The gentlest revealed his strength and the strongest let us see his weakness. Of course we fell in love. We all did.

Yes, there was one whom I loved more than all the others. That's what all David's prodding and prying was really about. Yes, I fell in love. I loved one of those wounded men. Even in that crowded, frenetic, heart-breaking space where too many men came to die or to be partly mended, there was one whom I loved with all my heart.

He was married and so was I. It was a long time ago. There was a war on.

NAIROBI
1952–1954

Chapter 14

Mombassa 1952
David

My breathing came fast and hard because I could see her, I could see her crushed against the railings of the ship, staring out, scanning the mass of humanity on Mombassa dock to left and to right, searching the swarms of khaki-clad men who were waiting like me. I had removed my hat – I always did at the first opportunity – so stood bare-headed and in shirt sleeves. From where she stood it would have been impossible to make me out, to differentiate one soldier from another in the sea of uniforms. But still I waved like mad, hoping she would spot me. Perhaps I was too much changed. My skin, naturally dark, was burnt dark brown in the sun and my hair was a crew cut. I could see that she was carrying Clara and was holding Eve's hand. Mary. Mary. I called her name. I waved and yelled.

It was noisy and chaotic and damn hot on that quayside with a sun so fierce it was melting the concrete. Everywhere you looked there was agitation and movement. The strings of soldiers left the ship first, marching down the gangplanks, disembarking with their mess kits slung over their shoulders. I welcomed them, silently, because those of us already stationed out here needed reinforcements. Family members followed, more hesitant, shading their eyes from the blinding light with pale hands and scanning the crowd for the one or two people who should be there to meet them. On the quayside, the natives, the black ant workers, the only ones immune to the punishing sun, never stopped their dashing up and down, up and down, dragging trolleys and makeshift carts as they fell over one another to jostle for the job of relieving someone of their luggage. It was ninety-five degrees in the shade and whilst I was by now used to it, those coming out from home would have found it utterly enervating. Imagine the embarkment scene in the film of the *Titanic* and that's what it was like – apart from the added military presence here in Mombassa.

Just the *Atlanta* came in that morning but even before it finished docking, the derricks started up with the grinding of metal against metal to take the military cargo off in huge nets. Caught like fish were containers of army equipment and fire arms and ammunition. I prayed that Mary would be too distracted to notice the guns. I didn't want her first reaction to be one of alarm. Don't let her think she has come out to trouble, I prayed.

That day while I stood on the quayside in my sweat-stained khaki shirt, I pushed to the back of my mind the rumours that circulated in the mess. There was always someone keen for a bit of stirring gossip but I had long ago learnt to ignore bad news until it arrived in the form of an official memo. On the other hand it was damn obvious that alarming news had reached England because here was our government responding by sending out all these service corps bods – the medics and ordnance chaps – who were disembarking from the same ship as Mary. It was probably a precaution, I told myself, so that the infrastructure would be in place if, or when, the fighting corps followed. There were whispers that the tribes in the mountains were becoming more restless, but for my part I didn't think it would come to anything. I had heard from the white settlers during our last cricket match against the colonial team from Naivasha that there had been a few nasty incidents up in the Aberdare Mountains, but it happened from time to time and I can't say I was worried by what I was told. It seemed to me that they had such a long-established and settled way of life, those wealthy white farmers with their armies of native servants, that any disruption or change was inconceivable. What chance would a few hysterical natives have against such strongholds?

Down the gangplank now came the soldiers of the Black Watch, not the full regiment but a single battalion to supplement those already stationed up in the hills. God, they must have been horribly hot, however resplendent their tartan uniform, although they do say that kilts are ideal for hot or cold weather. I remember thinking, I hope a bit of a breeze gets up the legs. After the soldiers came the civilians, looking pretty shell-shocked and shielding their eyes against the white-hot glare of the sun. I wasn't interested in any of them. It was just the backcloth. I had eyes only for one lovely lady and her two small daughters.

Mary still hadn't found me but I could see even from a distance that she looked weary and pale. No wonder. She must have been at her wit's end during the crossing from Southampton to Mombassa alone with two little girls. Later she would tell me that Clara hadn't been old enough to stray far from her side, but my strong-willed, mischievous Eve had run off again and again, to be found later, skipping all over the decks and poking her white-blonde head through the railings to stare down at the ocean. Like her mother, she was mesmerised by the sea. Mary told me later that her heart had been in her mouth for the entire voyage with the almost certain prospect of Eve falling overboard.

Finally Mary spotted me and I saw on her face an expression of sheer relief. As she twisted through the crowds towards me, an awkward passage with one child in tow and another in her weary arms, I likewise pushed forward to meet her. When we were within a yard or two of touching she called 'David!' and threw Clara at me. The child hung in the air for a few seconds but my reactions have always been fast, so instinctively I reached out and caught her safely in my arms. Like a cricket ball. It was an unusually strong and defiant gesture for Mary but one which spoke volumes. Take her. Take one child from me. I suppose it was just her way of telling me that she had been without me in England for six months and could not cope for one moment longer. If we had not been in such a public place I know she would have burst into floods of tears. I was moved almost to tears myself with love and joy and pity. The girls were caught and squashed in our first embrace. Clara squealed. Mary and I kissed briefly. We looked into each other's eyes, and not yet seeing there the person with whom we were once familiar, we looked away again. We turned our attention to the children.

Since the harbour master had been instructed to deal with Mary's two trunks – we travelled light in those days – all we had to do was walk the short distance to Mombassa train station and then wait on the platform to make sure that everything was put safely on to the train. There we stood, for a while awkward and silent, a family that was not yet a family. The girls clung to their mother, particularly Clara, who sent me quizzical little looks from behind Mary's skirt as if she was not quite sure who I was. Eve took my arm but her excitement was draining away and soon she was subdued and silent. I remember thinking how strange it was that being with Mary did not come naturally after the first relief of recognition on that quayside, not after being apart for so long. There was a hesitation and a formality in the way we addressed each other, like strangers who do not know how much they can give away or how much they dare risk. While we waited for the train, Mary talked mostly about her voyage. I let her talk. This was extra luggage she needed to shed before we could move forward again.

Chapter 15

MOMBASSA 1952
DAVID

The train journey from Mombassa to Nairobi would take about four hours, which was fine because Mary and I needed time to get used to being with each other. The railway line, hacked out through dense forest, would wind slowly uphill from ground level at Mombassa to five thousand feet above sea level at Nairobi. Someone described it to me once as a scar across Africa. I don't know why. Mary and I sat slightly apart, quiet in each other's company, staring out of the window. Was she taking note of the shifting landscape or were her thoughts still back in England or on the boat? The train rattled on through the Rabai Hills and then the dirt-dry Taru Desert, something of a shock coming so soon after the fertile coast. The red dust disturbed by the train's wheels drifted in clouds close beside the carriages and put a filmy screen between us and the barren plains, so that we looked out through rose-coloured spectacles. I chatted to Mary, telling her where we were, and while she nodded and smiled, I could see that she was far too tired to be as stunned as I had been when I made this same journey on my own for the first time. After a couple of hours we would arrive in the foothills of Kilimanjaro, a powerful, dramatic presence of ever-shifting colours and contours, and soon after that we would enter the marshy flats at the southern end of the Kikuyu uplands, one degree south of the Equator, which led to the purple slopes of the Ngong hills.

Along the route we occasionally caught a fleeting glimpse of a native encampment of small mud huts thatched with leaves, half-hidden by trees, and then, perhaps ten miles or so further on, another encampment, another tribe. At first Mary asked me about the people but honestly there were so many different tribes in East Africa that I could not give her any intelligible answers. I hadn't concerned myself with the natives. So we settled to silence. I was beginning to feel a bit disappointed that Mary was not even managing a pretence of excitement. Stupid of me, I know, to expect her to feel at ease just because she was back at my side. I had imagined that she would be curious to learn about her new country, her new home, but instead she was listless and wan, and I sensed a coolness that I interpreted as her way of punishing me for leaving her alone for so long, even though it had all been planned and agreed beforehand. I let her be. Said nothing. Women are such emotional creatures and Mary had always been a sensitive flower. We travelled on beneath a sky that would remain an almost cruelly bright blue until the sun dropped suddenly below the horizon. In Africa sunsets happen fast.

Only once did Mary become animated. Something caught her eye and she leant forward to stare out of the window. I looked where she pointed but all I could see was a black woman standing in a clearing. More or less naked. Well, Mary would see lots of women without clothes. Men too. To be honest, I felt a bit embarrassed that she was calling attention to a scene that was of so little consequence and, well… so primitive and savage.

'Oh look, David… the native girl…' Mary said, turning to me. It was the first time I had heard warmth in her voice. 'What tribe is she from? She is beautiful, don't you think?'

'Sorry, no idea. As I said, there are dozens of tribes. Can't tell most of them apart,' I replied, letting her know that I wasn't really interested. Mary gave me a quizzical look – almost a frown – but then put her head on my shoulder and dozed.

'Relax now,' I said, changing the topic of conversation. 'Not long now. Everything can wait until we get to the bungalow. I've arranged everything. There's nothing for you to do and I hope you'll be very pleasantly surprised.'

She slept on and off for the rest of the journey. Occasionally her eyelids opened and she glanced out of the window. It must have felt unreal. Don't rush her, I thought to myself. She has only just arrived in Africa.

Clara too was fast asleep, leaning sideways against her mother and making little snuffling noises through her open mouth, her dark hair sticky on her forehead. Unusual little girl, I thought. So dark and self-contained. She slept through the entire journey. But I remember that Eve was wide-awake again and wide-eyed, her spring over-wound, missing nothing as we swayed along the tracks. I let her chatter away, nodding my head in the right places, remembering all over again how to be a father to a bright fluttering butterfly of a little girl.

I was feeling a bit tense and unsettled myself by the time we finally drew into Nairobi station. I had thought about the reunion with Mary and the girls so many times during the months I had been out here alone, telling myself how it would be, but in the end nothing was as I had imagined it. I had pictured the two of us close and happy as we travelled together, yet we hardly seemed to know each other. She was with me but not with me. When I saw my good friend Harry Frame waiting on the platform as the train slowed down I felt a flood of relief to be back in Nairobi with a familiar face wearing its familiar expression of rueful amusement, as if he found the world permanently and inexplicably funny. There was my tall friend Harry scanning the windows for our faces. I felt a pang of guilt. My poor wife was exhausted and unsettled and I had reacted with such intolerance, expecting her to be affectionate and chirpy. I squeezed her hand.

'Mary, we're here. Look, there's Harry waiting to meet us,' I said to her as we gathered up one sleepy child and one fractious one. One of the natives on the platform would deal with our luggage. 'You'll like him,' I continued. 'He's the most versatile man I've ever known. Can take a car to pieces, has a degree in history from Oxford University, a bridge correspondent for *The Times*...' But Mary wasn't listening. Ssh, I told myself. Let her be. Yet for me it was so important that she liked him. He was a staunch ally, a good friend, and not a bad cricketer either.

We must have looked a bedraggled crew as we climbed down from the train, but Harry rushed up and greeted Mary warmly, taking both her hands in his.

'I am so very glad to meet you at last. David's missed you so much, you know. He never stops talking about you and the girls,' he said.

I smiled at his tact and blessed him for his white lies. The truth, as well he knew, was that I had quickly adapted to living in the officers' mess and had been too busy and delighted with my new job and the cricket to mope after Mary. Anyway, you had to make the best of things. It wasn't going to be forever.

'I hope you will be very happy out here. It's a wild and beautiful country,' Harry continued. 'And if there is anything my wife Marjorie or I can do to help you settle in, you have only to ask.'

Mary smiled. 'Thank you,' she said. 'I'm so glad to be here at last.'

Why ever had I worried that they might not get on? He was a charmer and very good with the ladies. Not like me; I'm more comfortable around men. Always have been. To be honest, women don't have much to say that interests me and I've never been one to flirt. Can't see the point.

'You and David must come over once you've settled in. We have a house in the city centre. I'll point it out to you as we drive along Delamere Avenue. Marjorie is very content and settled out here and she'll be able to tell you anything you need to know.'

'Thank you,' Mary said again, her face softening. It was going just fine.

'Right, let's get you home. It's a twenty-minute drive to your bungalow. You must be tired. I'll just go and organise someone to follow with your luggage.'

Off he went, striding along the platform, whistling 'We'll meet again, don't know where, don't know when,' while our little procession followed on behind. At last, Mary gave me a sweet smile and I snapped back to my old self.

Unlike me to worry. Not my style. Either sort it out or let it be was my motto.

Chapter 16

MOMBASSA 1952
MARY

Our ship slowed down, kicking out flurries of water as it edged its way alongside the dock. We were out on deck, a motley crew of excited, worried, dizzy and weary people who had been at sea for six weeks, all of us lined up against the railings, looking for the person who should be there to meet us. My ears would sing and roar and my body would suddenly veer sideways for several days once we set foot on dry land after the constant motion of the ship. My muscles had been making small involuntary adjustments every moment I had been awake so that I could keep my balance and prevent myself from keeling over, but from now on they would have to adapt to land that stayed still beneath my feet. I leant out, not too far because I was holding Clara in my arms and Eve was at my side and given half a chance she would find a way of falling over into that cloudy whirlpool. While murmuring 'Yes' and 'No' to Eve's outpouring of questions, I was actually in a daze, mesmerised by the perpetual motion of men in khaki uniforms who were elbowing and pushing their way through the crowds to reach our ship. And the army of natives in threadbare shirts with bare feet running, running, running.

Then came a mechanical roar and a grinding of wheels that sent shudders across the decks under our feet while we stood waiting for the gangplank to be set in place. The derricks were moving and natives were running up and down the quayside ready to grab and anchor the bulky nets of boxes and crates that swayed overhead. What was all that military paraphernalia that was being offloaded? I had no idea it was on board. It looked as if they were preparing for war. The crates had rifles in them; I could see them through the cracks. What has David not told me, I wondered.

I put up an arm to shield my eyes from the sun and I spotted him. I sighed with relief that I wouldn't have to stand amongst that packed, heaving, sunburned mass of black and white humanity waiting for him to turn up. That was all.

It was our turn to walk down the metal gangplank after standing for an eternity in line while Eve slid her fists along the wire railing back and forth, back and forth, squeak squeak squeak, until I thought I would scream. My anger, as I stepped onto land and threaded my way through the cram of bodies to meet David, took me by surprise because it was so unreasonable and unkind. Why did I feel that fury when there he was, present and correct, in his khaki shorts and pressed khaki shirt, tanned to a mahogany brown, more muscular than when I last saw him, and so obviously relaxed and at home there in that foreign country? I was in tears as the distance between us closed; he ducked expertly through the mob with a wide smile while I brushed away all evidence of the upset I felt. I hurled Clara into his arms, trying in that gesture to throw away the hostility I felt towards him because there was no need and no explanation for it. I was angry with myself more than with him because we had waited six months for this meeting in Mombassa, the start of a new life that we had planned in detail late at night while we were trapped in a curtain-twitching village under my parents' roof, whispering together in the bedroom with only a thin wall between us and sharp maternal ears. This was exactly what we wanted.

Call it female intuition but I knew he had thrived out there without me. He would have been at home in the mess, amongst men, talking about the things men talk about, and equally happy with the sweat and hard graft of exercises up in the mountains. Knowing David, soldiers would like him and he would command their respect. It's something to do with their shared background of hardship, which most privileged officers cannot begin to imagine. Them and us. That has never been David's way. I wondered, not for the first time, whether I had married a man who glowed with satisfaction and pride only amongst men – on the football pitch, in the cricket grounds, training his men in battle skills, never in my arms or in the heart of domesticity. David was at ease with men, something which in the first blush of love I admired, but which puzzled me now and threw me off balance. Once he told me that he didn't really like women and found their company stifling. He told me I was the exception, which simultaneously put me on a pedestal and hurled me into exile. He once referred to our lovely girls as 'two useless daughters'. Perhaps in that crystal-clear moment, with every sense heightened and nerves exposed, in that painfully bright light, even lies had nowhere to hide.

Our embrace was brief, buffeted and nudged as we were on all sides. In the handing-over of Clara I had a moment to compose myself and let him believe that my frayed nerves were the result of our long crossing. I didn't let on that I made a friend on the ship, a young married woman called Judith who was on her way out to meet her newly married husband serving with the air force. What with her excitement and impatience and boundless energy, she was only too happy to have something to do to occupy her time so she helped me out with the girls, sometimes giving me a whole blessed afternoon to sleep while she entertained Eve and Clara. There she was, a small figure further down the quay with a tall man whose arms were wrapped round her. We promised we would stay in contact but I wondered if we would.

So we were a family once again, although by the way she was

leaning away from David and struggling to get out of his arms, I wondered if Clara even remembered her father. For once, because it served me well, I let my naughty Eve take centre stage and ignored her outrageously flighty behaviour with her father. There she went, holding his hand and skipping along beside him in her white socks and blue shoes; she gazed up at his face, oh such a sweet little angel. I loved her with all my heart but I was not seduced by her charms.

Everything was a blur of perpetual motion as we made our way through the crowds to Mombassa station and climbed aboard our train. I didn't have time to register that new place, that new continent, because there were too many people blocking my view and swarming all over the platform, nudging me, brushing against me, and leaving a residue of spice and sweat in my nostrils. The sheer mass of humanity was dizzying.

The train snorted a couple of times to warm up. A whistle. Then I felt the gathered-up physical effort of the engine as it first dragged its dead weight of carriages along the track and out of the station before its momentum began to pick up. We were on our way to Nairobi, and again I felt unreal, unsubstantial, as I leant my head against the seat and stared blankly out of the window, giving David just enough attention to keep him from puzzlement. He seemed as pleased as punch to have us back and was eager to tell me everything at once. It must have been exhaustion. What else could have turned my mood tetchy and sour?

I remember I was staring out of the window, shockingly indifferent because I was too tired to pay proper attention to the constantly changing contours and colours of the plains and hills, when my eye was caught by a smudge of black against brilliant green. The smudge became a person and the person became a tall, willowy young black woman, who, from the inky smoothness of her skin and the upward tilt of her high, pointed breasts, was probably not long into adolescence. She was naked apart from shimmering gold rings around her neck and ankles. It was the way she was standing that jolted me out of my stupor. She was a statue, as still as a stone, but also, I fancied, quietly tuned in to her surroundings like a deer alert to the rustle of a wild cat. She was as much a part of the landscape as the trees and rocks and blades of grass. This was her land. This must sound naive – the white woman's romantic view of the native – but I don't mean it like that. I just wanted to acknowledge her right of possession because she and her ancestors had lived here and owned and worked the land for centuries long before we white folk came along, and I was uncomfortable with the absolute separation of them and us. Of black and white. I also felt in some way her inferior because I, supposedly educated and sophisticated, was lost, in my marriage and in myself and in this new country where I had just arrived, while she seemed to possess the gift of belonging, which was apparent even in her proud bearing. While I watched, mesmerised by her grace, she bent down, picked up a huge basket that was at her side, and, balancing it on her head, walked on with a liquid sway of her hips.

'Look…' I was tugging at David's arm. 'Isn't she lovely? What tribe is she from?'

He had no idea; in fact, I don't think he was the least bit interested. For him she was just another native woman like a thousand others. Later I would find out from Harry that she was probably a young Turkana woman down from the mountains to collect water. Holding close to my heart the image of her confidence and certainty, as a possibility I suppose for myself, I dozed again until the train pulled into Nairobi station.

*

It was that war-time song that finally broke open my carapace and made me smile – 'We'll Meet Again' – because it conjured up memories of Vera Lynn singing for the troops in Burma while huge insects, attracted to the bright stage lights, dive-bombed her accompanist's piano keys. Ironically that was the time when I, like other women I knew, felt most fulfilled, and most confident and sure of myself. How did he know? He was striding ahead of us, but after looking into my eyes, really looking, not just the usual polite glance, I knew quite well that he was whistling that song for me, to welcome me, to cheer me up because he had correctly read my uncertainty. In that first meeting on a railway platform in Africa, I guessed that here was a man who cleverly hid his wisdom and emotions beneath an easy charm so that his real character was unfathomable except to those whom he allowed to see it. I guessed that, chameleon-like, he adapted to his surroundings and his companions, showing them one facet or another but never his wholeness and entirety. Where David was straightforward, he was complex. Where David was transparent, he was opaque. I wanted to know this man who could guess a woman's past from one look into her jaded eyes.

I should say clearly here that I had no thoughts beyond getting to know Harry and perhaps finding in him a friend. He was someone I warmed to immediately, that is all. I am not writing a romantic novel; I am being honest. Anyway, imagine the scene. There I was, new on Kenyan soil after crossing an ocean, tetchy and tired, reunited with my husband who, after six months' absence had become a stranger, with two little girls in tow, one clinging like a limpet and one who, despite total exhaustion, was so unable to keep still that I had to watch her every move in case she dashed off and threw herself under the next train. Between my husband, who now chatted easily to Harry, catching up on the news, and my children, who wilted at my side, and while trying to push away the thousand new impressions and sensations that came at me from every corner of that noisy station, there was the comforting, still presence of a tall man to whom I wanted to cling as to a liferaft. There was no hint of flirtation. How could there be? He was there to meet us. That was all.

Harry opened the car doors. David climbed in beside him, very much at ease and talking cricket now in his official army voice – no Liverpool vowels. I was in the back between the girls. David was asking Harry the score of the latest cricket match, which he had missed to collect me, while for my benefit pointing out hotels and offices and streets that meant nothing to me. I blocked out his tourist commentary and formed my own first impressions of a city centre that looked more European than African, with its wide avenues lined on both sides by arching palm trees. It was a luxurious city, I thought. A wealthy city. There was a crazy mix of architectural styles just in the areas we drove through; I spotted grand colonial, Arab, and mock Tudor. My first thought was that there was nothing there that marked the place out as African. I saw no Africans! The city bustled with white folk, and African Indians and Pakistanis. Where were the natives? Would the native girl with the gold bangles ever come here? Did she even know that the city existed?

Occasionally I stole a glance in the driving mirror, where Harry's face was half visible. Once he caught me looking at him and smiled. It was a smile of sympathy.

Chapter 17

NAIROBI 1952
DAVID

From Nairobi Station on the edge of town, we drove through the city centre, and as we drove along Delamere Avenue I imagined looking at it through Mary's eyes. She would be impressed, as I had been, by the grand hotels, the excellent range of shops and the department stores that compared well with any in England. The main avenues were wide and clean and lined with waving palms, which broke the sun into dazzling dots of light on the tarmac.

I suppose I was pleased to find out that Nairobi was a predominantly white city; in fact apart from the heat and eternally blue skies, you would hardly that know that you were in Africa. I was telling Mary all of this as Harry drove us home.

'About seventy-five per cent of the population here is English or European,' I said, twisting round in the front seat. 'Quite a lot of Pakistanis too, who have set themselves up as shop keepers. They live in their area of the city and we live in ours. Pretty segregated, so we don't mix much.'

Mary said nothing. Was she listening?

'Of course, I meet them on the cricket pitch. They're cricket mad. Always have been. Our bungalow is rented from a wealthy Pakistani who owns a printing firm. I was a bit disappointed to find there were no married quarters here but I think you'll like what I've found.'

'What do you want married quarters for when you can have your own house and garden?' Harry asked. 'Dreary places. The same all over the world. You wouldn't know from looking out of the window if you were in Africa, Portsmouth or Cyprus.'

'Nonsense,' I laughed. 'I like the security of housing in barracks. And because everything you need is there in one place.'

'I'd rather feel part of the place I've come to, not caged in behind high walls with a security guard to salute you in and out.'

'You're different.'

'Why?'

'Not really army at all.'

Harry laughed dutifully at this tired old joke.

'I know… I know… never been in a fighting corps in my life…'

'You know I respect you Intelligence chaps. I'm not belittling you.'

'Yes you are.'

'And it's no good appealing to Mary for sympathy, old man, because she is not allowed to hold views that are different from those of her husband.' I was joking, of course, but I had seen him glance at my wife with a wry expression as if to say, 'Sorry about this banter.'

'You won't see many natives,' I said to Mary, ignoring Harry and returning to my previous topic. 'They hardly ever come down from the mountains. You'll see a few wandering around wrapped in their blankets in this smothering heat. Don't know how they can bear it. There are natives in Nairobi but most of them work as servants in the hotels and as domestics and cooks in the homes of the white folk. We are lucky that way. Servants cost next to nothing here.'

Again I saw Harry tilt his head, just slightly, to look at Mary as if to gauge her reaction to what I was saying. His views about living in the city were somewhat different from mine, not that we talked about it much. I guessed that he was a bit of a liberal. Mostly we chatted about cricket. While I was grateful that the social order was well established and worked efficiently, I think he considered that the natives deserved better. Well, that was his point of view but I could think of a number of arguments why giving the natives more control and money would not be a good idea. So we agreed to differ.

Harry sped along Delamere Avenue, perhaps showing off for Mary's benefit in the Mercedes, which he knew I admired. Although I knew in my head that this wasn't the time for touristy chatter, I was just too excited at having Mary with me at last to refrain from pointing out the five-star hotels and the fabulous houses which belonged to the upper echelons of the forces. Harry, sensible chap that he was, and not full of emotion as I was, remained quiet, perhaps understanding that Mary and the girls were too tired to take anything in. From the kick-kicking of small feet through the back of my car seat, I knew that Eve was too exhausted to keep still. Her eyes were too bright and her cheeks were stained with bright burning circles. That girl was about to collapse. Clara didn't even try to keep up with it all. Bless her, when I glanced over my shoulder, I could see her leaning against her mother, her eyelids heavy and half-closed, in her own little world. We would soon be there – otherwise I could see that a grown-up female head would soon be toppling sideways too.

They must have heard the car approaching. Either that or they had been sitting outside keeping a look out. When I had left, long before daylight, they had seemed genuinely pleased and excited about my family's arrival. Anyway, as the car pulled into our drive, I felt such pride that we had three servants and that for Mary housework and cooking would be a thing of the past. As we got out of the car, they stood to attention: Niangueso, our cook in his chef's white hat, who had a liking for pombe and who, a few months later, would be sacked for chasing the houseboy all round the garden with the meat cleaver while Mary and Eve and Clara screamed and screamed. Next to him was our cheerful young houseboy, Malinge, who would do all the cleaning and other domestic tasks. And finally our part-time gardener, Thomas.

'Jambo hanare.'

'Hello, how are you.'

A bow from each one. Big, eager smiles. How do they manage to have such excellent teeth, I wondered, not for the first time, when they only push a twig through them and don't know what toothpaste is? Their teeth were a darn sight better than mine. White teeth and jet-black skin. That day their faces were washed and shiny, but from the neck down they were as shabby as ever. They only seemed to have one set of clothes each – shorts and a shirt in the wrong sizes and always torn. No one mended anything for them.

I watched confused emotions flash across Mary's face, puzzlement then anxiety then astonishment. If looks could speak! She was sending me glances which said, 'OK, why didn't you tell me about this?' Of course she couldn't display her ignorance in front of everyone by admitting that it was all a complete surprise. At her side, Harry smiled in sympathy as she struggled to maintain her composure. Then he took his leave, just touching Mary's arm as if to reassure her that it was all going to be fine.

'I'll leave you to it. See you again soon,' he said quietly. 'And jolly good luck!'

'I hope so. And thank you for everything,' Mary replied.

After Harry had left and I had signalled to the servants to carry on with their work, we took a walk around the grounds, arm in arm.

'Why didn't tell you me we would have servants, David! Three servants!' she asked when out of earshot.

'I wanted it to be a surprise,' I smiled.

'I wish I had known… I'd have behaved more appropriately instead of gawping at them so rudely.'

'You weren't rude. They were just delighted to meet you and the girls.'

'But David…'

'It's wonderful, isn't it?' I interrupted. 'I don't even have to pay them. The army takes care of that. You've always hated housework, haven't you, and now you won't have to do any.'

Mary was quiet, staring at the ground, perhaps gathering her thoughts and catching up with so many new experiences.

'Do you remember our first lunch in Coopers…'

'Of course I remember.'

'…and how I almost dissuaded you from marrying me because I wanted to make sure you knew that I might not be able to offer you a high enough standard of living?'

'Why are you bringing this up now?'

'Oh, I'm just struck by the contrast between my expectations then and how things have turned out. I never thought then that one day I would be able to offer you a house like this. And three servants.'

'But David, I don't need three servants,' she said with her usual modesty. 'It's too many.'

Bless her. How little she knew about the way things worked out here. It was no big deal to have a cook and a houseboy.

'Most whites of my rank have more. It's what we are allocated. You just enjoy it,' I replied, still amused at her astonishment. 'I know we're privileged but that's the way it is.'

'But what will I do with myself?'

'Whatever you want. Have Eve and Clara all to yourself, as you wanted. Without grandparents to spoil them. You can do some sight-seeing. The officers' mess organises all kinds of trips and outings and there are coffee mornings, I believe, for officers' wives.'

Mary was biting her lip and fussing with a strand of hair that kept falling over her eyes. I had hoped she would show more delight – more gratitude – but she was oddly silent. I told myself to give her time. She was exhausted. She would be fine in the morning.

Mary would take to life in Nairobi like a fish to water, I thought to myself. She was born into the wrong social class.

My wife stood under the shade of the jacaranda tree with a puzzled look on her pretty face, trying to take it all in. Then she roamed the gardens and explored the house and veranda, exclaiming and commenting on it all, before she went off to wash and change. Later, wearing a pretty cotton frock I had not seen before, and seated in a wicker chair on the veranda while the girls ran wild around the garden, she still looked bemused. Malinge brought out two gin and tonics with ice and slices of lime, and a bowl of salted nuts and crisps.

'It's like being in a hotel,' she sighed.

'This is nothing, I assure you, compared with how the colonials live up in the hills. I'll drive you up into the Aberdare Mountains later on, when you have settled in, and show you the estates and farms. This is quite modest. Honestly.'

'But the servants, David... I'm still not sure...' she began again. 'I mean... won't they spoil our privacy?'

'Not at all. Don't worry. I know how you like your privacy.'

'Where do they sleep?'

'In their own quarters at the back of the house.'

'Them and us.'

I looked at her sharply. This tone of voice was something new and for a moment it worried me. Once again, I told myself to give her time. She had only just arrived.

As I keep telling Eve now, in those first few months we lived a life of luxury in Nairobi and I revelled in it. Very early in the morning, while Mary was still asleep but I was already awake, there would be a polite knock at the bedroom door and Malinge would bring in our tray of tea and biscuits. We rose early because I had to be at work by eight to get as much done as possible before the heat became too enervating. We stopped at twelve for lunch, and while more sedentary souls slept, I returned to the bungalow to eat and change, and then I was out on the cricket pitch until evening. Mary sometimes accompanied me, especially in the early days. Later, she preferred to go off on her own to explore the city, or took the girls to the market, or read under the mosquito net and the quiet hum of the fans.

I was a good and fair boss. Firm but friendly. Our three servants would do anything for us and we grew to trust them so much that on the occasional day when Mary was unable to meet the children from school herself at lunchtime, Malinge would go instead. Clara's kindergarten and Eve's primary school were very close together, both only a ten-minute walk from the bungalow. The three of them would walk slowly back, engrossed in conversation, sometimes stopping to examine a stone or a plant or an insect, a small white hand in each of Malinge's black ones. Other officers and their wives said we were foolish to trust a native to collect our children, particularly once the rumours began, but not once did it occur to me that our servants would do anything to abuse our kindness. In those innocent days I never imagined any harm could possibly come to any of us. We were immune.

Halcyon days. Mary and I were blessed with an easy life in a beautiful country. On my days off we would drive to Nakuru, sometimes in the company of Harry and Marjorie, where we ate five-course lunches at a palatial country club, waited on by dozens of native servants. Or Nivasha, where Eve and Clara stared mouths-agape at the flamingos, which would suddenly take flight as if a gun had been fired on the ground, hundreds soaring upwards, a spreading pink cloud in a bright blue sky. You can see in the photographs how carefree Mary is, tanned and smiling.

If only I could flip back the pages of the calendar and keep her there with the warm breeze lifting the hem of her pretty frock while she laughs and lifts her face to the sun.

*

'I was naive. Too kind. But that was your mother's influence,' my father says to himself, turning to me with eyes that look through me, and I don't want to interrupt his memories to ask for an explanation. He is miles away, lingering in his Nairobi garden. 'Our bungalow in Nairobi,' he says after a long pause. 'Of course, you won't remember it.'

Chapter 18

Nairobi 1952
Eve

Oh, but I do. I can still feel the burning boards of the wooden veranda beneath my bare feet and I remember that Clara and I were forever getting splinters that Mother pricked out with a fine sewing needle dipped in Dettol.

I am wearing a white sun-frock with smocking in navy blue stitching and a straw hat tied under my chin with white ribbons to keep the sun off. Red sandals with straps and buckles. It is lunchtime and Mother, Clara and I are walking home from school. It is a long way when you are thirsty. Noisy Nairobi. People everywhere bumping into me. Hot, dusty Nairobi. I want a drink. Wait, Eve, until we get home. I'm very thirsty. You have to wait. We turn from the road and walk along the dirt track with long blades of grass that tickle your bare legs. I can blow on a blade of grass and make a squeak. Clara can't, though she tries until her cheeks are bright pink. We walk past the gardens of other houses in our road. I like the dry dirt. Kick. Kick. I leave the toe of my sandal in the dirt and drag it along, making a little white line. Step and drag. My red sandal is scuffed and grey with dust. Stop it, Eve. Stop dragging your feet. You'll spoil your sandals. I drag my feet all along the path beside the fence, which is very high, shutting in our house, shutting in all the houses in our road. It is safe. No one can get in. Once we are alone I must remember to tell Clara we are safe from the lions because I know she worries. Once I told her the lions prowl at night close to the fence and she cried and clung to me in bed because she was so scared. It is easy to make Clara frightened and then I am sorry for teasing her. In the fence there is a gate for each house but we have to find the right one. Clara does not know which is her house. We have been in Africa for ages but she still doesn't know where she lives. I am six now. Clara is three. She is small for her age but I am tall. One bungalow. Another bungalow. Another bungalow with a veranda like ours. My bungalow has large cactus bushes near the fence, and through the gate our garden path sort of curves round past our rope swing made from a car tyre. Lots of big trees. I know which is my bungalow. I bend down and ask, Is this your house, Clara? She looks at me and I know she does not know and then she says, Tiny bit like. I look up at Mother and see her eyes creased at the corners, twinkly and smiley. We get to the next house and I ask the same question and Clara says, Tiny bit like again but her big grey eyes are filling with tears and I know soon she will cry. I could save her but I don't. She says Tiny bit like at our house too and Mother and I giggle and Clara's mouth turns upside-down and the tears spill and roll down her cheeks and Mother picks her up and kisses her and tells her not to cry because it is all right and one day soon when she is a bit bigger she will know which is her house. She must know in case she has to run away from something dangerous. Or someone dangerous. Mother says, Sorry, Darling to Clara and strokes her hair and wipes her tears with a white hanky and promises her a chocolate biscuit, but I am not sorry. Clara must learn where she lives or she might get lost one day. We are in Africa. She is not safe.

Clara is afraid of lions but I know that lions can't get into the garden to hurt us because I have walked all the way round looking for holes in the wire fence and there are none big enough for a lion, only the right size for a mouse. But black tribesmen might cut their way in. I haven't told Clara what I know because she would only have nightmares. I can be very quiet when I listen at the kitchen door. I hear Malinge and Niangueso talking. Niangueso says, Trouble ahead. Big trouble. He says, My people in the mountains very angry with white men. Want their land back. White men are bad. White men cruel. Lots of men go and oath. He asks Malinge, You go? and Malinge says, No. No go. No go and oath. He says, Memsaab good to me. Like Memsaab. They talk about oathing. Has to be, says Niangueso. Time is come. We are ready.

He means loathing – I know that word. Do the black people loath the white people?

We are not safe in Africa.

Chapter 19

Nairobi 1952
Mary

My heart did a double beat when we turned into the gravel drive and I saw the bungalow for the first time. It was a single-storey, timber-built building with a large, shady veranda. I could see sliding gauze doors from the veranda into the house, some of them open, letting in the air. The garden was large and untamed and I was grateful for that; a house like that needs a wild setting. I noticed on the way there the suburban rose gardens and little manicured plots that some white people had cultivated like a mark of national identity. Why uproot the succulents and oleander that belonged there? Why create a little England in the middle of Africa?

The sun sprinkled dancing light through the leaves of mature trees on to rust-red soil. A white curtain, caught by the breeze, waved out of an open window. Eve was off and running around the garden the minute the car came to a halt, and why stop her? Clara swayed beside me, looking through sleep-heavy eyes. Warmth stroked my bare arms, my bare legs, my face, until my forehead softened and I smiled to tell the house that I was happy to be there. I was reminded of Bangalore and Singapore. I have always been at home in a hot climate.

The servants were another matter altogether. David was all puffed up with pride as he introduced Malinge, Niangueso and Thomas, and had no idea what my raised eyebrows meant when I sent him warning signs that this was not a pleasant surprise at all and that he should have told me, or at least asked me, if I wanted to be in charge of three natives who would be constantly under my roof. That would have to wait, because the three men were so delightfully welcoming, and I could not bear to offend them. I could tell from the way they grinned at Eve and Clara that they were genuinely glad that a family had arrived to fill the spaces. It was my problem, not theirs. I couldn't bear the roles of master and servant, mistress and servant, with their assumed inequality. Heavens, I find it hard enough to sit in a restaurant while someone waits on me; I want to jump up and ask them to leave me to get my own meal because of the falseness and fawning and formality.

Of course, David couldn't understand any of this. The machinery that oils the army is rank and that oil lubricates each man's actions and those of his commanding officer. Now a captain, he took orders from those above and gave orders to those below. As an army officer's wife I was expected to slot into the same kind of hierarchy. But I knew all this before he said he wanted to rejoin the army after trying civilian life and finding it dull, so I just had to keep my mouth firmly shut. Sometimes I thought I had been absent without leave since the war ended, like the princess asleep in her castle, somewhere in a foreign country where I remembered men who endured terrible loss and pain and were grateful for the smallest act of kindness, men so traumatised by what they had seen and what they had done that their priorities were as re-shuffled as a dropped pack of cards. In that country, rank was meaningless; or rather, the ranking was different: there were the dead, the dying and the barely alive. There were those whose lives were forever changed by their injuries.

Why was I thinking about that now, my toes peeping from open sandals and already burning brown on red Kenyan soil? After six weeks on a ship travelling the ocean, I felt as if I had opened my eyes as you do after an anaesthetic, when you watch things gradually come back into focus. You watch the hands of the clock on the wall until you can read the time. I looked at the blurry green shapes to my left until they clarified into cactus plants with wickedly hurtful spines.

'Mummy… Mummy!' Eve pulled me back.

'Eve, stop tugging my arm. What is it?'

'There's a swing in the tree. A tyre. Can I play on it?'

'Yes, Eve. Take Clara. Off you go.' It will probably be two minutes before you fall off or push Clara off and she will come running back, weeping, with a cut head and you running ahead of her to insist it wasn't your fault.

'Be careful, Eve,' I called after her. 'Gently. OK?' My words evaporated, a drop of water on hot ground.

'The tyre was already here when I came,' David's tone was pedantic, as if he was lecturing to a room of foreigners. 'The house belongs to a wealthy Pakistani businessman who owns one of the printing presses in town. He lets it out to army families. There are no army quarters for married staff here. Unusual really. I thought we'd be starting army life together in barracks. I'd have preferred that. Everything tickety boo.'

I most certainly did not want to live in the stifling security and isolation of military barracks. 'It's lovely, David,' I said. They were only words and it cost me nothing to offer them.

'I'll say goodbye…' Harry murmured. He had been standing quietly in the background watching the proceedings, refraining from comment. 'You have plenty to do so I'll leave you to it.' Then he touched my bare arm. Just a touch. 'See you again soon, I hope.'

'Thank you for everything,' I replied, aware that my cheeks were flushed so that I had to look away. For heaven's sake! I admonished myself. You are thirty-two years old and blushing because a handsome chap puts his hand on your arm. It must be exhaustion. Or the heat.

Or these sudden restless flashes from the past. 'Goodbye. See you again,' I said.

For the first month I was busy with my new home where I could make my own decisions away from prying, disapproving maternal eyes. A weight was off my shoulders, so that I could shrug them again. The last five years under the family roof were best described by the words TUT TUT, written like that in capital letters. How my mother and I argued constantly over petty things, which in the end became a dozen elephants in our living room. Now I could have my potatoes as soft and fluffy and as extravagantly buttered as I wanted. I need never eat another apple pie for as long as I lived. I could leave the house without being halted: Where are you going? What time will you be back? And Eve was safe from being ground into the road under my father's motorbike and sidecar. What's more, I could take that daughter of mine in hand. Every time my back was turned, there was my mother slipping her sweets from a pocket in her pinny or encouraging her to dip her fingers into raw cake mix. There was my father leading her to the garage while I waited to see if she would emerge again with both hands and all ten fingers. Yes, I admit it. I was resentful that when I was a child I was deemed unworthy of their affection, yet their first, beloved granddaughter had them wrapped round her little fingers.

And yet… I was still not as free as I wanted to be.

'David…' I said tentatively one evening a few weeks later. He had come home from work bang on time, dropped his hat in the exact same spot on the hall table, handed his shoes and Sam Brown to Malinge to be polished, changed into civvies and settled himself with a whisky in his chair on the veranda while we waited for our evening meal.

'David… do we really need three servants?'

He looked at me with a raised eyebrow, as if I were a naughty child.

'I mean, there isn't enough for them to do, and I'd be quite happy to do more of the housework myself.' The truth was that I wanted to be alone. I wanted my privacy. If the penalty was housework, then fine, I'd take it. The other truth was that I was ill at ease being waited on by three native men who belonged there in Nairobi while I, a visitor fleetingly passing through their country, gave them orders.

'Why don't you just enjoy the luxury while we have it?' he said, predictably. The subtext was: I have worked hard to reach this position, to gain a commission, to become an army officer, and I am still climbing up the promotion ladder as far as I can go, away from the poverty of my childhood. 'Anyway, you'd never manage the garden. It's heavy work, men's work.'

'Yes, of course we need Thomas, and anyway he's only here three afternoons a week and I see very little of him. But we don't need a full-time cook and a full-time houseboy.'

'I don't know a single officer whose wife does her own cooking and cleaning out here.' He really was disappointed in me. I was not behaving like a captain's wife. I had not grown into my role.

'It's a luxury to have meals prepared… sometimes. But every day… four times a day… we don't need Malinge on duty at six in the morning, bringing us tea and getting our breakfast. How about asking him just to prepare the evening meal…'

'I think it's splendid!' David interrupted. 'We lie in bed listening to the birds and in comes Malinge with hot tea and biscuits! What's wrong with that?'

'It's an intrusion. It's not right.'

'What do you mean, "not right"? It is our right. All the officers have servants. You should see the staff which the settlers have… whole armies of servants.'

'So? That doesn't justify us having more than we need. I've heard quite enough about the way the settlers live in Happy Valley to make me wary of any example they set. I mean, Kenya once belonged to the tribes before colonialism, not those rich white men…'

'Mary, wake up! What century are you living in? That was a hundred years ago. The colonials have brought civilisation to a backward country. They have transformed Kenya. The natives are hopeless… ignorant and uneducated… they know nothing about modern farming methods…'

'That's one version of events.'

'So it would be fine if we had white servants?' He was twisting the conversation away from what I was trying to tell him. He was good at that.

'Better.'

'You're talking nonsense,' David answered. That was his stock reply if he disagreed with me. 'They are grateful that we employ them and treat them well. They need the jobs.'

'I suppose so. Perhaps.'

'What do you mean, "perhaps"? There's no perhaps about it.'

'But I feel awkward giving them orders. I was talking to Marjorie about it the other day. She, by the way, has one houseboy and does do some cooking herself, so that puts paid to your previous argument. I would have thought you knew that, knowing Harry so well.'

'I don't pry into his domestic arrangements.'

'Well, Marjorie said something that stuck in my mind… she said she tried to give him some dignity.'

'Then talk to her about it. She's been out here long enough and can tell you what you need to know. But Marjorie is no example for you. She is an artist, not just Harry's wife.'

By implication, I was just David's wife. Somehow the kernel of the debate was lost and my attempt to describe my discomfort around the native servants had slipped sideways into my inability to be a good army spouse who managed her servants with confidence.

It was a mistake to mention Marjorie. I didn't dare tell David that my first meeting with her in a cafe in town had not been a success and that I was worried that we did not have much in common. I wanted so much to like her because of David's friendship with Harry, but she talked with a cool intelligence about art and culture while I, out of my depth, lamely chatted about my children. I could see that she was trying to be kind but in the event our two monologues crossed the table and went their separate ways. Could I approach her for support or advice?

To be honest, I was a little bit afraid of her.

Chapter 20

Edinburgh 2005
Eve

When my mother died two years ago, my father was presented with a choice of two cities – Edinburgh or London. Myself as companion and carer, or my sister. A fellow football fanatic or someone to partner him in card games and Scrabble. A reluctant cook or an accomplished one. The daughter who leaves at 7 a.m. to catch the tube every morning to work in the city or the one who teaches part-time at the art college and spends hours on her own making glass panels. In our hearts neither Clara nor I expected him to survive long after the loss of our mother, and each of us believed that this mighty upheaval would lead to a transient, short and final phase in a long and active life. Still in Folkestone in those early, grief-soaked months, out of reach of conversation and unable to make the simplest of decisions, my father procrastinated while we phoned to check that he was still alive. In the end, the matter was decided of its own accord when a modern flat, very close to my own, came on the market. Still my father hesitated because without his wife, where he lived was of no consequence. In the end, we made the decision for him.

It was quickly arranged. Clara, as competent as ever, and secretly relieved that her filial duties would be fraught but short-lived rather than ongoing, stayed in Folkestone for a few days to sleep in Mother's recently vacated bed while she sorted things out. That I could not have done; the floor would have been preferable. After a lifetime of army postings, she reported back to me, our parents had precious little worth keeping, something that saddened each of us. My father requested only that his reclining chair should go with him, a chair which came with its own story of being spotted centre stage in a store window before the summer sales, queued for at dawn, and snapped up as my father hurled himself through the glass doors the minute they were opened. So he and the chair would travel to Edinburgh. He was, in effect, starting over again.

It was a warm autumn day but I was chilled to my bones as I walked across the zebra crossing and through the doors into the airport terminal. Still I shivered as, half an hour early, I waited for his plane to land. There were two of me standing at the arrivals gate, one waiting and one watching to see if the waiting one was behaving appropriately. What is appropriate, the frozen me asked the hovering me. There is no protocol for this. I am meeting my elderly father, who will arrive without my frail mother walking loved and protected at his side. Yes, I expected him to look pretty bad. Clara had warned me. No, I was not prepared for the bent old man who emerged in slow motion from the arrivals corridor hanging on to the arm of an air hostess who carried his bag. He came to a halt at my side. His face was grey, haggard, furrowed, and when I put my arms round him, tears from red raw eyes flowed silently down his cheeks to the foyer floor.

'I'll look after you now,' I said, shocked and shaken. Don't show it, the hovering one warned. I won't. I won't.

'I'm going to cry,' he said. But he already was crying.

'Then cry,' I replied. 'Why shouldn't you cry? You have every reason to.'

One year later, his stoicism and incredible physical strength have seen him through. From my window sometimes I catch a glimpse of him walking down my street to get his paper, marching to a sergeant's barking commands or a military tune scratched forever into his memory, the needle stuck in the long-playing record. Left, right. Left, right.

*

'Do you remember how you disgraced yourself when we went to lunch with Harry and Marjorie for the first time a few weeks after you had arrived in Nairobi?' my father asks, skipping the social niceties and settling himself into his usual chair.

Here we go. No hanging around. Straight into the next chapter. As I had predicted, the narrative of his army life occupies and preoccupies him. Several times a week he arrives full to bursting with words. We are seated side by side in my study, my father staring into space while he talks and me rattling away at the keyboard trying to keep up with him. My pieces of glass lie abandoned and dusty on the floor above because his story is absorbing so much of my time and energy.

'How could I forget? What a fuss you all made. It's one of those ghastly childhood incidents which stays with you forever. It probably did psychological damage for life,' I tease.

Because I can tease him now. I can look him in the eye and watch for the sparkle. From the age of thirteen he was a distant, authoritarian figure with whom I barely spoke more than a few predictable, censured words. 'Here's your mother', he would always say, if by chance he was the one to pick up the phone. Yet here I am in my fifties pushing back the boundaries bit by bit and forming – dare I say it – a good relationship with this man whom once I feared.

'Go on!' my father retorts, poking me in the ribs. 'Damaged for life! You had a wonderful life as a child.'

I neither agree nor disagree with him, but nudge him to continue instead. 'They didn't have any children, did they?'

'No,' my father replies, then goes silent. For a moment he looks confused and troubled. 'I never knew why. It's not something Harry and I ever talked about. I only know Marjorie was a very clever woman, first class degree in fine art from Glasgow University, obviously a very keen painter and of some reputation I believe, and always seemed perfectly content...'

'...and so never wanted children.' These days we often finish one another's sentences.

'No, that's not true. That's not what I was going to say,' he says. 'Harry once let slip that they had wanted children.'

'She certainly didn't like them!' I say. 'She was hopeless with us. Bossy and unsympathetic. I remember once she met us from school when Mother was unwell and she dragged us along the pavement much too fast, so poor Clara was tripping over her little feet, and Marjorie's mouth was set in a grim straight line. When I asked if we could stop to buy our sweets from the Pakistani shop near our road, like we always did, she said, "Certainly not!" and gripped my wrist as if she hated me.'

'Well...' my father says, again stuck for words. Unlike him. 'Maybe it was her way of coping... pretending she did not like children. Actually I don't think she did like you. I expect she thought you were spoilt and undisciplined.'

'I wasn't.'

'Let's say you were a bit of a handful sometimes. Rather wild. You certainly shamed us that day we went to lunch with them. Your mother cried when we got home... you won't remember... because she felt humiliated. Word always got round, you know.' He seems relieved to get off the topic of Marjorie's childlessness, quickly filling the silence with the anecdote he's been trying to get out since he arrived on my doorstep.

'Yes. Army quarters. Army barracks. Living in a fish bowl,' I retort.

'You had a wonderful childhood,' my father states. It is fact not opinion.

I choose not to reply. He has no idea what I really think on this subject, nor do I have any intention of filling him in at this late point in his life. I return to his story instead. 'Anyway, it was ridiculous. It was an accident. Two little girls being made to sit through a formal lunch with adults they didn't know!'

'Things were different in those days. Children were expected to behave themselves. It wasn't asking anything special of you, because we all took our children to lunch at the officers' mess and the country clubs.'

'Clara was only three then and I was, what... just six?'

'Old enough. Your behaviour that day made it very difficult for Mary and Marjorie to be friends. They were always strained with each other. Fortunately it made not the slightest difference to Harry and me.'

'They would never have been close friends anyway,' I say. 'You can't blame that on me. She was not Mother's sort. Too sharp and clever by half, I imagine.'

My father shrugs, then adds, 'They became very close friends later...'

His comment hangs in the air.

'Later? I didn't know that. When?'

'Later. Right at the end, when it mattered. When Mary needed her, Marjorie was wonderful...'

'When?' I repeat. This is news to me.

He does not reply. I have no idea what he is talking about. I leave him to his memories because I have been pulled into mine.

*

Mummy is unravelling like a ball of wool rolled across the floor. I think her nerves are frayed, that's what she says when I ask her what is the matter. Frayed. Afraid. I am putting on my white shoes as fast as I can. No, I can do it. Let me do it myself. Mummy, stop tugging my hair. I don't want a bow in it. She pulls my hair too hard and ties in a blue satin ribbon. My frock is blue and white gingham with lots of gathers across my chest. Smocking, that's the word. Smocking, smacking, shocking. Clara and I are in the back of the car. Stop wriggling, Eve. Sit still. I am wriggling because my dress is scratchy. Mummy is stiff in her seat like my frock, like someone starched her. Leave Clara alone, she nags. But my sister is on my half of the seat. There is an invisible line down the bench and you must NOT cross it. Not with even a finger. Move over, Clara. Stop sticking your elbow in me. Stay on your half of the seat, you bad girl. The hot red plastic seat sticks to the back of my legs so to get out of the car I have to peel myself off. Ouch. Will I leave my skin behind? Their houseboy answers the door. A red fez. Hello. You must be Eve. You must be Clara. Come inside. I don't like her. She uses a different, slower voice for children and another quick one when she talks to the adults. I want to take off my shoes and squiggle my toes in the white carpet. In our house we have wooden floors and lino. What ARE you doing, Eve? Put your shoe back on! I stare. Clara stares. There are paintings on the walls and carved statues of wild animals. There are pieces of glass. I want to touch them. Rough or smooth under my fingers? They are having drinks now and they are talking. They all sit on the edges of their chairs in case there are insects hidden down the cracks further back. Cockroaches. Snakes. Mummy's smile is not her real smile and her voice is too high. I think she is unhappy here too. Clara and I are sunk and stuck in white leather armchairs, our legs sticking straight out. I can't reach the floor. We have lemonade with ice in it. Sit still, Eve. I can't sit still. I can't touch the floor. I want to run around. Clara gets out of her chair and stands by Mummy. Baby! Spoilt baby. We are sitting round a table with a stiff white cloth. The thick napkins are rolled up with carved wooden rings on them. I slide the ring off and on. Off and on. Eve, says Mummy. It's her warning voice. Stop swinging your legs, Eve. Behave, my father growls. I hate that word. I hate it when he says that. That one word

means a lot more than a whole sentence of words. I don't like Auntie
Marjorie, as I have been told to call her. She is not my auntie and if
you touched her she would be hard and icy. Here she comes with a
big silver bowl and a ladle. It's tomato soup. You like tomato soup,
Mummy says. I don't like tomato soup, Clara says. Just eat a little.
Mummy aims a spoonful at Clara's mouth but she turns her head
away. Mummy sighs. It is not comfortable sitting here because they
are stiff as sticks and everyone is on their best behaviour. Maybe
that's what Daddy means, that I'm not on mine. Oh Eve! OH. OH.
I have spilt tomato-red soup on the white cloth and my dish is upside-
down. A big red stain on the white cloth. Tomato-red soup dripping
blood on the white carpet. It's all right, says Auntie Marjorie, but
she is telling a lie. She runs quick quick quick in her high heels and
comes back with wet cloths. Mummy has jumped up too. They dab
at the carpet. Auntie Marjorie pulls everything off the table, Daddy
and Uncle Harry are helping her, and then she whisks the cloth away
and fetches another one. The soup is cold. I can't remember the rest
of the meal. I go away inside my head. No one speaks to me. When
we leave that house Mummy slaps me on the legs and says, You are a
naughty, naughty girl. Daddy says, Steady on, Mary. I am sent to my
bedroom when we get home. I can hear Mummy crying.

*

My father leans back in his chair.

'Coffee?' I offer.

'Yes please,' he says with a wink because it is a joke between us,
the fact that only I can make his coffee as hot and as frothy and as
sweet as he likes it. It takes a coffee machine, a microwave, a pan
and a milk-frothing gadget to achieve the exact temperature and
consistency, all of course hidden away in the kitchen so he thinks
I just do it like magic. Or does he?

'Better get started,' he says, as he takes a sip from his mug and
signals that I have got his drink just right again. 'Where was I?'

'Well, you've been telling the story about lunch with Harry and Marjorie, but you haven't got us back to the bungalow after our journey from Mombassa yet!' I tease.

'Jumped the gun. Doesn't matter,' he says.

Chapter 21

Nairobi 1952
Mary

It wasn't exactly an ordeal – lunch with Harry and Marjorie. So why was I on edge? Perhaps because Marjorie and I had not talked easily when we had first met. Perhaps because this was my first formal social engagement as an army wife and I was uncomfortable in that skin. Perhaps it would grow to fit me, but I doubted it. It would always be too tight or too loose. I am not good at roles or rules. 'Please, Eve, please,' I begged, 'be helpful and put on your socks and shoes' (she could manage this perfectly well but today chose not to), and when I gathered up a bunch of her silky blonde hair to tie a bow in it, the ribbon took on a slippery life of its own and I had to tie the knot really tight, hurting her. Meanwhile Clara had vanished. David was pacing up and down the hall. We are coming, truly we are. Yes, I know we are late. Where is Clara? David, please look in the garden for Clara. Where? – under the biggest cactus probably. Come on, Eve. Don't you dare try and pull that ribbon out!

Of course I had bumped into Harry a couple of times at the barracks or in the cricket club, and each time he had been impeccably polite, and so had I. We knew how to conduct ourselves. Army life, as I was quickly learning, had rules to cover every occasion and eventuality, and these I was doing my best to grasp. Smile sweetly to those of higher rank and say nothing that will ruffle their value system or their sense of superiority. I could manage that. Be cool with those of lower rank and maintain an adequate distance. Harder. And with the natives, be haughty and bossy and wear your thickest mask so that you give nothing away. Hardest of all. I wasn't at all sure I liked these games, but I had to play them, or David would not advance in his career. An army wife must never be a liability. Going to lunch with one's husband's superior and his wife (Harry was a colonel, one rank above David) no doubt involved some subtle combination of respect and friendliness, but damn it, Eve was squirming about on the back seat on the car, digging her sharp little elbow into her sister's soft flesh, and if anyone were to disgrace herself this afternoon I'd lay wagers as to which of the three of us it would be.

The front door opened and I was immediately put in my place because Marjorie's houseboy sported a red fez. Make a mental note – get a similar one for Malinge. Fortunately I had offended very few people with our servant's lack of appropriate headgear since the visiting and entertaining had not yet begun. Because I was new to the army and new to Africa, I had had a stay of execution.

It took about ten seconds for me to do a recce of the Frames' abode and to realise that I had entered a foreign world – excuse the pun. For a start there was the white carpet. No one with children who are not tied up or caged would commit themselves to such a hostage to sanity. Second, there were the objects. Glass, sculpture, wood carvings and original paintings adorned this home, some actually on plinths, each one asking for little racing feet and flapping hands to bump into them and knock them over. The lounge and hall were a bit like a museum, and I was going to have to say 'Don't touch' about a hundred times in one afternoon. I had long ago put away my very few valuable possessions because each one of them was an accident waiting to happen. Third, and this I admit took a few more minutes to establish, Marjorie did not seem to like children, nor did she know how to deal with them. Eve and Clara picked up the patronising note in her voice immediately, and noticed the woman's nervousness around them, which made me nervous, which made them nervous. Just talk to them as you would to anyone else, I wanted to say, and please stop sounding like Joyce Grenfell.

Since I had already gathered from my first meeting with Marjorie that we had little in common, I wondered what on earth we could talk about. She was clever, as in clever clogs, clever dick, but not warm and not very sensitive. While I am someone who trusts my instinct and intuition, everything she did struck me as a conscious act. We got off to a bad start because I was waiting for something dreadful to happen, and of course it did.

If you have ever walked on egg shells trying not to crush them with your great big feet, you will have some idea of what lunch was like. David was the only one who seemed truly oblivious of the vibes in that room as Marjorie and I awkwardly sipped our drinks and made several abortive attempts to talk about Nairobi. My mouth was shaped in a rictus of a smile while my eyes and ears were totally distracted watching the children, especially Eve, so no doubt I appeared a complete moron as I nodded and grinned in all the wrong places while hissing at Eve to keep still, stop wriggling, stop edging towards a large and beautiful bowl balanced on a very small and precarious table. Yes, I know the colours are seductive and it is shiny and bright, but don't you dare touch it. Harry looked at me a couple of times with what I interpreted as kindness, and asked a few innocuous questions about settling in. And Eve, a sponge when it came to picking up atmosphere, responded by spinning out of control because she was not at ease with these people.

When Marjorie left the room with us all seated like marionettes around a table covered with a starched white cloth and rolled white napkins, drinking gin and tonic from fine-stemmed vessels of cut glass (the girls were given green plastic beakers), and returned carrying an enormous silver tureen, my heart gave a bit of a shudder. At home I gave the girls their meals ready on their plates, obviously a left-over from my working class origins. When she ladled tomato soup out of the tureen (it was out of tins and reheated by the fez-wearing servant, by the way) into fragile little dishes, I knew we were doomed. Minutes later, Eve jumped up like a Jack-in-the-box, noticing something that caught her attention, and the soup dripped its orange stain deep into Marjorie's white carpet. After the mopping and the repeated 'It doesn't matter one bit,' said between gritted teeth, we made a heroic attempt to resume our meal, and our conversation. Despite trying to mobilise it, my face had set in a concrete mask, rendering muscle movement impossible. My eyes stared out as startled as a rabbit's caught in the glare of headlights, while my mouth made talking and smiling movements. I don't think I heard one word of what was exchanged.

I cried on the way home because I had let David down, because my children were not brought up properly and did not know how to conduct themselves in company, because I had been hoping in vain that I would find a friend in Marjorie, and, dare I admit it, because I had made a fool of myself in front of Harry. Poor Eve bore the brunt of my shame and humiliation. I should not have shouted at her. I should not have smacked her. My poor Eve. It was not her fault.

Chapter 22

Nairobi 1952
David

Watching Mary during those first weeks in Nairobi was like watching a flower open its petals to the morning sun. Her skin turned golden brown, her hair was full of pale streaks, and her expression relaxed and softened. I was delighted to have her back at my side where she belonged. This place suited her. She was meant to be here.

My girls were thriving too. Eve, who had worried me because she was pale and delicate, always asthmatic and poorly with colds, grew strong and robust. I watched her running around outside in the fresh air. Her skinny legs were finally putting on a bit of muscle and I dared hope that she might make an athlete yet. That would make me proud. Clara sat and talked to herself and ate soil; although Mary tried everything from bribes to scoldings to dissuade her, there she would sit staring into space in a corner of the garden licking dusty fingers after digging them into the ground, a diet of red dust apparently necessary for her childish dreams. But when she developed neither typhoid nor diphtheria nor polio we left her to it and to this day her immune system is healthy. 'Useless daughters,' I sometimes said to Mary, mostly in jest. 'Can't play soccer. Can't play cricket. I wanted boys. Why didn't you supply me with boys? A whole football team would have been perfect.'

And me? Well, I was in my element, even before Mary arrived. I was happier than I'd been since my war years – at ease amongst my men, especially the NCOs, happy in uniform, glad to be outdoors or driving around much of the time, and overjoyed of course to have so many opportunities to play cricket and golf. This life suited me down to the ground.

The only thing that occasionally troubled me was a sense of inferiority. OK, I didn't perhaps look born to lead as the other officers did, but was there any need to make a point of letting me know it? Was my own very different background really leaking through my khaki uniform and leaving a visible stain? They had such confidence and arrogance, those other young officers who had followed the traditional Eton–Sandhurst route into the army, the sons of landed gentry, many of them following their own illustrious and high-ranking fathers into the same profession. They felt superior. They knew how to command; it was wired in. They had a swagger which I would never acquire, and drawling, barking voices, while mine, if I were not careful, spoke of my Liverpudlian origins. So I had some covering up to do, some rubbing out of an upbringing that did me no good out here. It wasn't that I was ashamed of my past but I felt I had to compensate for it to prove myself their equal, or more than their equal, because of my modest beginnings. It was a matter of pride.

*

I warned Mary to keep quiet about my employment between the war years in Libya and this posting to Nairobi because there's not much kudos in being a teacher in a small village school. I was bored. I was restless. We could not afford a home of our own so we lived with Mary's parents – a splendid house with a large garden but oh how we suffered from a lack of privacy and independence. Maud and Mary argued incessantly. Their bickering over trivial nonsense drove me mad. I would hear the raised voices contradicting each other about the number of minutes it took to boil potatoes or whether butter or margarine was better for shortcrust pastry. One day I overheard them bitching about the lamb chops – something about how much fat to trim off – and I understood that two women in a kitchen is one too many. Village life was closing in on us too, the gossip and the smallness, the strain of being friendly to everyone, and all that stopping in the road to politely and pointlessly pass the time of day. It's true about the twitching of the lace curtains. Everyone knew us and we knew everyone. Mary and I felt trapped.

As for Eve, well, in her grandfather's eyes she could do no wrong. 'You are my flaxen-haired fairy,' he would tell her. 'Hair like spun gold. You are the apple of my eye.' No wonder my elder daughter was turning into a spoilt little madam, with poor little Clara living in her shadow. Mary and I wanted our daughters to ourselves. After four years of village life with my in-laws I was like a caged tiger. I was sick of routine and full of resentment and pent-up energy. I yearned to get back into the army.

'I want to apply for a commission,' I told her. 'To be an army officer. I think I have it in me. I want to work with a regiment of men again, be part of a team, like I did in the war, and having been asked to sort out the mess left by some useless officers… well, I think I could do the job better. Of course, some of them were superb leaders, but others hadn't a clue how to communicate with the men. I understand those men and their backgrounds. I think I can do a good job as a commanding officer.'

'Then do it,' she said, and I was grateful.

'I suppose the war changed all of us.'

'I know.'

'I can't wait to get back to that hard exercise and discipline. I'm a fit man, Mary, and I feel useless here.'

'You're not useless. You contribute a lot with the lads, training them and playing football. But I can see that it doesn't satisfy you. You are restless, David.'

'Is it that obvious?'

'Yes.'

'You don't mind being uprooted?'

'I want to be uprooted.'

'You don't mind leaving all of this…'

'There is nothing to mind. Nothing to miss.'

We walked together, arm in arm, to slip the letter into the postbox at the bottom of the lane. Mary was all nerves, her hand trembling as she took the letter from me and slipped it into the box. I hadn't realised how much she too needed to escape.

'Good luck!' Mary seemed a bit out of control. Verging on the hysterical. But then I was offering her the chance of a completely different life. 'Fingers crossed. Touch wood.' She picked up a twig and stroked it.

'Where might we be posted?' she asked.

'Could be anywhere,' I replied. 'Cyprus, Aldershot, Germany, Malta.'

'I hope it's somewhere warm. I want blue skies and sunshine. And the girls… what a way to grow up… a different place every two years.'

'I can't wait to get them away from here.'

'There's not much for them here,' she agreed. 'It's stifling.'

On that issue, we were absolutely in accord.

Chapter 23

DORSET 1950
EVE

Ragwort is like its name, raggedy with tiny yellow flowers. Old Man's Beard is soft and tassled. I run my thumb and fingers up and down the silky threads hanging from the stalk. Ragged Robin is tall with bright pink flowers. We snap off stems of Ragged Robin until we have a fistful each to take home and put in the yellow vase. In and out of the shade and the sunshine along the grass verge. Nice and slow. Granny never rushes me. Lady's Mantle. Dock leaves that you rub on your skin after stinging nettles. We pick dandelion leaves and pretend we have stings. The leaves become slimy as you roll them, and cool. Forget-me-nots. Primroses. She is plump and round and wears a flowered pinny and makes apple pies because Grandpa loves them. One magpie is unlucky. Don't walk under a ladder. A black cat crossing our path is good luck. Never, never catch a glimpse of a new moon through glass or you have bad luck for a month.

Nearly home again. Back down the lane. C-lip c-lop behind us. Penny pulling the cart with our milk in metal churns. I give Penny half an apple from my pocket. Penny's brown velvet nose. Stroke it. Rub it. Rubbery lips, so soft, but green slime all over the bit. She is crunching down on the metal in her mouth. It hurts her. Take her bit away and let her eat her apple. Granny fetches the blue jug and a cup. Four pints every day in the jug and warm milk in the cup for me. I hate warm milk. Makes me gag. Milk's good for you, Granny says, but she is not cross like Mummy is when I don't drink it. You'll never get plump if you don't drink your milk, she says. Carrots help you see in the dark. Don't ever ever catch a glimpse of a new moon through glass. Once a month, Granny and I sneak out of the house at night with our hands over our eyes just in case we catch a glimpse through the window. In the garden we scan the sky, searching, searching for the new moon. Hard to find when there is cloud. If one of us sees the little silver sliver we both shout in triumph. A whole month of good luck and nothing will harm us.

Granny's hair was once her crowning glory, she tells me. When she was young it was thick and glossy and auburn with waves and curls that shone in the sun. She misses her young hair because now it's a thin grey plait wrapped round her head and held in place with two tortoiseshell combs. In the evenings, she lets me take out her bobby pins so that I can unravel the three strands of the plait and brush her hair. I pull the comb through it, sometimes making a bun, sometimes re-plaiting it, sometimes just playing with her long long hair while she sits still at her dressing table and tells me about when she was young.

Grandpa has a motorcycle with a sidecar. Mummy says he's too old. Let me come for a ride, Grandpa. No. Your mother says I'm not allowed to take you. Please. Please. Come on then, apple of my eye. Slither thee down into the sidecar, into the leather seat and hold tight on to the little handle. I'm flat in here, almost on the road. Hold on tight. Fast. Faster. He roars away down our lane wearing his sheepskin and leather hat with the flaps over his ears. I am riding in the sidecar at last. The vibrations start in my feet and purr up my legs and into my bottom. The hedges are blurred, the noise in my ears is a roaring animal sprinting alongside us. I look up and see Grandpa's black gloves on the handlebars and his goggles over his eyes, his black scarf flying behind us like ribbons. We tip sideways round the corners. I am pressed against the cold side of the car but I am not afraid.

Oh. Later. Angry loud voices in the kitchen. Mummy is shouting in a high voice. Grandpa is barking back. She's perfectly safe with me. You could have killed her. I have told you never never take her with you. Stop your fretting, woman. You're over-protective with that girl. She's only four years old for heaven's sake. You could have had an accident. You know you are too old to ride that thing. Stop your noise, woman. She's my child. You won't get another chance to risk her life. It's time we got away. It's time. We are leaving. We are going far away. Going. Away.

Clara is sitting in the garden chewing soil and singing. How can she do that when her mouth is gummed with dirt? She picks out a worm and stares it in the eye. Do worms have eyes? She spits out the gravel and the stones. I am picking raspberries with Granny. My mouth is all stained purple but Granny says it doesn't matter. My toes are dirty because I am not wearing shoes. You can help me make the pastry for a raspberry and apple pie. Cut the apple peel in one long green curling piece and throw it over your left shoulder. When it falls on the floor it makes the shape of the first letter of the name of the man you will marry. I will marry someone beginning with S. Last time it was N. Granny's pinny is faded and flowery over her round tummy, straps criss-crossed at the back and tied in a bow. At the kitchen table we squash little blobs of margarine, squeeze them into the soft white flour, make lumps until our fingers are crusted. Then cold water. Knead with knuckles then press and push fingers in and make a ball, roll with the rolling pin, and into the pie tin. Apple tart. Tart apples make your mouth pucker.

Bird's legs, Granny says. She used to have skinny legs like me. My socks fall down all the time when I walk and run, horrid when they slide into my shoes and make lumps to walk on. Olive oil will fatten my legs, Granny says, rubbing my calves while I lie face down on her bed. Old pink eiderdown which puffs feathers into the air and makes my breathing tubes go tight. When I am older, a doctor will tell me I have asthma. Granny's bed is made of violets. Not really, but there are little bags of faded flowers under her pillow which smell dry-sweet.

When we go to market Granny spends some of her housekeeping money on plants but don't tell anyone, she whispers, it's our secret, little pots of pretty-faced violets hidden in a brown paper bag with soil at the bottom so that they do not die. We catch the bus home. Quick, into the flower beds and no one will notice. I know they are there. Mummy doesn't have green fingers. Mine are getting greener.

Mummy and Daddy are going away for the day. A new hat with a bunch of cherries and one hard green leaf is out of its tissue paper and on to Mummy's head, and new gloves, and new silky stockings with lines up the back and shiny high-heeled shoes. Mummy looks so pretty. Where are you going? Aldershot. Why? Daddy has an interview for a new job.

Where's Aldershot? I don't want Daddy to have a new job. Next year I'm going to school here, the same school where he is a teacher. We will walk to school together and Granny will meet me in the afternoons when Daddy stays behind to play football or cricket with the boys.

I have lived here in this house since Clara was born. I never want to go anywhere else.

Chapter 24

ALDERSHOT 1951
DAVID

I'm not the sort of chap who notices what his wife is wearing. Men don't, do they? Yet I remember the hat she wore the day we took the train to Aldershot for my commission interview, not her usual style at all, in fact quite a cheeky hat with a bunch of red cherries. I had never seen it before. I teased her a bit and called her Cherry Ripe, mainly to make her smile and put her in a good mood ready to meet the colonel.

There had been a bit of a row in the kitchen the previous day because Robert had hauled his motorbike out of the garage and taken Eve for a ride down the country lanes, our precious little girl in the sidecar. Afterwards, Mary had lashed out at her father. I don't think it was quite as bad as she made out but maternal anxiety is a powerful brew and Robert, in his seventies, was becoming accident-prone. Not long ago he came off his bike taking a corner too fast and broke a few fingers. Could have been much worse. This time Eve was unharmed but we made it clear that he must not take her again, and of course if today goes well, the situation won't arise. Problem solved.

It was a cheerful journey. I was in a confident mood and Mary was quietly excited. When we arrived at Headquarters, she waited on a hard chair in a corridor while the duty sergeant showed me into an empty room. There I sat, back straight, shoulders back, staring out of the window. Ten minutes passed. Not what one expects in the army. Punctuality is everything. Was this the right place? Where was the colonel who was going to interview me?

Then in he charged, sweating profusely and dressed in tennis shorts.

'Hope you don't mind,' he said, chucking his racquet in the corner.

I said, 'I don't mind,' presuming he referred to the unconventional attire.

He said, 'Are you a sportsman?'

I said, 'I play a bit of cricket. Due to play in a benefit match tomorrow, Sir, against a full Somerset side. Four English players, Willard, Tremlett, Redpath and...'

'Batsman or bowler?' he interrupted.

'A bit of an all-rounder, Sir. I make a few runs, I take a few wickets and I catch a few balls.'

'Excellent. Well done.'

After that the interview went very well indeed. We talked a lot of sport, especially cricket. I had heard all about the colonel from others and felt enormous respect for him. He had suffered at the hands of the Japanese and been tortured in a prison camp. Of course he never mentioned his injuries but I had heard that he was in constant pain – yes, even (or perhaps especially) when he played cricket.

Over lunch in the canteen he chatted to Mary about her Red Cross training when the war broke out and after I had left for Libya. He listened intently and sympathetically as she told him about her subsequent posting to Edinburgh, where she worked as a nurse, meeting the wounded straight from Dunkirk. She told him how later she had been posted to Singapore, where she had accompanied the injured and shell-shocked Australian troops back to Brisbane. She told him about going ashore with those wounded men on stretchers and on crutches. Men who had lost their sight or their hearing. Men who were half-mad with what they had seen. She stayed with them until they were sufficiently recovered to leave the nursing home. Probably the colonel identified with those young men; he nodded his head and leant in to listen as if he knew what they had gone through. I was a bit surprised to hear my Mary talking so confidently and obviously making a good impression on such a senior officer. She was almost a different woman from the one I knew.

It puzzled me that she didn't want to talk about that period of her life. It was as if she had filed it away in a safe and thrown away the key. Perhaps it was too painful. I learnt more that day over lunch as the two of them talked together, and I admit I felt a twinge of jealousy that she confided in him in a way she had never done with me. She never told me how she coped with those torn and mutilated men. How was she able to touch their disfigured faces and bodies? What did she talk to them about? How did she comfort them?

'Well done,' the colonel said, 'for sticking by them. I bet you did a grand job and were a wonderful comfort to them.'

She demurred, turning the subject adeptly away from herself and back to the courage of the men, telling him how she had watched them learning to walk again with artificial limbs, to get around without sight.

'They were so brave,' she said. 'And so very young. Most of them persevered with their terrible disabilities until the medical corps declared them fit to re-enter civilian life. Some never recovered. What they had seen and suffered would never fade. Many remained shell-shocked.'

I can't quite square Mary's wartime experiences with what I know of her. My Mary, modest and gentle, nevertheless coped, and by all accounts coped superbly, with men who were brutalised and damaged. Other women, and men too, would have been too upset to go near them. There was a steely core buried deep within that slim, willowy frame, out of sight, hidden behind her pleasant manner and her kind, unobtrusive way with others.

Those years remained forever hidden from me. For each of us they were some of the most vivid and significant years of our lives, but because they could not be shared, they remained invisible and private. I have few clues to help me picture her and imagine her life, just as she could only reconstruct, from my stories and from the photographs I brought back from the desert, my six years in the 8th Army in Libya.

We went our separate ways during the war years and perhaps our experiences changed us more than we acknowledged. We parted and it was not smooth coming together again. After several years, it still felt as if we were trying too hard to re-enter civilian life and the relationship we began when we were so young.

Chapter 25

EDINBURGH 2005
EVE

It's beginning to worry me that my father's narrative reads like a Karen Blixen memoir about the last golden age of colonialism. He's painting this romantic picture of benevolent white farmers with willing natives tilling the red soil of Kiambu and Nyeri while the army chaps play cricket in the sun and teach African children how to count to ten. Of course it's his story and I have no right to interfere. If this is how he remembers it, so be it. And yet…

…he misses out so much. Why is there no acknowledgment of the increasingly harrowing plight of the Kikuyu people and their long battle to reclaim their land and their livelihood? Should he not just mention in passing that by 1940 one in every eight Kikuyu had been forced to work as a tenant labourer on land that had once been their own? The squatters, as they were called, worked from dawn to dusk for a pittance while thousands of others were banished to reserves in the west where the land was too barren to offer them a living. For the young men this meant the severing of their independence. Normally after adolescence they would move to their own shamba, then marry and become independent of the previous generation. There were not now enough patches of land for them to claim their own. Did my father know that 60,000 acres of land in the most fertile central belt was owned and occupied by whites?

When my father arrived on that quayside in Mombassa to meet my mother, surely he was aware that in the mountains above Nairobi, the Kikuyu were gathering to plan their desperate and doomed revolt against the whites because our laws and our government had made their lives untenable. They were oppressed, dispossessed and land-hungry.

Perhaps I am being too hard on him. This different perspective has emerged fairly recently and so my father would not have been party to anything other than the official version of events – how the vicious and barbaric Mau Mau were planning to rise up against a benevolent, paternal white government. Decades later, Clara and I dug out accounts that clashed with all that we had been told. We became absorbed and haunted by the place in which we had lived briefly as outsiders. Of course we were only children in Nairobi, and I know not to trust my own filtered memories, but round our dinner table, talk was limited to the domestic, the trivial, the inconsequential happenings and the latest cricket scores. Nor is the real story missing only from Nairobi. Looking back now on our army postings to Kenya and Libya, Malta and Cyprus, Germany and Gibraltar, I see lost opportunities to observe and to understand people and cultures that were different from ours. Why did my parents take so little interest in the countries in which we were sojourners?

My father's answer now is that it was none of our business, certainly none of his business. You don't join the army to dabble in the politics of the countries in which you are stationed. You don't try to be absorbed into a foreign culture. You have a job to do and you get on with it. If you are an army officer, an army wife, an army child, your duty is to exist within the bubble of the barracks and not to question what goes on outside. And so we did. In army cars driven by army drivers, we would halt at the red-and-white-striped barrier where the soldier in the hut saluted my father and lifted the bar. Out we went, like tourists venturing out to stare for a few hours at a different place. We went to safe places. Tourist places. Hotels and restaurants and shops where the British were known and welcomed. Then we returned to the safety of the enclosure where the striped barrier closed behind us.

Am I being unfair? I am exaggerating to some extent. The countries were obviously distinct and my sister and I took away memories of the dust and beauty and animals of a Kenyan National Park, the white sand and palm trees of a Tripoli beach, the barbed wire and sandbags which divided the Greek and Turkish areas in Cyprus. And yet… the very English way we lived meant that each of my twenty-seven homes belonged securely in a little British oasis, a mirage of life back in the UK.

I remember the brutality of barracks, the acres of concrete, the men in uniform, the colour khaki. I was sent to seventeen schools, never mind if the choice of subjects changed with every one or if the language of the teaching was foreign. I remember in Tripoli, Clara and I were taught in Italian by nuns and from the first day to the last, I understood nothing. I remember all of us singing Italian songs when, on Friday afternoons, our coach left for the beach, waving off our mothers, each child in a white cotton cap to protect us from the sun. We sat in a circle in the sand under a palm-roofed shelter, confined to the shade. There were exchanges between the nuns and the children. Perhaps questions and answers, perhaps stories or nursery rhymes. I don't know. I will never know. At tea-time we bit into salami-filled crunchy baguettes and slid our tongues around soft sweet cakes. We had beakers of warm orange squash. Then finally we were released. As if a starting gun had gone off, we raced from the cool shelter to the sun-scorched beach, our feet skimming over the red-hot grains of fine white sand. We were allowed twenty minutes of splashing and swimming in the sparkly sea that for hours we had watched with longing. I remember sitting at the edge of the sea while the gentle shallow waves broke over my legs and washed the sand and stickiness from my body. I lay down to savour the salt water sliding over my face and soaking my hair. I remember running along the shoreline, kicking and splashing with feverish freedom until the nuns shouted me back and chastised me.

For my mother, it was a case of moving from one married quarter to another, unpacking our trunks, getting directions to the Naafi and the library, and settling down to a routine that was not all that different from the one in our previous posting a thousand miles away. During their later postings, after Clara and I had left home, our parents gave up unpacking the trunks, so that when my mother died, Clara and I found buried in yellowed newspaper folded saris from India, lace tablecloths from Cyprus and carved wooden animals from Kenya. Tourists' trinkets.

Each time we arrived in a new country we females spent the first day with the quartermaster going through the inventory of the furniture and crockery and cutlery and sheets in the standard-issue house or flat with its standard-issue buff-painted walls on which army children must not put up posters or pictures in case they scratch or mark the surface. Knives, fish, six. Forks, fish, six. Tureen, soup, medium, one. Tureen, soup, large, one. I wonder why my mother never felt the need to make the house more her own, as some army wives did by shipping across bits of furniture and buying lamps, even putting away the drinking glasses, plain, one dozen, in favour of something that was their own. I suppose Father, being a skinflint, would never have opened his wallet to pay for fripperies to decorate a house. The combination of Mother's acceptance of her surroundings and Father's indifference to them meant that Clara and I existed for our entire childhood in houses, flats and bungalows which were more or less identical. Beyond their hedges and gates there would be the Naafi where we went shopping, the army church with its army padre for births, weddings and deaths, the army library, the children's playground in the middle of the barracks, and always the lines of expressionless soldiers in khaki berets marching, marching, marching, or running in the heat with backpacks while the sweat soaked through their shirts and ran down their faces. If we came across a stray one who had somehow lost his parade he would snap his hard boots together, salute my father and shout Sir!

Remember I am thinking back over twelve years of moving on. My life was measured in three-year spans and I thought of my growing up in terms of being aged five, eight, eleven, fourteen. Only at seventeen did I break the pattern when I escaped the three-year globe-turning by heading back to the UK and Glasgow School of Art. A four-year posting, not three. Sometimes in my memories places become jumbled, like our three different postings in post-war, re-built Germany, all in the space of three years. Clara, I ask sometimes, was it in Hanover or Bielefeld that we had a flat next to the army veterans' hospital where I became traumatised by the missing limbs and burnt faces? Where I lay face down in the sand of the Blau See because I could not look at the man at the water's edge pointing with just a stump?

But I must not give the impression that all places had the same significance. Africa was special. The point I am trying to make is that we never really got under its skin.

Chapter 26

Nairobi 1952
Mary

My husband had become morose. Instead of bouncing in each evening full of the day's events, he returned in a foul mood and after dinner lay flat on his bed watching the wooden blades of the fan go round. Maybe he was thinking. If he was, he disclosed none of his meditations to me. More likely sulking, I suspected. The girls stayed well out of his way. Even Eve gave up after a few failed attempts to penetrate his smouldering bad temper. 'Go away and leave me alone,' he snapped at her. Clara knew better than to try.

'Whatever is the matter, David?' I asked after a long and tedious succession of these evenings in which he seemed to be punishing someone. Maybe me.

'You know what's the matter,' he snarled.

'I'm only asking.'

'The bloody job. What else?'

'But brooding doesn't help.'

'I'm angry.'

'OK, you're angry, but this helps no one. You're making us all miserable.'

'You'd be angry if you had to sit in an office all day shuffling papers.'

Well maybe, but I wouldn't take it out on everyone else. 'Are there no compensations?'

'For God's sake, Mary. For eight months I've been driven around the countryside by my sergeant, dropping in on the units where we teach English to the black soldiers in the East African Rifles and inspecting the schools for the Askari children, and now I'm stuck behind a desk.'

I put a hand on his arm. 'What was it you loved so much?'

His voice softened. 'White toothy smiles in black faces. Their appreciation. The discipline. My freedom. The children chanting "Umbile mara tatu ninane". "Twice one is two." Very rewarding work, I can tell you.'

'Mmm,' I muttered in encouragement.

'And being with my men. My troops.'

'Why the sudden change?'

'Panic, nothing else. A bit of trouble up in the Aberdare Mountains and the colonel decides we need a garrison to monitor the situation. Damn idiot. You'd think there was a bloody war on. It's nothing.'

'But why you?'

'I just happen to be the only chap with a Signals and education background.'

'So what's coming through? Is it serious?'

'Nothing's coming through. A few tedious reports and nothing remotely serious. There have been a couple of attacks by a few natives up in the mountains and they set up a garrison. I haven't enough work to occupy two hours a day. I do the crossword. I stare out of the window. I have coffee with Harry. Damn it, I joined the army for some action and I'm being paid a handsome salary to run up and down the cricket pitch because I haven't any other way of occupying my afternoons.'

Yes, he had his cricket. Every afternoon, the other David, the one who was full of bonhomie and team spirit, strode out on to the cricket pitch to cheers from the men watching. Given how much energy he put into every single toss of the ball and swipe of his bat, I was surprised his frustration had not dissipated.

It was all the same to me. I had been in Nairobi for two months and my thoughts too were elsewhere those days, although, unlike David, I tried to disguise my mental and emotional absence. One day soon after we had lunch with the Frames, I was quietly reading in my deckchair to one side of the pavilion, well away from the other wives, who wanted to chat and gossip and complain about their servants, when suddenly there was Harry crouched beside me. Eve and Clara were somewhere. One of the joys of that posting was that the girls were free. They ran wild and I knew they were safe because the cricket ground was surrounded by a high fence and they knew every inch of it. We went there often enough! Most of the children ran around without adults supervising them.

That afternoon, as soon as we arrived, the girls made a beeline for a line of tight-spaced acacia trees, out of the sun, where they stepped into other worlds invented by Eve and loved and inhabited by Clara. I knew that Eve was telling Clara some rambling yarn, one episode at a time, which Clara followed with her mouth agape. Whether Eve had the whole adventure loaded in her imagination, or whether she made it up as the mood took her, I have no idea, but from the snippets I overheard there was excitement and sentimentality in spades and Clara often wept. I believed it best to leave them to it. Maybe other wives and mothers thought I was too careless and lenient but I didn't care. I wanted to give my daughters the freedom I never had when I was young.

'Oh, you made me jump,' I said, laughing. 'I was miles away.'

'Sorry to surprise you,' Harry replied. 'I've been looking for a chance to come over and apologise.'

'For what?'

'For putting you and the girls in an impossible situation the other

Sunday. Marjorie and I didn't think it through. It was our fault. You see, we are not used to children.'

'Oh,' I said, stunned, because I had replayed every minute of that awful afternoon and had chastised myself for not managing better. I had naturally concluded the fault was all mine.

'Do you fancy a stroll?' he asked. 'I can't talk here with all those eyes on stalks and female ears flapping. If you follow the path round the back of the pavilion it leads to a nice walk through the woods. I'm out. Disgraced after only ten runs. David will have harsh words for me if ever anyone manages to bowl him out, so I need a break before I face his wrath.'

A good excuse, I thought. He's been working on that one.

'Of course,' I replied. 'I'm only biding my time until David is ready to come home. He likes me to watch him, although I confess I don't. I just look up if there is a roar.'

'Then we have at least two more hours to ourselves.'

At first we wandered in silence until we reached the trees where the sun flickered in and out of immensely high branches, between leaves, now bleaching us with dazzling light, now casting us in shade, so that my eyes didn't have time to adjust to the sudden change, and everything was blurred and dark. I felt comfortable walking there with him.

'I have been thinking about you,' he began. 'I was worried we may have frightened you away for good. I need to talk to you and to explain.'

'There's nothing to explain, surely?' I answered. 'My girls… well… Eve… behaved badly, and of course it annoyed Marjorie after all the work she had put into that lunch. You see, we have been living with my parents ever since Eve was born, and she has been allowed a long rein. Grandparents are allowed to spoil their grandchildren, I suppose, but they treated her like a little princess. It was one of the reasons I wanted to get right away.' Or was that a rationalisation?

'I don't think she behaved badly,' Harry said vehemently. 'She behaved like a six-year-old child, that's all. She was excited…'

'But she must learn some manners. I must take her in hand.'

'No, don't break her spirit. She's strong and very much herself.'

What a lovely thing to say. I looked at him with surprise and gratitude and for the first time really spoke my mind. 'To be honest, I couldn't break her spirit if I tried. Nor would I want to. And I'm hopeless at being strict. David is always telling me I'm much too soft. He says that what those girls need, especially Eve, is a good spanking. But I can't do it. I slapped her legs after we left your house and then cried my eyes out because I felt so bad about hurting her. She didn't deserve it. I'll have to use cunning and guile and bribery instead so that we can go out into polite society.' Here I looked up at him and saw by his smile that he understood perfectly my irony. And my dilemma.

We had reached a circular clearing where the sun poured straight down, like a searchlight down a tunnel. All around us were trees so tall that their tops formed a canopy against the sky. Beneath our feet the grass was coarse and smothered with a tangle of spiky undergrowth. The background music was loud – the crickets, which never ceased their scratching noise, and the softer hum of a thousand invisible insects in the grass.

'Let's sit down for a minute,' Harry suggested, dropping to sit with his back against the trunk of an old, scarred tree. I noticed that his legs, stretched out in front of him, were long and lean. He patted the grass beside him. 'May I offer you this green cushion, Madame? Here…' and he raised his hand to help me settle down beside him. 'You've made your excuses, and very poor ones they are if I may say so. Now I need to make mine.'

What was so lovely about that afternoon was that there seemed to be no tension and no need to monitor what I said because this poised man had a gift for putting people at their ease. Of course, I saw the charm and I was not fooled, but at the same time I felt warmed and cosseted by it. I closed my eyes and let the sun gild my cheeks and eyelids. There, I'd kicked off my sandals and was curling my toes in the hot grass tuffets. I tucked my skirt round my legs. Our arms touched. Our shoulders were an inch apart. We were both quiet.

'If Marjorie seems ill at ease around children, it's for a reason.' He looked to check that I was listening. I was. I could listen to him all day, and more. 'This is what I've come to tell you. I want to tell you so that you will understand the other afternoon.'

I liked his directness. No beating about the bush. But I was not prepared for the intimacy of the story he narrated without drama. Without any play for my emotions.

'When we first married, after the war, like you and David, we wanted a family. We tried and tried. For several years. We went to doctors and they sent us to specialists. The specialists turned us both inside out to find out what was wrong. I remember the day we were given the results. It was in a corridor, a cream-painted corridor with windows too high to see out, on a hard wooden bench, the two of us sitting rigid waiting for the verdict like criminals after a court hearing. The doctor could not look either of us in the eye as he told us that Marjorie could not have children because a childhood illness had left her infertile. She did not cry. She just sat there in silence. She sat there for a long long time after the doctor had walked away.'

'Oh, I'm so sorry…' I blurted out, but he lay a hand on my arm to let me know he had more to say.

'After that, it was as if a door shut. Marjorie never talked about it again. I tried but she silenced me until I understood it was easier for her that way. Let the wound heal and grow a hard scab, and don't ever touch it again, she was saying. Behind her door, she seemed to strip out and discard all her softness as if there was no longer a use for it. She fell on her work like someone ravenous. She painted with a raw, angry energy, and that's more or less how it's been ever since.

Her paintings are her children.'

There is no facile comment after a story like that and rather than insult him with one, I simply nodded my head, and sat in silence beside him. I let my hand rest on his for a moment. Where words are useless, a gesture may serve.

'And so,' he continued, 'she is not very good or very happy around children. She chooses to mix with other childless couples, mainly with other painters and artists and writers, with whom she is at ease. Which is why I said it was our fault. It was careless of me to think it could have been any different. We should have invited you and David to dinner.'

'I felt the atmosphere,' I admitted. 'As soon as I walked in the door I knew something was wrong, but I thought maybe she was having a bad day. But I wouldn't dream of blaming her, Harry, I just feel so sad for her. Anyway, I was nervous too'.

'Female instinct?' he teased, leaving the story on a light note.

'Something like that,' I replied.

Don't ask me how long we sat there that afternoon; all I know is that I was oblivious to the hours passing and only the increasing coolness and creeping shade alerted me to the fact that afternoon was slipping into evening. As we rounded the corner of the pavilion, David had been bowled out, but he was so deep in conversation with another cricketer that he did not notice us approaching, and the girls, thank heavens, were twirling upside-down, heads hanging like mops, knickers on display to all the world, round and round the poles that surrounded the veranda while someone's little boy stared at them with his mouth hanging open. I noticed that Clara's knickers were damp and stained grass green.

Chapter 27

Edinburgh 2005
Eve

'How are you today, Father?'

My morning phone call must be punctual at 9.30 a.m. or he roars, 'Too late!' Today I am on time and he replies, 'When are we doing our writing?'

'Tuesday and Friday are our writing days,' I remind him, having tried to instil some kind of routine so that I know which of my days are clear…

'Oh.' Disappointment is thinly disguised. 'There's no sport on. I need to go to the library. That Josephine Cox book was rubbish, and the Catherine Cookson was not up to scratch so I didn't bother to finish it, and as for that other one you picked, what's his name…'

'Er…'

We go to the library twice a week so I cannot keep up with either what he takes out or the plots that he insists on telling me, blow by blow. 'Ian McEwan? Ian Banks?'

'One of those. Utter rubbish. I don't want any more books full of sex.'

At this point I am tempted to join in the next verse of his chorus because I know exactly what he is going to say.

'What matters to me are the characters. The characters have to be believable and interesting and likable. I'm not interested in some homosexual who… Why did you choose a book like that for me? You know me.'

There are filters I apply to all the books I choose for him, but I must have slipped up here. 'I'm working on my glass today. I can take you to the library tomorrow,' I say.

'Can't wait until tomorrow. Nothing to read. Oh, I'll go by myself to Morningside.'

It's emotional blackmail because he knows I can't let him stagger all that way. Although he never complains, I am aware that he is just a bit more frail than he was eighteen months ago, and whereas once, without a moment's hesitation, he would walk the mile across the nearby hospital grounds, dragging his tartan shopping trolley across the hummocks of grass before emerging at the noisy High Street, he now prefers to be driven there by me. I understand. When you are ninety and one eye is blind, it must be reassuring and comforting to go to bed at 8 p.m. with a book and the electric blanket turned up full. Except we can't often find good books. I read all the reviews and ask the utterly patient librarians for recommendations – for they see us coming in the door and smile – but if we get a single hit out of five or six, we are doing well.

'OK. Let me get some work done this morning and I'll pick you up at two and we'll go to the library.' I sigh silently. I was hoping for a rare full day at my bench.

'And then do some writing,' he adds.

Really! He is incorrigible. And I am a bit of a pushover.

*

'Where was I?' he says, squinting at my computer screen with his good eye.

I get the file up, scroll down to our last entry, and then have to jump back up a bit because I wrote my own thoughts after he left last time, and these he mustn't see. I would not hurt him, not for all the world, by hinting that my growing up was anything short of ideal. He needs his story of our lives, and I need mine. To shatter his memories – or what he decides to remember – would be to break him. Luckily he has no idea what I am up to with the mouse and keyboard and soon we are back on the page which he last dictated.

'You were saying how happy you and Mother were in Nairobi. "Halcyon days" you called that period. You wrote: "If only I could flip back the pages of the calendar and keep her there with the warm breeze lifting the hem of her pretty frock while she laughs and lifts her face to the sun." I was wondering afterwards when I read it through why you had written that because it sounds as if everything was about to change.'

'Well, it was. You know that,' he says gruffly.

'The Mau Mau?'

'Yes, that. But more than that. You don't know. We never told you.'

'What didn't you tell me?' I ask, only half attending as I get ready to continue typing. Since there is evidence aplenty in his tale of a poetic licence over-writing reality I think no more about it.

'You'll find out when I get there.' Then he turns away. 'She was happy. She had a happy life.' His voice breaks.

'I know. You must miss her so much,' I say, putting a hand on the scratchy tweed of his jacket.

'Every day of my life.' He turns his back to shield me from his tears. I reach for the box of tissues but he is pulling his checked handkerchief from his pocket, the square of cotton fabric that during my early childhood was my consolation. How many times did he pull out that handkerchief smelling of tobacco and coins and him to wrap a cut finger or to wipe away my tears? Now we are both reflective, quietly together but isolated in our own thoughts.

This time it is me who jumps.

'On we go,' he says. Stiff upper lip. Steady under fire.

'OK. I'm ready,' I say.

*

One day I was twiddling my thumbs in the garrison when a memo landed on my desk alerting us to a fresh incident in the Aberdare Mountains. Now, I knew those mountains well from training my troops up there. All that dense scrub and cover was ideal for teaching soldiers how to deal with ambushes because it was difficult terrain, sodden and dark with hardly any light filtering through the trees. It could feel very threatening and my men were often tense even though it was only a training exercise. A few of us would set out the hidden traps, using our own men of course as the enemy. The essence was to move through that dense forest without being seen or heard. The soldiers knew that somewhere in the tangled, knotted undergrowth were pretend enemies and if you stumbled into one of the traps, you were dead. I showed my soldiers how to move with stealth, quietly, always listening, listening. The Ghurkas proved absolutely brilliant at it in the desert. Slithered along like snakes. The thing is… we were working across a vast uncharted region above Nairobi and it was almost impossible to get a mental map of the place, and it was easy to get lost. The natives of course had the advantage of knowing it like the back of their hands and used a hundred different paths through the forest which we never found. For all we knew they were hiding in the bushes watching us pretending to be them.

Until the memo came in that Monday morning, there was nothing extraordinary about the mountain training; it was routine. I loved working with my men and watching their skills and confidence grow. I was a good leader, though I say so myself. On another posting to Loch Earnhead decades later, I would take my men up the Scottish mountains to train them in exactly the same way.

At that point I wasn't worried. I was aware of rumours, of course, but there are always rumours in a place like Kenya. For a couple of months before Mary arrived I had heard on the grapevine that this tribe or that tribe was causing a bit of trouble, but it came to nothing and I paid little attention…

*

'Father, this won't do,' I interrupt, finally exasperated. 'You want me to type "a bit of trouble"?'

'Yes. Why not?'

I give him a quizzical look. 'You want to describe what was happening up in the mountains as "a bit of trouble"?'

"Yes. That's all it was. Nothing more than a few minor incidents. Tribesmen had struck a few times, destroying settler property and killing some animals, that kind of thing. Brutal lot.'

'But you can't skate over history like that. That's so patronising. The natives had been beaten into submission… they were losing their own land… their own country… this is not just about you, it's about them too. This was a turning point of huge significance.'

I have over-stepped my daughterly boundaries. This is not how one speaks to a father like mine.

'You are wrong,' he growls. 'As far as we knew everything was fine during our first few months in Nairobi. Maybe the government at home knew more, maybe the Intelligence Corps knew something, but the ordinary army personnel out in Kenya did not know, nor was it our business to know. You don't go around poking your nose into affairs that don't concern you.'

'Don't concern you!' I repeat.

'Exactly.'

'But Father… you write as if this is nothing more than your personal story… the story of your time in Nairobi.'

'It is. That's what we are writing, isn't it?'

'Yes, but against a very particular backdrop… it's not just about you and your family… it's about a whole generation of white people who still lived a dream and had not woken up… about collective blindness to the politics of a country that was not theirs and collective amnesia about the plight of the people who owned and belonged in

171

that country… and who had been robbed of their way of living…'

'Oh, be quiet, clever clogs! What are you on about? You sound just like Harry when he heard about the murders. Harry and I had something of a falling out that day, a bit of an argument, which had never happened before.'

So we return to the personal – the only thing that interests him.

'Come to think of it, you and Harry would have got on very well. Neither of you is afraid to say what you think.'

'Mother always called me intolerant and tactless because I had to tell the truth,' I remind him.

'I know,' he replies. 'You were. Still are.' He gives me a little shove.

'OK, I'll stop interrupting. Please carry on.' This is his story, not mine, as I have to keep telling myself. I was only a child when this happened.

'So… shall I continue?'

'Of course. Please do,' I reply.

*

Well, as I was saying, I was in my office one Monday morning in early November when a memo came through from the Black Watch stationed up in the hills. It said that a white couple living at the edge of the Aberdare Forest, near Thomson's Falls, had been attacked by natives. We all knew this particular couple. Ideal type of settler. None of your Happy Valley philanderers. They cared deeply about their adopted country. They loved Kenya.

'Have you heard the news?' Harry burst into my office.

'Appalling,' I replied.

'I know the Meiklejohns well. Such decent folk. Liked and respected by everyone. Jock is a retired naval commander, isn't he, and his wife a retired doctor.'

'It's an isolated incident?' I was asking him for reassurance.

'Not exactly. There have been others, sporadic I grant you.'

'What happened?'

'You really want to know the details? We're trying to keep it quiet. The colonials want to take the law into their own hands and are already organising vigilante groups. God help us.'

'Can we wander outside and you can tell me?' I needed some air.

'Fine, but I warn you, it's not pretty.'

'No need to spare me.'

We lit cigarettes and settled ourselves on a wall in the sun. Harry began.

'OK, this is what I've been told... the Meiklejohns were sitting down to their after-dinner coffee on their veranda when they were attacked by about a dozen natives with machetes. We think one or more of their servants were involved, or at least gave the tip-off. Apparently Jock tried to load his revolver but collapsed, probably from a heart attack. He's in intensive care and not expected to survive. His wife... well, they mutilated her. They cut off her breasts. Somehow she too has survived.'

'Good God,' I said. 'This is a new turn of events.'

'Nonsense. The only new and worrying development is that the Mieklejohns' servants were implicated. They're beginning to desert in droves while pretending to remain loyal. You know and I know that the Mau Mau are fast becoming a serious threat. Listen, David, and this is for your ears alone – don't tell anyone yet, though it will only be a matter of time before it gets around – this isn't the first incident. We hushed up a previous attack in October in the hope that it was a one-off. The last thing Intelligence needs is unnecessary panic. You know Erik Bowker?'

I nodded. I had heard of him. A veteran of both world wars.

'His body was discovered in his home. He had been disembowelled – a telltale sign of a Mau Mau attack, as is this latest attack on the Meiklejohns. One attack we can treat as an isolated incident, but not two. I'm just waiting now for all hell to break loose as the news spreads, because the settlers in the Highlands are already frightened and twitchy. Many of them are such a long way from neighbours and miles from any police assistance.'

I was stunned. 'Such brutality. Why? I don't understand.'

'That's a bit naive of you, David.'

'What do you mean?'

'Surely you understand. The younger sons of British aristocrats arrived here fifty years ago with the encouragement and blessing of the good old British government, helped themselves to the most fertile regions of Kenya, robbed the Africans of their traditional way of farming, turned the tribesmen into servants in silly hats and white gloves... you don't expect the Africans to say thank you, do you?'

'As far as I'm aware, the settlers have treated the natives pretty well. Provided them with jobs and decent living conditions...'

'And driven them off their own land! Not only that, spoilt the land with over-cultivation until it's infertile. The Kikuyus are up there now building terraces without pay to try to stop the soil eroding any further. Not a happy story, is it?'

I must say I was a bit taken aback by his vehemence. I had no idea Harry felt so strongly. He had never spoken about it until now.

'Why did you accept the posting if you object so strongly to the way of life here?'

'Like you, I knew little about it until I got here, but since then I've kept my eyes peeled and my ear to the ground. It's my job, after all. You learn things. I'm paid to learn things.' He paused and looked at me, as if wondering whether to continue.

'Go on,' I said.

'It stinks. And the fallout, when it comes, is going to be epic. The whites have taken Africa for their own. The blacks are working as labourers on land that was once their own. It's explosive.'

'I'm sorry, but I don't agree. I treat my three servants very well indeed. They have nothing to complain about.'

'For God's sake, David, you can't reduce this to the personal. We're not discussing you and your servants, we're talking about the myth of the great white settlers bringing Christian values and better living conditions for the natives. It's crap. What do they do, these Brits? They play polo, hunt wild animals, drink themselves senseless, snort cocaine – it's not called Happy Valley for nothing, is it? You've seen them at their all-night parties in that Muthaiga Club in the city, the Moulin Rouge of Africa, playing cards all night, and drinking pink gin for breakfast after waking up in bed with someone else's wife. The English aristocratic lifestyle transplanted to Africa, old chap. A pleasant sight for the Africans, don't you think?'

'It's none of my business what the colonials do, Harry. I'm here to do my job, to train my men, and that's what I do.'

'You're wriggling.'

I was feeling a bit out of my depth by now. Obviously Harry was party to a lot more information than I was and that was why he was ranting on. The way things worked was that the garrison received all the incoming messages, including those from MI5 for the Intelligence bods. The high-security information was all in code. Just rows of numbers to me. MI5 had to prevent anything finding its way to the troops, especially the King's African Rifles, who might easily have been infiltrated. Whitehall was hugely complex, with personnel from a number of departments who didn't always agree among themselves, and these were the folk who were communicating directly with Harry. Some of the information eventually reached the rest of us. Some didn't. We were told what we needed to know and no more. Intelligence was regarded as the elite, of course, while we were just the fighting soldiers. Their role was vital; I would never deny that. Once they deciphered the messages, they forwarded them straight to the top, to Monty, who would decide what action to take. All well above my head.

'The settlers are responding to the two attacks predictably,' Harry said, breaking into my thoughts. 'Right now they are forming vigilante groups all over the Rift Valley and here, around Nairobi. You know what will happen next, don't you? They're going to take the law into their own hands and take revenge on anyone they decide is suspicious. Not just participants in the Mau Mau movement but anyone whose face they don't like. They will act on impulse. Mark my words, David, things will get very uncomfortable.'

'They must feel threatened,' I said.

'You know, David, none of this is unexpected. The settlers have been talking about "the night of the long knives" for a long long time and OK, it may have arrived. But if both sides carry on reacting the way they are doing, it is only a short step to civil war, and you and I will be in over our heads. I can't say any more. There is more… but… you know… classified information. All I want to say now is please be careful. Be very careful. Take care of Mary and the girls.'

And with that he left, slamming my door.

Chapter 28

NAIROBI 1953
DAVID

A couple of months passed without further incident. Mary was working three mornings a week in Nairobi now, having pleaded boredom, and either took the girls somewhere in the car in the afternoons or went walking in the city, sometimes alone, sometimes in the company of Marjorie. Less frequently she came to watch me play cricket. I was still not inclined to worry much about the political situation because what filtered down from our departing Kenyan governor, Sir Philip Mitchell, was that there was no need to take the Mau Mau restlessness too seriously. Harry, more tense and preoccupied than I had ever seen him, had a different perspective.

'You're not playing much cricket these days!' I joked with him one day. 'Sometimes you don't turn up at all. Sometimes you bat for ten minutes then give me some feeble excuse for running off. I seem to be losing one of my best men. What's that all about then?'

'Sorry, David. I've let you down there.' He couldn't even look me in the eye. 'Been a bit busy lately, that's all. I can't concentrate. Can't keep my eye on the ball.'

I knew it was an excuse but I didn't want to push him. His work was explanation enough. Who knows what he was having to deal with.

'More developments?'

'They've arrested Kenyatta,' he said, 'and it's a corrupt business. You won't believe this, David, but the court sessions are taking place in Kapenguria, just about the most remote outpost in Kenya. There's no rail service, no hotel or restaurant, no phones and no running water.'

'Why there? Why not Nairobi?'

'To avoid publicity and demonstrations, of course.'

'So what's the outcome going to be?'

'No credible evidence for a conviction, despite colonial officers picking over a ton and a half of documents from Kenyatta's house. On the slimmest of evidence, then, I suspect the government will charge him with managing an unlawful society, or, to you and me, "fomenting a revolution". It was rigged from the start. Judge Baring set himself up for the duration of the trial at that damn Kitale Club, the most exclusive club in town, where apparently he spent every evening and every weekend hobnobbing with the wealthiest landowners. Now, what did they have to say to one another, I wonder? What's more, the landowners have taken to arriving at the courthouse as if for a day out, bringing picnic lunches which are served by their white-gloved African houseboys. A picture of impartiality, don't you think?'

I found Harry's politics increasingly intrusive and distasteful. I suppose I was humouring him by allowing him to talk as he did. Perhaps I should have been firmer and told him I wasn't interested, but instead, to keep the peace, I just dropped the odd acquiescent word in the spaces he left for me to fill. I didn't want to jeopardise our friendship. While he was exercised, I was calm. You see, up until then, the attacks by the Mau Mau were still sporadic and restricted to the remote farms in the mountains, while in Nairobi itself nothing had changed. It honestly did not occur to me then that we were on the brink of something serious. If I had known more I would have told Mary to leave her job and stay at home. Like a shot. Eve and Clara were still being taken to school and brought home by a native. Perhaps I was naive, but if I was, then so were many other servicemen stationed out there. We did not know about the scale of the desertion by our servants and other workers to the Mau Mau training camps, nor how organised and concerted was the growing native movement against the whites. Harry knew more. He tried to tell me, but I wasn't listening.

Then the Kenyatta trial began and on the first night of the court's adjournment – I remember the date clearly, it was January 24th, 1953 – my composure was finally shaken. On a farm, not far from where Erik Bowker had been murdered, a family were hacked to death in their beds. I use that language not to sensationalise the event but because it is an accurate description. Roger and Esme Ruck, and their six-year-old son Michael, died of multiple machete wounds, killed by their own servants, who up till then, as far as anyone knew, had been trustworthy and loyal. We learnt that one of the servants who had massacred the family had, only a few days earlier, tenderly carried the little boy back to the house after he had fallen off his pony and hurt himself. Now the child was dead. Butchered in his bed.

This time when Harry poked his head around my door, I was ready for him, and I was fuming.

'So,' I said, not giving him time even to pull up a chair, 'I hope you're not going to lecture me on the rights of the Mau Mau.'

He looked at me in surprise. The mild man had finally spoken.

'I don't defend any kind of atrocity,' he replied. 'I say the situation is more complex than some people in power are willing to admit.'

'Don't talk to me about complexities. It looks very simple from where I'm standing. The Mau Mau have decided that there is only one course of action. Violence. They don't want negotiation. They don't want discussion. OK, the whites have taken their land, but are they willing to talk about a gradual, civilised transfer of some of it back to them? No. The natives are acting true to form. Barbaric and brutal.'

'You think the natives have the opportunity to discuss their situation with the colonial…'

'No, don't interrupt, just listen for once. The Tullochs, old and infirm and isolated, cut down with machetes. Bowker – hacked to death in his bath. The Meiklejohns, attacked while reading after supper. Ian found later trying to assemble his shotgun, delirious and so dreadfully injured that he was unrecognisable. Died the next day. Anthony Gibson, a British war veteran, taken prisoner during the North African campaign, killed in Nyeri… there are others… and now the Rucks. The very best kind of settler. Esme was medically qualified and ran a clinic on her farm for the Africans! Their little boy Michael played on the farm with the Kikuyu children who lived in the labour lines below. He was hacked to death by one of their own servants. Ruck treated his servants as well as or better than any. Believe me, Harry, this time the Mau Mau have gone too far. The murder of the Rucks will prove a watershed.'

'These are personal tragedies… I agree… but they don't change either the history or the plight of the Africans. I am not talking about the personal, David, however much you keep returning to the individual case. The Kikuyu people are dispossessed. The whites have robbed them of their way of living.'

'After what they have done, I don't give a damn if the Kikuyu are lined up against a brick wall and shot!' I exploded. 'The death of the Rucks… it's pure savagery. Have you seen the photographs of the child's blood-spattered nursery? Mark my words, Harry. The whites are baying for blood and I sympathise with them.'

Harry was silent. I was spent. It's not often I am pushed to express myself so vehemently. So we just sat there for a while. I suspect that Harry realised that there was no common ground.

'Shall you send Mary and the girls back home now?' he asked quietly.

'I don't know. I haven't spoken to Mary about it yet.'

'Perhaps you should. Look, David, no matter how different our political views, please believe me when I say I have only your best interests at heart. We don't know how far things will escalate. I have already spoken with Marjorie, who of course refuses point-blank to go anywhere. She says she'll sleep with a gun on her bedside table and blow out the brains of anyone who dares interrupt her sleep. Or her painting. She would, too.' He paused then and looked at me. 'But your Mary is altogether more sensitive and I'm not sure how she will cope.'

'It's very good of you to think of us,' I replied with cool irony. 'But Mary may well surprise us.' Once more he had managed to raise my hackles. Damn it, I knew my own wife. I was bridled to have Mary described to me as sensitive as if I, her husband, did not know that already. Damn cheek. Yes, she was a gentle soul, wouldn't hurt a fly, but she was made of sterner stuff than he implied. What made Harry think he knew more about her than me?

'If you will excuse me, I have work to do,' I said, pretending to gather up some papers on my desk. Harry took the hint.

'Fine. I'd better be on my way too.'

And with that we parted. Not a good note.

Afterwards I calmed down a bit and rather regretted my outburst. Harry was a good friend whom I could rely on. One of the best. We'd probably get over it. Despite our differences, I took what he said seriously and decided to talk to Mary that evening. Her time in Nairobi was probably drawing to a close almost before it had begun.

Chapter 29

Nairobi 1953
David

It was an African sunset. The sky was the colour of ripe black grapes and the sun a hanging disc. On the balcony, Mary stood with her back to me, in silhouette, gazing at the garden. She was watching the spectacular mauve light in which everything was back-lit: the spines on the cactus bushes and the pale pink and cream oleander flowers turned to damson and plum. No wonder she had not heard me come in.

Eve and Clara were sprawled on the floor of the living room playing with little felt figures, as absorbed in their world as Mary was in the melting colours outside. When Clara concentrated, her little mouth hung open and sometimes she mouthed words to herself. Eve frowned and scissored her legs up and down, up and down.

I didn't want to break this perfect picture by barging into it. Especially as the bearer of bad news. Eve was the first to notice me. 'Oh, Daddy! You made me jump.'

'How can you jump when you are lying on the floor?' I teased.

'Like this,' she said. My quicksilver Eve was on her feet, her arms flung round me. I was rooted to the spot with a girl's thin brown tentacles binding me. Clara lifted her head then and smiled with her wonderful grey eyes. Mary did not turn round.

'Mary,' I called.

She jumped, turned. Smoothed down her soft hair, and slowly smiled.

She walked towards me with a lingering backward glance, unable to let go. 'Could anywhere be more beautiful?'

I sighed. I was about to tell her she had to leave, that this beautiful country was becoming dangerous. 'I need to talk to you later. After dinner.'

Mary finally gave me her attention. 'What about?'

'The situation here.'

'Oh, that. There's a lot of scaremongering, isn't there? The wives are having a field day working themselves up about this Mau Mau business. How bad is it really?'

'I'll tell you everything I know. Later. When the girls are in bed.'

She nodded, and while I went through to the bedroom to remove my Sam Brown and tie and to change into civvies, I could hear bursts of laughter and my three little women singing 'Ten Green Bottles'. A few moments of pleasure cut short by a stab of guilt. I was about to disrupt all of this.

The bedtime routine continued while dinner was being prepared by Malinge in the kitchen. I settled in a deckchair on the veranda with a glass of whisky, watching the sun sink to a red semi-circle, then a rim, and finally a scarlet and violet light show. After the bathing and powdering and singing, Eve was back to claim her elder-daughter privilege of sitting on my knee. I noticed her hair was almost white from the sun, and her long thin arms and legs were an even brown. My delicate Eve was thriving. Another pang of guilt because soon she would be either confined indoors or on her way back to England. Mary came to sit beside me. I had denied it for as long as I could but the truth was that this beautiful country was on the verge of war. My heart was a stone.

'Time's up, my sleepy Eve,' Mary said quietly. 'Back to bed now.'

'Not yet,' Eve mumbled into my chest.

'Yes,' Mary said firmly, prising away arms and legs. 'Bedtime.'

I watched as Mary gathered up my soft-skinned, white-haired child in her strong arms and, holding her close, carried her off to bed. That evening, just as the sinking sun had illuminated every single flower and leaf in the garden, so I experienced my life as if it were fresh and new. As if I had not been looking before. What a good mother Mary was. How golden she looked after the months in the sun. How much I loved them all.

When Mary came back, she kicked off her sandals and curled her legs under her as she always did. She waited for me to begin.

'It's not good news, Mary. I'm afraid things are about to change out here,' I began gently.

'It's OK, David. I know what's going on. I do get about. And if you are about to suggest that you send us home, please forget it because I don't want to go. I want to stay here and see it through.'

So there was to be no beating about the bush. Her vehemence caught me off guard because I had prepared a different speech to introduce her to the idea of a swift departure. Her face was flushed, two little pink circles on her pretty cheeks, and eyes drilling into me to know the truth.

'We need to talk this through,' I said.

'There is nothing to talk about. I don't want to leave,' she repeated. She was twisting a strand of hair round and round her finger, a familiar sign of anxiety, but she was also fierce and brave and bold. I remembered Mombassa, when she had hurled little Clara at me. Again I wondered if I truly knew my wife or whether she had changed and hardened – in a good way – during the years we had been apart.

'You don't have to stay for me,' I said. 'When I brought you out here I had no idea there was going to be any kind of trouble. My priority is to make sure you are safe.'

'I'm not staying for you. I'm staying for all of us.' Then she added,

'I'm staying for me.'

What did she mean?

'I'd prefer you to leave,' I said. 'For all our sakes.'

'I'd prefer to stay.'

Deadlock. I had two choices – to exert my will immediately and tell her that she had to go or to leave things for now. Eventually she would have to give in. There was no other option.

'Some of the wives are making such a drama of it, talking about the Mau Mau breaking in at night and killing us all in our beds,' she continued. 'Only Marjorie scoffs at it all and says it's utter nonsense. She won't be leaving Harry and running away to England, I am quite sure.'

'No. Marjorie's a tough cookie. Harry said she's carrying on painting as if nothing is amiss. You know Harry and I had a bit of a set-to the other day about the Mau Mau, but I think it's blown over.'

'Did he want Marjorie to return home?'

'No, no, not at all. We didn't talk about her. No, we think so differently about the political situation. He's a liberal. Even expresses some sympathy with the Mau Mau movement. He says I should open my eyes. We nearly came to blows.'

'Not really.'

'No. But it got heated.'

Mary flushed. 'Well, I'm with Marjorie. I'm not going home.'

'Marjorie is not a mother.'

She bit her lip. I watched her struggle. 'How dangerous will it be for us?'

'Hard to tell,' I told her honestly. 'Not very, here in Nairobi.'

'Is there any chance that the girls might be hurt? David, tell me honestly.'

'They will be safer here than anywhere else. If we were up in one of the isolated farms in the Aberdare Mountains, or down in the Rift Valley, I would have you booked on a plane tomorrow. I'd insist.

In fact, the families who live in the remote regions, civilian and army, are all coming down to stay in the city, in temporary accommodation. There's quite an evacuation going on. So that tells you that Nairobi is safe enough. The trouble is all up in the mountains.'

'And you?' Mary asked. 'What will you be doing?'

At this point, I remember, I held back for a moment, not wanting to reveal a quick adrenalin rush at the thought of active service again. I would be a soldier's soldier again and I bet almost every other officer and soldier out there was feeling the same. That's what we were trained for.

'I shall be out of the bloody garrison and on active service with all the other soldiers and officers. I'll be training the native soldiers.'

'So black could end up fighting black.'

I had never heard Mary so sharp. So primed and perceptive. 'Of course. The East African Rifles are all black. I've only a handful of white soldiers in my squad.'

'Won't they desert?'

'Different tribes, Mary. Chalk and cheese. They are loyal to us. The worst would be infiltration but we vet all the soldiers so thoroughly…'

'So it's civil war?'

'In a way, yes.'

Mary was lost in thought for a while.

'Headquarters is drawing up a rota,' I told her. 'Four or five times a week I shall be out with my men during the day. And several nights a week.'

'Armed?'

'Yes, of course.'

She nodded and became quiet again, turning her head away to stare out at the darkness. I let her absorb what I had said before I put my question to her one more time. 'Are you sure you wouldn't rather go home?'

'Tell me the truth, David. How likely is it that the Mau Mau will attack us – Eve, Clara and me – here in our bungalow?

'I would say not likely at all.'

'Then we'll stay.'

*

'Not likely at all.' These words have haunted me for the rest of my life. That evening I told Mary she would be safe and she trusted me.

For a moment I cannot continue with my story, nor can I explain to Eve, who is looking at me slightly impatiently with her fingers raised above the keyboard, because she does not know. We never told Eve and Clara what happened because they were much too young, and somehow afterwards it slipped away into the past, or we never found the right moment. They still do not know.

With an effort I drag myself back into the present. On with the story; there are a few months yet before we get to the unbearable part. To heartbreak. And then I may not be able to carry on.

Chapter 30

Nairobi 1953
Eve

If I stay very still I can hear most of what they say, especially Father who can't whisper in his deep voice. Mother's voice is too quiet to hear clearly. My warning sign is when the ice stops clinking. Why shouldn't I listen? Why won't they tell me?

I know about the black men with machetes hiding in the forest up in the mountains because Christopher and Steven at school told me. The boys are stupid and noisy. They play the Mau Mau game, which is rushing around the playground with sticks chopping at each other's heads and jumping out of bushes. Oy Oy Oy I'm a Mau Mau warrior, I'm a black man, and I'm going to chop you to pieces. Chop off your hands. Chop off your feet. Chop off your legs. Chop off your heads. Mrs Lester shouted at them yesterday and told them not to be so very silly but they just carry on when she goes inside.

At home Clara and I play Mending Michael Ruck. We take turns to be Michael on my bed or on cushions on the veranda. On a tray we have a bowl of warm water, cotton wool, a tube of Germolene, a bottle of aspirins, bandages, plasters and a needle with white thread for stitching. The cuts on Michael's body are so bad it takes a long time to clean and stitch and bandage. The other day Clara fell asleep while she was being Michael because it took me such a long time to make her better. If Mummy comes in we say we are playing Nurses, which is not a lie. One of us is a nurse and one of us is Michael. We don't want to frighten her.

Daddy is talking again. Arms? Oh, armed. A gun. Daddy will have a gun. Shall I tell Clara or not?

Clara and I sit in the dust behind the acacia tree. No one sees us there except Malinge and he would never tell on us. He is our friend. The grass is all burnt. If we bring out cushions we can prop ourselves with our backs against the tree trunk. We quickly take off hot socks and shoes. Later we undo the buttons on our dresses and take them off too. It is hot and sticky. Clara looks soft and plump in her white vest and knickers, and I love to hug her. I am telling her a story about a family of jam tarts, one chapter every day. The mother is called Mrs Short because of her temper, because she has too many children, about thirteen at the last count, and growing every time. The Granny in the human family makes pastry for an apple pie every day, and gathers up the scraps to make one or two little jam tarts. Then both families move to Nairobi, the Shorts in a Peek Frean biscuit tin with a tight lid so they don't get damp and die. In Africa the air is thin and hot so they soon crisp up once they are out of the tin and on to a plate, although they nearly die of fright when they are lifted out by black fingers. That man needs a good wash, says Mrs Short. And then, because the man has not just black hands, but a black face and black everything, the smallest tart, Plum, becomes scared and runs away. She rolls along the garden, under the wire fence, along the path and then sticks herself to the bumper of a car. The car climbs out of the city into the mountains, past the beautiful houses. I don't know what will happen next. Usually I make it up as I go along, but maybe Plum sees a group of black men plotting to kill some white people and she has to get back to the house to warn her family and the human family before they are all attacked and the Shorts become crumbs, which is the worst fate that can happen to a jam tart because they can never become whole again.

Chapter 31

NAIROBI 1953
MARY

It became a habit, our walk through the woods when Harry was bowled out or, increasingly, when he made a polite excuse not to play at all, and I began to look forward to my afternoons at the edge of the pitch instead of dreading the tedium. He had already told me that he played cricket not because he was passionate about it like David – his enthusiasm was all show – but because it was a tolerable way for him to mix with the men. Easier than smooching with the officers and colonials in one of the private clubs in Nairobi. Less painful than getting legless in the mess.

On one warm day in early November I was in such high spirits that I was playing chase with the girls, having first kicked off my shoes to be barefoot like them. Round and round the pavilion we went. Not very dignified, but so what? Eve was wearing a white sun frock and a straw hat tied under her chin with a white ribbon. Clara had removed her dress and was racing about in her vest and pants, her olive skin a deep, rich brown and her limbs gorgeously baby-soft and plump. She looked foreign, maybe a little Indian girl with her short bob of dark brown hair, until you noticed the incredible grey of her eyes. When I caught Eve, she squealed and wriggled, her slight body a worm that was impossible to hold, and so she slipped out of my reach and was off, starting the chase all over again. When I caught Clara, the silly girl, she didn't even try to escape, but put her arms round my neck and said, 'Mummy I love you,' and I said, 'Clara, I love you too. With all my heart.'

On the veranda, I saw that Harry was watching us. He leant on one arm, and on his face I thought I caught a look of such tenderness that I stopped in my tracks and, leaving the girls, the game and everything, walked across to greet him.

'What a picture you make.' He walked down the steps and came towards us, reaching out with his hands to take hold of mine. 'Pink cheeks and tousled hair and playing like three puppies. I wish I could paint, but that's Marjorie's bag and...' he stopped, so I finished the sentence for him.

'...she has far more interesting projects than this one!'

'That wasn't what I was going to say,' he said quietly. 'Mary, can we talk? Something has happened.'

'Mummy...' Eve interrupted, handing me her hat. 'Clara and I are too hot. We're going inside for a drink and then we are going to do our story in the woods and then we'll meet you back here.'

'Yes, that's fine, Eve,' I replied, distracted. 'Just make sure you are both back here by the time they put out tea. No more than an hour, OK? Are you listening to me, Eve?'

But Eve and Clara, one pale blonde sister and one dark one, holding hands, were gone.

Rose Red and Rose White, I thought. I must get that story out when we get home, and read it to them.

'I am feeling concerned for you,' Harry said. He seemed restless and instead of slowing down when we reached our clearing, he carried on into the trees on the far side. Here there was only shade and dark, rough undergrowth; in places a shaft of white light pierced the green canopy overhead.

'For me?' I asked.

'I don't want to jump the gun, or frighten you when there may be no need, but has David talked to you about the Mau Mau?'

'He's mentioned it, that's all. He told me he has heard rumours but he thinks there's nothing too much to worry about.'

'I don't agree,' Harry said. 'I think there is going to be trouble and I'm not just talking about the memos which land on my desk. Nairobi is like a pressure cooker which has been on the boil until it is almost dry and about to explode. This is my personal view.'

'Can you explain it to me, Harry?' I asked. 'David tells me so little. I think he believes that politics are for men and that we women are too dim or too sweet to understand any of it. I keep my eyes open and I worry that sometimes he sees what he wants to see. It's as if he has blinkers on to stop him seeing the whole complex picture.'

'Very few of the soldiers show more than a superficial interest. I don't blame them for that. They're trained to fight, not to question the rights and wrongs of a country's past. Their job is to obey, give orders, react. It's black and white, if you'll excuse the dreadful pun. Partly they are kept in ignorance because the rules dictate that what comes down the lines from MI5 is absolutely confidential. I'd be court-martialled if I passed any of it on. Nor can I tell them what I get up to when I'm theoretically off duty. I spend a lot of my free time driving Marjorie up into the villages and settlements so that she can paint the natives, thus killing two birds with one stone because I use the time to talk to people. I have contacts. I watch. I listen.'

'I do wonder why you are in the army at all. You don't seem the type,' I blurted. 'I've been puzzling over it ever since we met. You know, almost everyone I talk to here trots out the same account about the whites coming to Kenya to tame the ignorant black savages, so I keep my mouth shut. With David too, because he sees the natives as inferior and in need of discipline. He doesn't despise them or anything, he just toes the official line. Actually, I don't think he gives any of it much thought, so I need to talk to you about it… but back to my first question… I do wonder why you are here.'

'Increasingly I wonder myself.'

'Why are you here?'

'Well… it seemed like a good idea at the time.' His tone was rueful, self-critical. He paused for a moment as if collecting his thoughts. 'When Marjorie found out she couldn't have children, she said she wanted to travel and to paint people in their own habitats. I told you… she threw herself into her painting. I think I was feeling numb and all I could think of was how to give her what she wanted. So I joined G branch – Intelligence – hoping the undercover work might suit me, at least in the interim, and in many ways it does… and here we are. Marjorie is busy and occupied. And I…'

'And you?'

'I find myself here in Kenya, aware that life for many of the Africans is intolerable. They are in despair.'

'I'm ashamed that I know so little,' I replied. 'Will you tell me?'

'I don't want to lecture you, Mary.'

'I want you to lecture me. I need to know the truth.'

'The truth,' he repeated. 'Whose truth?'

I looked at him, admiring and perplexed. This was a new kind of dialogue because I had never met anyone who sifted through his thoughts until the grains of truth – he would say 'his truth' – were caught in a net. Other people just gave me their instant answers.

'OK. I accept that there are different versions of what is happening but I'd like to hear what you think about the Mau Mau situation.'

'Well… it's complex, Mary. The problem is people don't look back far enough. To understand what's happening now in Kenya you have to go way back to the 1920s, when the first rich white settlers began arriving in southern Kiambu to claim great swathes of fertile land for themselves. I'm talking thousands and thousands of acres. The younger sons of landed gentry, old Etonians, retired army officers. Those chaps wanted to create here a way of life that they knew damn well was dying out almost everywhere else. Last-gasp colonialism. Anachronistic and privileged. An escape from change and modernity… sorry, it makes me so angry.'

'It's fine. Carry on. Please.'

'Well, at first the Kikuyus stayed on as squatters, working the land for the whites and helping them build their vast, productive farms. What a cruel irony. Each native family continued to work its own patch of land – its shamba – but unwittingly they became tenant farmers to their white landlords when new laws forced them to sign contracts as paid – very poorly paid – labourers. Then came more laws restricting the number of cattle they could own. Without cattle they had no way of paying bridal dues…'

'I don't understand, David. Bridal dues?'

'When he came of age each son would move out of the family shamba and claim his own patch of land and start farming. But the whites refused to let the men move on. Without land, a man cannot marry, cannot pay for his bride. What's more, 100,000 Kikuyu have been forcibly repatriated. It's a good word with a bad meaning. The natives have had to carry their possessions on their backs and on carts to other parts of Kenya where the land is almost infertile and very difficult to farm.'

'That's terrible,' I said, inadequately.

'And so we have the tale of two cities. The white story: Happy Valley, land of luxury, economic prosperity, cheap black labour, gin slings and all-night orgies. And the black story: dispossessed Africans, poverty, oppression, land hunger. The whites hold political power because the Africans don't even have political representation. The whites have thrown the scraps to the blacks.'

It was a lot to take in. It was a shock too, because David has told me nothing about Kenya's history or politics. No, that's not fair. It was my responsibility to find out, and I hadn't bothered.

'I've been walking around wearing earplugs,' I told Harry. 'I am ashamed of my ignorance.'

'Don't blame yourself,' Harry replied. 'It's me who is stepping out of line here. Others either don't know or don't want to know. That's army life for you. Most folk are used to living in barracks and army quarters where they can literally remain shut behind the barricades away from the country they inhabit, if they so choose. It's unusual here because all of us are living in the city. We can be tourists and visitors, not just army personnel. There are opportunities to get under the skin of the place.'

'What's going to happen?' I asked.

'I think it's going to get bloody. There have been a number of attacks, mutilations, on the cattle and livestock owned by the settlers...'

'The Kikuyu are so brutal...' I blurted out.

'I know. They are without mercy. Again, all I can say in their defence is that they have their backs against the wall...'

'I see that... I see all that... but the savagery of the attacks, Harry!'

'I'm afraid it's going to get worse. The Mau Mau have organised mass oathing ceremonies for the swearing of loyalty and allegiance. To our white sensibilities it's all a bit disgusting because it involves drinking goat's blood and so on, but that's the way things are done. The point is... the Mau Mau have started to turn against their own... against those who remain loyal to the whites... and they are killing their own people to terrify others into joining the resistance. And the settlers are becoming hysterical.'

Harry had his arm round my shoulders as we walked on, now in silence.

'I care about you very much, Mary,' he said while I was still miles away, thinking through everything he had told me. 'You know that, don't you? I couldn't bear anything to happen to you. I'm telling you all this because it might be best if you leave.'

I tried not to read too much into his words. He was my closest friend in Nairobi, and it was OK surely to admit that we cared about each other.

'What will Marjorie do?' I asked, aware of her absence in the conversation.

'Oh, Marjorie's tough,' he replied. 'I keep her informed and she carries on as usual. She won't leave even if things get nasty.'

'Then why should I?'

'Because…' and he hesitated. 'Marjorie is a survivor and she's always insisted on her independence, on making her own decisions.'

'Are you saying I can't make decisions for myself?'

'No… Mary, I'm sorry, I didn't mean that… I know you are a strong woman too.'

Now he was looking at the ground, avoiding my eyes.

'It's just that… I couldn't bear anything to happen to you. Or the girls.'

'Thank you,' I replied, blushing, as shy and silly as a young girl because he had turned back to me and his warm arm still rested on my shoulder. The hairs on his hand were bleached gold. He wore no wedding ring. It was a physical effort not to lift my arm and cover his hand with mine.

I looked at him. There was tenderness in his eyes and I couldn't pretend that it wasn't for me. Our relationship was honest. Then he was standing still and slowly twisting me round to face him, wrapping his arm right around my shoulders, and I didn't shake it off or pull away.

'Why are you telling me this?' I asked, doing my best to carry on a normal conversation in a normal tone of voice.

'Because I couldn't bear anything to happen to you.'

Only for a fleeting moment did we stand there, frozen in the thick heat at the edge of the precipice while my heart beat like some crazy over-wound clock and a trapped butterfly marked a frantic tattoo with its wings deep in the pit of my stomach. I lifted my arm and placed my hand over his to thank him for his concern… no, delete that. I put my hand on his because I had to. Because I wanted to touch him. And at once his other arm was around me, pulling me to him while he stroked my hair and touched my neck and my forehead. I had one silly image before I was lost in some other place where there were no thoughts. I am like Alice, I thought to myself, falling down a deep pit and nothing on this earth can stop me. Then thinking and images were gone and all that remained was my skin, which had grown a thousand times more sensitive, feeling in fine grain each imprint he made with his fingers. His touch was exquisite. His hands were sure and skilled as they moved down my back and around my waist. I was all shivers and goose bumps. My body sang in a way that was new and startling. My bones were liquid. My eyelids heavy, closing, then opening to see him looking at me. Lips met, at first barely touching, only a taste, because given such a heady brew, a sip is enough. Another kiss, longer this time, surprise and inevitability colliding. More kisses, deep and sweet and hungry. I had never felt like this before. In the space of a few minutes I was alive and trembling from head to toe with an impossibly urgent need to explore this man's body the way he had begun to explore mine.

When finally we pulled apart my cheeks were scarlet and my lips swollen. As the old me and the new slowly peeled apart, I became dizzied with the conflicting feelings of pleasure and censure, joy and alarm, sensuality and shame.

'Don't,' he said, reading my thoughts, and kissing me on my cheek. 'Don't try to work it out. Accept what is happening.'

Anything I said would be inadequate and trite, so I said nothing. Holding hands, we slowly walked on.

When we emerged from the trees and circled the pavilion, David was still batting. Everything was just as it had been. Nothing had changed – and everything.

Chapter 32

Nairobi 1953
Mary

David and I had exchanged places. He was whole again, a man comfortable in his skin because when he left each morning it was to drill his men in the art of warfare and to prepare them, and himself, for battle. He was action man, all muscle and reflexes and polished brass buttons. As the tension built inside and around Nairobi and all of us who remained there felt increasingly insecure and unsettled, so David's confidence and sense of purpose grew. I knew that if we were not there to distract and worry him, he would be in his element. Above all else, David was a soldier. This was a David I had not seen before because while he was away fighting his war in the desert, I was occupied in Scotland and Singapore and Australia. Now, like then, he wore his uniform with pride and told me that at last, and to his utmost satisfaction, he was doing what he joined the army to do. He was needed here. He was a useful man. He was a man who would make life-or-death decisions if the conflict escalated and the Mau Mau decided on a full-scale attack. Did he look forward to being at war again?

I was two people in one skin. The first wore the mask of a wife and mother – one which fit so closely that sometimes I forgot that I was wearing it.

The second was a dreamer who sleepwalked through her days like some wayward adolescent who has fallen in love for the first time. The dreamer's mask was not yet familiar and sometimes she felt the need to remove it, but it possessed a magical capacity for self-renewal, which was in the power of the man-magician whom she met sometimes by chance in some ordinary social setting and sometimes alone in secret places. It only took one look, she noticed, or a hand brushed against hers, and this mask snapped back into place, fitting her more tightly than ever before.

Then there was a third mask that David had handed me just recently. It was that of the wife of a soldier on active military duty, whose permanent preoccupation was the protection of her children. I wore this mask with deadly seriousness. One day David took me to the firing range because every wife had to learn to use firearms in case the Mau Mau attacked Nairobi itself. It could happen to any one of us. I was reaping the downside of living away from barracks, which until now, and especially recently, I had so enjoyed. In army quarters we would have been safer, but the curtains would have twitched and the mouths would have spread the word that Mary Dell was often seen in the company of a married officer. In Nairobi I had more privacy and some anonymity. I could come and go as I pleased without other wives spying on me.

'One reason for getting used to handling a gun is that we can't trust our servants anymore,' David told me as we drove towards Headquarters and turned off towards the training ground at the back of the sports buildings. 'Many of them will remain loyal whatever happens but they are under constant threat by the extremists. They are being intimidated. Some have already gone to the mountains to join the Mau Mau rebels. This is no simple war of black against white. It's black against black, too. It's very messy.'

'I can't believe any of our servants would hurt us,' I replied.

'You can't rely on anything, Mary. You can't trust anyone.

If someone threatened to kill a loyal native's wife and children if he didn't join the movement, he would have no choice but to go. And they're already using these scare tactics. They have killed to persuade those who hesitate. They will kill a lot more to force loyalists to join their cause.'

'You know, Clara has formed such a touching attachment to Malinge.' I had stopped listening because David was being over dramatic and pedantic. I knew all this. 'Sometimes when I walk out on to the veranda I can hear them playing cards together and laughing, or just talking and talking. Malinge is teaching her games which he played as a child and teaching her Swahili. He's like a big brother. It's inconceivable that he would harm her.'

'That's probably what the Meiklejohns said before their servants hacked their little boy to pieces in his bed,' David retorted. 'Sorry, Mary, but from now on, you trust nobody. Not Malinge. No one. Always be on your guard. And no more leaving Clara and Malinge together. Do you understand?'

'With my mind, yes, but with my heart, no,' I replied.

'That's good enough.'

While David found his keys and went inside the building to unlock the ammunitions store I waited outside, feeling guilty and chastened because sometimes I chose to be blind and deaf to what was going on around me. David made me feel a neglectful and irresponsible mother. While the grapevine carried the fear from family to family and the tension was cranked up day by day, I was slipping away to meet another man because he made me feel beautiful and giddy with love. I was self-absorbed and foolish. Put a stop to this selfish nonsense, I told myself. Grow up. What do you think you're playing at?

When David returned I was eager to try my best because I was contrite and angry with myself. But as soon as we reached the firing range, David's manner began to grate because he patronised me in his assumption that I would find this difficult and strange. I found myself playing along, falling back into the role of docile wife in need of his masculine protection because that was how he liked things to be. Because it was easier that way. I allowed him to think I didn't want to touch the gun. In some ways it was true, but while he interpreted my disgust as female sensibility in fact it was abhorrence at the prospect of perpetrating violence on any living creature.

It was too easy to slip back into the paler shape of the young woman I was when we first met, before the war, before the hospital in Edinburgh, before Singapore, before the hospital ship that sailed for Australia. I didn't blame him because he didn't witness the changes in me during the six years when I grew strong and independent and became someone who – dare I say this even in a whisper and in secret – might not have married David if I had my time over again. In this I know I am no different from many other women who returned home knowing what it was like to feel valued, confident that they too had contributed their best. Many, if pushed to tell the truth, would admit that those years were among the best and most productive of their lives. And when it all ended that precious past was crossed out as if it had never happened and the skilled women were sent back to their baking and dusting without any renegotiation. Our men had seen and suffered the unthinkable and we women had to forget that we had too.

'You're not concentrating,' David said crossly. 'Are you listening?'

'Yes,' I lied.

'Then do what I've just told you to do. Take the safety catch off, then on. Off and on again.'

I complied.

'OK. Next stage, Mary. Safety catch off. Fire. Don't wait to aim. Fire. Don't aim at the head because a head is easy to miss. If it moves, aim at the stomach.'

I did as I was told and did not disappoint him. He thought I had never handled a gun before, but before we boarded the hospital ship in Singapore all the nurses were taught how to use a gun, and I always carried mine in my bag when called out at night. But it was much too late to tell him that. The game must go on. And a bit of revision wouldn't hurt as it had been a while.

'Not bad at all,' he said, patting my shoulder. 'You see, the trick is to stop your hand and fingers trembling. A lot of people think that it's a sharp eye that determines how well they fire a gun but it's not. It's all in the very gentle squeezing of the trigger. You have to have a steady hand.'

I know that. I know, David. Don't lecture me like a hopeless wife. We stayed there going over and over the same series of movements until I knew I would be able to perform them in my sleep. Which was the whole point. To give him his dues, David was an excellent teacher and I knew I was in capable hands. If anyone could prepare me for some crazy Mau Mau native crashing into our bungalow one dark night, he could. I told myself that I should be content and grateful.

In the car on the way home, he was sufficiently pleased with me that I risked one clumsy stab at putting the record straight.

'I sometimes think you forget I worked through the war,' I said, taking it gently, not wanting to rile him. 'I may seem a bit soft but I can be tough too when I need to be.' Save my knowledge of guns for a bit later, I told myself. Don't shock him.

'I'm sure you'll cope in an emergency, Mary, but I want to make sure that you are as prepared as you possibly can be. I would never forgive myself, never, if anything happened to you when it had been in my power to prevent it. I hate the thought of you using a gun as much as you do but soon I'll be out on patrol at night and I want to leave the bungalow knowing that you can protect yourself. And Eve and Clara.'

He had touched my raw spot. I changed from a woman fighting the patronising manner of my husband to a lioness ready to show my claws at any hint of a threat to my cubs. We parked the car and started to walk towards the bungalow.

And right on cue, before I could say anything else, two wild things burst from the bushes and tumbled out in front of us.

'Saw you coming!' sang Eve. 'We've been waiting for you for ages and you didn't know we were there!'

'Been on our tummies. As flat as worms. Wriggling and slithering...' Clara added breathlessly. 'Or maybe snakes.'

'Oh, you two naughty girls! You gave me such a fright!' I cried, not angry at all, but stunned by their sudden timely intrusion upon our scene. Straight from the firing range where I had just learnt to use a pistol to protect myself and, much more importantly, to protect them. Because I was hugging them close it took a minute for me to notice that my younger daughter was more or less naked.

'Clara, where's your dress?' I gasped. That girl! She was turning wilder by the day, almost a native girl herself.

'Hidden behind a tree. Animals don't wear frocks,' she answered as she curled her legs around me, smearing dusty red soil all over my legs and my clean, pale-almond dress.

'Mary, you can't let Clara run about like this...' David began.

'Oh dear... I know... I'll try and make them more civilised.'

'I mean it, Mary...'

But Eve came running at me snorting wild animal noises, her hands scratching the air like pointy claws. I seized her too and held onto her. 'I'm a bigger, wilder animal and now I've caught you, I'm never going to let you go,' I breathed into her tangled, hot hair.

Suddenly my eyes filled with tears, but in bending down to hug my elder daughter I managed to keep them hidden. I would truly kill anyone who dared to try to harm them, with or without a gun. What had I been thinking about? Tomorrow, when we met, I would tell Harry that it couldn't possibly go on.

Chapter 33

NAIROBI 1953
MARY

David came home, changed into his cricket flannels, and left again for the sports grounds, not even asking about my own plans for the afternoon. Fine. Eve and Clara had been invited to tea with friends, which gave me about three hours.

As winter turned the corner into an early spring, we women were still free to come and go, although with more caution, and always alert for anything out of the ordinary. Life went on. Those of us who had chosen to remain in Nairobi heard the details of each new attack on a white farm and each new attempt by the army to close down a Kikuyu camp, but in the city, so far, we had not been involved. We walked more quickly and glanced more often over our shoulders. We carried a bit more adrenalin, just in case.

To cover our tracks Harry and I usually arranged to meet in a cafe or a shop on some insignificant street corner, several blocks back from the broad, buzzing Delamere Avenue, where traffic flowed all day long, cars parked haphazardly and people thronged the pavements. We stayed well away from the hotels and restaurants and bars where businessmen sat and talked all day over tiny cups of bitter coffee and where Harry too had often parked himself to make contact with someone who knew something. We were careful and cautious.

Harry's habit of wandering casually around the city listening to a conversation here, an exchange of words there, made him an ideal partner in crime and I was learning fast to behave like a spy. He knew the labyrinthine streets like the back of his hand and prowled there like a cat. At least, that was the picture I had created of him going about his work. Harry was a professional and told me very little because to do so would be to jeopardise his safety and mine. He was an Intelligence officer. What he knew he did not share.

I made my way quietly along the back streets carrying my shopping basket over my arm and keeping my eyes cast down. I stopped to buy a few lemons or a twist of ground coriander. I was invisible, or if not invisible then at least doing nothing to draw attention to myself. Just another colonial wife out on her own to buy something she needed. My chosen route, a track that any white woman might follow and where I hoped I would bump into someone who knew me, thus providing an alibi, took me through the open street markets, where I pretended to linger. This was our familiar Saturday morning territory – stalls piled high with melons sliced with butcher blades into neat and even slices oozing juice or festooned with ropes of cheap wooden bangles and glass beads that twinkled in the sun and drew Clara and Eve like a pair of magpies.

'Mummy, I want…'

'Mummy, please can I have…'

'Oh, just this once…'

Sometimes I gave in and bought several child-sized bracelets of gilt and sparkly blue glass or pretend diamonds that they slipped on to their small brown wrists, circles of shiny promise to twist round and round and transform them into princesses. Then, of course, it was even harder to get them home because one of them, usually Clara, would stop dead in the midst of a crush of people to stretch out her arm and admire her new jewels. I worried that Eve or Clara would slip away and vanish in that heaving concentration of humanity and be lost forever.

'Eve, keep hold of my hand,' I would nag.

'Clara, don't just stop like that because I may never find you again.'

I kept my voice light-hearted, although my fears were heavy and real enough.

I was thinking of my little girls as I threaded my way through the stalls, thinking too that I had to keep up my guard because you never knew who you might bump into, literally, in that aggressive market area where stall keepers harangued you and reached out to grab your arm or force something into your palm and where everyone was pressed so close together that I always returned home with the smell of mango and hot spiced sweat in my hair.

Behind the market the roads soon became dirty and narrow. It was brutal and ugly there, away from the imposing colonial facade of the city. Men stared at me, openly lewd, because few white women ventured that way. I walked faster. Two blocks back, a turn to the right, another turn to the left, and there was the small pavement cafe with a couple of tables outside. And of course he was there, leaning back in his chair, long legs stretched out in front of him, a half-finished beer on his table and a book in his hand. He was wearing sunglasses so that no one could make eye contact, and you would think, if you came across him by chance, that he was completely absorbed in his reading. But as I approached from a distance, he casually removed his glasses, winked at me and finished his beer in one long gulp. As I passed his table he was already getting up, his hand in his pocket fishing out some coins to throw on the table. He nodded to the waiter. They knew him there. This was the quiet English man who talked with foreigners.

Round the next corner his old blue Hillman waited. It took less than a minute for him to catch me up, open the car door and for the two of us to slip inside. But still someone might be watching. On the bench seat, sticky after being heated by a broiling sun, we stared straight ahead and did not touch. We barely acknowledged one another's presence until we were on the road out of Nairobi, when his arm went around me and I leaned my head on his shoulder with a smile and a sigh.

Nairobi is a gift for secret lovers. With its wide open parks and lakes and game reserves we could vanish into the endless space of a sprawling landscape. Our journey towards each other had taken us from the confines of the cricket pitch to the latticework of tall trees behind the pavilion and from there up into the mountains or to the shores of one of the lakes, where Harry surprised me again and again with some solitary, tree-circled piece of ground where we were truly alone and hidden from the rest of the world. Sometimes we sat for hours watching impala and wildebeest. We walked hand in hand along the shore of Lake Naivasha. We watched the sun set behind the purple and turquoise crags of Mount Kilimanjaro. I was not unaware of the ridiculousness of having such a Hollywood backdrop for our affair of the heart, a stage setting so exquisite and unlikely that I had to pinch myself to confirm that it was real.

On that day, because time was limited, we did not have the luxury of going far away. Harry slowed down outside the gates to a house that he knew was empty, its colonial owners having fled to England because they were afraid. Their native servants were dismissed and gone. The car wheels crunched slowly down the drive as if we were some ordinary friends of the owners who were calling on the off chance of finding someone at home. We just happened to be driving past. Casually we slipped out of the car and slowly circled the house and made a show of ringing the bell and knocking loudly on the door. We feigned surprise when no one came to let us in. My goodness, where are all the servants? While putting on that ridiculous charade, I imagined I was on a film set and the cameraman was behind us, recording our every move. While most of our actions were purely for show, Harry was literally checking that all the doors and windows were shuttered and locked and was glancing at the ground for signs of recent footprints in the gravel. Nothing. He listened, but there was only the sound of a hundred different birds singing their hearts out in the forest behind the house.

While I mounted the steps to the veranda Harry returned to the car for the blankets and cushions he had stashed in the boot.

Perhaps it was the necessary guile, the planning and subterfuge, the long breath-held wait, the holding back that gave our love-making such intensity and urgency. For now, for perhaps the next hour, there was absolutely no hurry. We snatched a single kiss and then he settled himself with his back against the end of the veranda while I reached toward him and pushed the first small pearly white button through its buttonhole, noticing as I did so a loose thread, which I bit off. Under the crisp white shirt his skin was honey warm and smooth and his shoulders were sprinkled with freckles where the African sun had scorched him and left a permanent mark. I sank my teeth into those beautiful shoulders, and his neck, and the tops of his arms, leaving little red crescents of love. The hairs on his forearms were bleached creamy-gold against the chestnut skin. An old scar wreathed his wrist and at the tops of his arms were coin-round blemishes from vaccines. For a while he was content to let me drop my kisses on his body, a slow, teasing prelude to the passion which would soon consume us.

Up on one elbow now, he flipped me over with one deft movement of his arms so that my back was in the cushions and his weight was on top of me and I could feel sharp splinters of wood pushing up into my spine. Pain and pleasure – it is all one. He held down my shoulders and kissed me long and hard. I imagined what we looked like from high above where a vulture circled in the sky; from its vantage point it would see synchronised movements, two fluid, sighing forms shifting and flowing together, now close, now teasingly apart, now tangled up like a hydra, now moving in a stately dance of love. When we settled again, my back curled against his stomach, his fingers felt for the knots – always tight beneath my shoulder blades – and kneaded away the tension until I was liquid softness. Until I found Harry I didn't know I possessed those pleasure points all down my back, nor the nerve endings which lay close to my skin so that when they were touched I shivered with delight. I closed my eyes so that I could concentrate on his touch. For a long time we were as slow as snakes. My sandals were already kicked away – one fell off the veranda, where it looked lost and abandoned in the long grass. A splash of white on green. Harry was unpeeling my clothes, skin from a warm fruit, dropping the flimsy layers like a pile of pale handkerchiefs on the wooden floor of the veranda. He twisted round to kiss the spaces between my toes.

I was asleep before and now I was awake. There was no choice. I loved him completely, totally, unreservedly. Any arbitrary rules which society threw at us went whizzing past. I didn't bother to catch them.

Chapter 34

Edinburgh 2005
Eve

It is Tuesday and my father has not yet arrived. Punctuality. That's the thing. Thanks to him I turn up for every appointment – hospital, hairdresser, lawyer, friend – at least fifteen minutes early in case I'm late. If I'm meeting a late person this means that I often arrive half an hour too soon. Some things you can't get out of your system, like your heart sinking when you see a single magpie or carelessly walk under a ladder. Every month I stand out in the rain and wind searching the night sky for the new moon and then, damn it, I accidently and inevitably catch the tiny silver nail-paring through glass and bring down bad luck for the rest of the month. The legacy of my upbringing.

Because he is writing his memories I find myself, when he leaves, drifting back to mine. In his history I am a bit player, not as important as my mother or the army or his sport. Before I fell from grace I was his favoured daughter, his Blondie. If that hadn't happened, perhaps now I would have a more important and sustained part in his narrative. While his role as father is so far predictably steadfast and unchanging I know that my role as cherished daughter breaks off very soon. Before and after. Loved and not loved. Of course, he has not reached the point in the narrative when he turns his face from me, nor will he come to it while he is in Nairobi. I have six more years of feeling secure in my father's admiration. But it is odd that he does not mention it, nor hint at the breakdown ahead. I long to ask him, Why did you stop loving me? Can we talk about it now, please, after forty years of silence? You did not like me, did you? Do you now?

I linger with my fleeting memories of a small thin girl with white-blonde hair running in the sun, running to her father when he arrives home, running for her father when he bets her she cannot race around the garden in three minutes, or the cricket pitch in five minutes, and she does it and is rewarded with a smile and a pat on her hot head. I was a little girl with a father in a khaki uniform and a handkerchief in his pocket for my injuries and my tears. His love I took for granted, as one does.

I read of traumatic, fraught relationships between fathers and daughters as they go on fighting and hurting each other until the father dies. Then the survivor writes her misery memoir. It won't be like that. From the age of thirteen until I left home at seventeen I accepted that he did not like me and in response I shrugged my shoulders, swallowed my pride and hurt, and got on with other things. His withdrawal didn't turn me into a crazy girl, although it probably wore away a good chunk of my confidence and self-belief. A girl needs to see reflected in her father's eyes unconditional love and approval to keep her grounded in her growing years. I saw disapproval and dislike, so I threw myself into the excitement and rewards of boyfriends and being a swot at school and my gang of weird buddies. Only, now I know what I missed. I read of women whose fathers have remained their friend and mentor – the trusted one – long after they have grown up. If I had slipped out of the house one dark night during my adolescence I think he would have breathed a sigh of relief and carried on as usual. For forty years he has remained absent in my life. Here's your mother, he would say into the receiver when I made my Sunday-evening duty calls. Our longest conversation was about ten words.

*

I lost my father's love one evening on a bumpy track called Lovers' Lane. Most small towns and villages have one. Excuse me, while I desert Nairobi to whizz the tape of my life forward about eight years. Two more postings – to Portsmouth and Germany – have come and gone and now we are living near Aldershot. Although in my own mind there was a single cut-off point when my father turned his back on me, probably it was a long time in the brewing, as he observed me morph from a biddable, pretty girl with pale plaits to a surly, clever teenager. More to the point, he watched the diagram of my world shift its major reference points until he, my sun, slid from the centre to the side and finally beyond the circumference.

The weed-clogged, summer-dry, dusty track through the fields was heavily rutted from the tractor wheels driven between the dairy farm and the shed in town where the fresh, frothy milk was poured into glass bottles which jiggled along a conveyor belt to be loaded in crates on to a couple of electric milk carts. I learnt a lot about milk production that summer – from cow to doorstep – when I was thirteen and my very first boyfriend had a part-time job after school and at weekends helping on the farm and delivering the milk. That is how I became the family disgrace. An army officer's daughter was going out with a common milkman! My mother, unable to cope with the shame of it before her wealthy neighbours, sighed frequently. My father pretended he could not see me. But wait, this is still mild.

Clara and I shared a bedroom, divided with an imaginary line as real as the one that cut the back car seat in two when we travelled about Nairobi. Her half of the room was coordinated in pink, with shelves neatly crammed with little ornaments and porcelain animals, which she dusted. Her only concession to her appearance was at night when she rolled her silky dark hair round huge pink curlers and I told her she would never find a husband if she looked like that in bed. My half of the room, by the window, was a dump of cheap C&A clothes pulled on and thrown off and little bottles of Rimmel cosmetics as I experimented with blue eye shadow and black mascara. Radio Luxembourg was the link-up for my generation but reception was so bad and our radio so old that the only place I could pick up a signal was in our draughty hall. So in the evenings, while my parents did I know not what in the lounge, and Clara amused herself in our bedroom, I lay sprawled on the lino, ear to the speaker, trying to pick up the faint and squeaky sounds of Cilla Black's 'Anyone Who Had a Heart' and Del Shannon's 'Runaway' and Elvis singing 'Wooden Heart'.

Early on Saturday mornings there would be a shrill whistle from beneath our bedroom window, which was over the porch, and the accompanying clink of milk bottles.

'Your boyfriend,' Clara would sniff from her bed as if announcing a bad smell.

At thirteen I was a radar beacon constantly monitoring the landscape for boys, including the one who lived in the big house opposite. I was spotted one day at my lookout post, leaning out of the window, by the boy who delivered the milk, and so began the early-morning flirting which my sister so disdained. Soon, given the ongoing rejection of the rich boy-next-door, I was going out with him.

After school, when the bus had delivered me to within walking distance of home, I stumbled along the rutted track with a fast-beating heart, dragging my satchel and tripping over tufts and stones in my haste to get to him. There was the black-painted gate into the yard where the cows mooed their way in and out for milking. Behind the cow-patted, urine-soaked yard was the dark cavern of a milking shed where my handsome boyfriend impressed me no end by being in charge of so much activity. After he had milked the cows

and turned them loose and swept out the yard, we would walk in
the fields, his hand in mine, his arm around my waist or shoulders.
He was well built for a lad of fifteen – probably all that carting of
milk crates and sweeping of cow dung – and in the heat he was often
stripped to the waist, sweating, pushing back strands of thick black
hair. I wasn't in love with him. I fancied him, I was thirteen, and
I wanted to learn about sex. It was a hot hot summer.

Most days I would sit on the gate swinging my legs, watching him
at his labours. One day he came over, held my head in his hands,
and kissed me. Just before I closed my eyes (I had seen that much
in films) I remember a cow lifting its great brown and cream head
to stare at us, its fat tongue lolling, and then the boy's tongue was
parting my lips, pushing into my mouth. I remember walking home
alone afterwards down the rutted track, feeling thrilled and exultant
that I had been kissed. I had been kissed. A French kiss from a tough
farmer's lad.

After that we spent as much time as possible exploring each other's
bodies. I was eager to learn. He was not very talkative but his hands
were eloquent and his work with animals made him, in my eyes,
earthy and much older than his years. We lay in long ripening grass.
His hands, hardened by work, made their way up my blouse and
under my skirt, sure and confident. My hands roamed his chest and
arms, his back and shoulders, and we kissed until our mouths were
sore. I remember the first time I curled my hands around his erection
and was shocked to feel hardness within soft flesh. I had never seen
my father naked. Until that summer day I had no idea what men had
between their legs.

It was innocent. Brand new and innocent. We were just a young
boy and a younger girl standing on a precipice, looking down into the
unexplored landscape of sex.

Wind the tape forward a bit and we have been together for about
four months. He is my boyfriend and we are going steady. At some

level I knew that this boy was not the love of my life but his warm and relaxed physicality was good for me and just what I needed as I metamorphosed bit by bit from child to woman. It was autumn and the leaves were falling. The grasses and nettles at the sides of the track were turning dry and snapped easily when we swished them, like children, with sticks. This day was mellow and golden. I remember we were just wandering along, bodies stuck close together, his arm round my shoulders, my arm round his waist, when we heard a car behind us on the track. Cars didn't go that way, but it could have been a farm vehicle. We didn't bother turning around, just moved to the side to let it pass. But it didn't. When it was almost on top of us, we heard the wheels skid to a halt. A door open. Heavy running footsteps. Someone grabbed my arm very hard and I cried out loud and… oh please no… the person hurting me was my father. Of course my heart sank. It plummetted all the way down a very deep well. My father was red-furious, breathing hard, and hurting me as he dragged me back to the car. His fingers made bruises on my arms.

'Get in,' he shouted, shoving me into the back seat and slamming the door. 'I never thought I would have to witness what I have just seen. You disgust me.'

He revved the car, wrenching it in a three-point turn, and back we went down the track, dust spraying out behind and words, ugly words, spewing out of my father's mouth. I was frozen. I stared straight ahead, not out of the back window at the figure left behind. I had been caught with a boy. I knew I would be in trouble when I was found out, that much was obvious, but I was terrified by the ferocity of my father's rage.

'That's it. Finished. That's the last time you see him, you little bitch.'

'We were only…' I attempted in a very small voice, my cheeks burning with shame.

'Don't you give me any "We were only…" Don't think you can

kid me. You're nothing but a slut! Now shut up. I don't want to hear another word.'

My father pushed me into the house and barked at me to go to my room. He didn't speak to me for a week, not a single word, and if he walked into a room where I was sitting doing my homework, he turned on his heel and left. He looked through me if we happened to pass in a corridor or on the stairs. My mother was cool for a day, then she seemed to mellow and was kind, at least when my father was not around. Clara washed her hands of the whole episode and pretended I didn't exist. Two out of three of my family were not acknowledging my presence. What had I done that was so terrible? My friends and I had often wondered what would happen if our parents caught us snogging and mucking around with boys. It was a constant background nag of worry, but we dealt with the threat lightly, thinking our new experiences well worth the risk. A couple of my friends had been caught and told off and grounded, but later they were forgiven and released and ran straight back into the arms of their boys. But for me a shutter had snapped closed forever. My father conveyed repulsion and rejection for months and months until it became the norm. There would never be forgiveness. He would not love me again.

That was the turning point. Never again did he touch me gently if I was sad or hurt, or talk to me, or teach me something I wanted to know. When I was thirteen I found my first boyfriend and lost my father.

*

The door bell rings, making me jump. Tears are streaming down my face. One leg is numb from sitting still in one place for so long. Upset and shaken at the poignancy and vividness of my own memories after all these years, I stumble down the stairs. Mustn't keep him waiting. Mustn't let him see me crying. For a brief moment I expect to see the father who was strict and cruel and uncomfortable with my developing sexuality. My transition from child to woman. Was it because he was never at ease with his own? I dread reaching the door and hearing the harsh voice bark its criticisms and put-downs.

But no. This is a different person, an old man who looks a bit grey and tired and says, 'Awful night. You shouldn't be making me write this story. Gives me nightmares. It's all your fault.' And whereas once those last four words would have been cruel and heartfelt, now they are only half-true and said with a twinkle.

'Oh dear,' I say. 'Do you want to carry on? You don't have to, you know.'

But he is already climbing the stairs. I notice that his breath is a bit short and halfway up he pauses to place his hand on the banisters to rest. I see an old hand with wrinkled paper skin and brown age spots. At the top landing I help him climb out of his bullet-proof sports jacket.

'I've been going over and over it… lying awake thinking… agreeing to let Mary stay in Nairobi. It was the wrong decision. I used to lie on my bed then, awake until the early hours, worrying about sending Mary and you girls home but in the morning whenever I raised the subject your mother was always adamant that she would stay. So much was going on at that time. A state of emergency. You don't remember, do you? Where's that coffee?'

Do I reply or rush to the kitchen?

'Go and sit down, Father,' I say. 'How much danger were we in? Really?'

'At that stage of the game, very little I think.'

'It was the beginning?'

'It was the beginning. Then the Mau Mau murdered one of their own. Waruhui.'

'Who?' I ask. I do not know this part of the story.

'Before I get to that… well… you have to understand the Kikuyu were taking revenge on their own people. The so-called loyalists…

because they stuck with us. There were some very powerful black chiefs out there who'd prospered and swore allegiance to us in return for privileges. One of the really big guns was Waruhui, who was nick-named "Africa's Churchill" in the British press because of his allegiance to British law and order and his unswerving hostility towards the Mau Mau.' My father pauses and gives me a quizzical look. 'This is all part of the story. Why aren't you writing it down? Shall I go on?'

'Please do.'

Chapter 35

Nairobi 1953
David

It was late afternoon. The date was October 9th, 1953. Afterwards the story spread like a bush fire and more people were afraid.

Dressed as usual in his smart suit, crisp white shirt and tie, Senior Chief Waruhui climbed into the back seat of his shining Hudson Sedan with a couple of his friends. He was to be driven to the village of Gache for a meeting. The car set off, past the pink stucco buildings and the manicured grounds of the Muthaiga Club and the three men talked about the possible implications of the current situation for them and other loyalists. They leant back, relaxed, as they passed acres of well-tended coffee plantations and swathes of banana trees whose leaves glistened a darker green with the first rains of the season.

It was no more than twenty minutes later that their car was waved to a halt on an empty expanse of road by three black police. Nothing unusual about that. Probably a routine road check. The driver pulled up and composed his features into a mask without expression while one of the police gestured to those in the back to roll down the window. The policeman stooped, looked inside, and asked which of the three passengers was Chief Waruhui. As Waruhui leant forward to identify himself, the policeman pulled a gun. Through the words still being spoken came the hard hurting metal of a barrel, and then the bullet that blew out the chief's brains. Threads of tissue spurted on to the windscreen, the windows, the other men, and hung there. The chief's body had jerked as the bullet was fired. A puppet on a string. Then three more shots at close range through the white shirt; three channels close to Waruhui's heart, which spurted red, soaking his companions. Waruhui died right there in his Hudson Sedan. They said afterwards that it was the first shot that killed him.

Three black men shot more bullets into the car tyres and ran off into the forest, whooping and screaming at one another. The other three black men, shocked and shaking, pushed open the car doors and stumbled away to flag down the next car, to raise the alarm, to get help. They shook off the bits of flesh and wiped their bloody hands on the leaves of the banana trees.

Harry heard the news and sent a string of memos composed in a tone that cleaned away all drama and shock. Then he set off to tell me because he wanted to discuss it without the formality normally demanded of him.

'God, what timing.' he said, pulling up a chair that looked much too small for a man of his height. He managed to fold himself into it.

'Nice start for Sir Evelyn Baring,' I agreed. 'The poor sod has only just arrived to take up his new post.'

'Governor of the colony. Replacement for Sir Philip Mitchell,' Harry said scathingly.

'You don't approve? He has the right credentials. Don't start judging already, old man. He's only been here ten days.'

'Not everyone knows this but he contacted severe amoebic dysentery in his previous post in India. Rumour has it that the illness has left him weak and depressed. Just the man to cope with a bloody native uprising. He won't have a clue.'

'He's not come out as a fighting soldier, Harry. Office job. High-up office job.'

'He'll still need stamina. Why not appoint someone who's fit? Over-Baring, I call him.'

I braced myself for another dose of Harry's cynicism.

'Nothing more than a bloody bureaucrat. He's got none of the right qualifications for dealing with what's going on out here. Do you know, David, no one told the poor bugger the truth. They kept it hushed up to make sure he came out. Poor sod. He was watching his servant hang up his shirts when they sent him a memo telling him that the Mau Mau had control of three Kikuyu districts and that the movement was spreading fast. Had he known, he would never have taken on the job.'

'Hang on, Harry. Give the man a chance,' I replied. 'He's got the best possible pedigree. I thought he looked very confident at the swearing-in ceremony, didn't you?'

'I do agree that not many men can wear an oversized white pith helmet topped with ostrich feathers and not look an idiot,' Harry said.

'Well, he acted promptly when Waruhui was murdered. I heard he immediately cabled the Colonial Office to ask permission to declare a state of emergency. He was responsible for getting Operation Jock Scott in place.' Why do I always find myself defending the actions of my superiors with Harry, I wondered.

'The thing is,' Harry continued, ignoring what I'd just said, 'I suspect that Baring believes that the situation here is being greatly exaggerated and that the Mau Mau movement will fall apart in three months at most. Flash in a pan. They don't have the skills, those backward natives up in the mountains, to organise a revolution.'

'Could be right.' I thought he was being serious.

'Rubbish!'

'So what do you think?'

'I think we are just settling in for one of the most savage and bloody periods in the history of Africa. I think it will be years before we see it through to the end.'

That silenced me. Harry had dropped hints enough that he thought we were in for a rough time but I hadn't taken much notice. But this was said with absolute conviction.

'I'm off. See you later,' he said with a nod as he left my room.

I thought about Harry's words a lot, and was still running the tape-loop of our conversation through my mind when I arrived back at the bungalow that evening, where I was surprised to find that Mary was not at home. It was the first time she had not come out to greet me. Malinge turned up in the hall looking concerned, as if he were somehow to blame, followed by Eve and Clara, barefoot, hot and dishevelled.

'Memsaab shopping. Memsaab not back,' Malinge said quickly.

I took off my hat and placed it with my keys on the side table in the hall. My first reaction was surprise and perhaps slight concern, but not anxiety. Mary went out and about still in Nairobi, although more cautiously now. She never stayed away for more than a couple of hours.

'When did she leave?' I asked.

'Bwana, two o'clock.'

'Mummy left after lunch to go shopping,' Eve said breathlessly, partly because she had been running about, and partly, I suspect, because she was picking up the tension and felt self-important telling me that her mother was not home. 'I wanted to go too but she said No. She said she had a lot to do and wanted to run round the shops quickly and she said Clara was not quick enough and would get too tired, and I said I was quick enough but she said I was to stay with Clara.'

'Quite right, Eve. OK, Malinge, nothing to worry about I'm sure. Memsaab has been delayed somewhere. Go back to the kitchen and prepare dinner.' When he had gone, I turned to my girls and was struck, as I often was, by how unalike they were, one so dark and one so fair. 'How about washing your hands and combing your hair, and I'll beat you both at Monopoly while we wait for Mummy to come home?'

I wanted to calm things down. I can't abide panic. Clara ran squealing down the corridor to the bathroom, and judging by how quickly she was back, I don't suppose she did more than run her fingers under the cold tap. A game before dinner was not to be missed. Clara loved every board game I could lay my hands on and was skilful at everything I taught her. She played as if her life depended on it. Her sister, though, turned up her nose and said cards and board games were boring. I'd rather read a book or draw, she'd say. But tonight the pair of them were eager, and we were not long into our game, with Clara trying so hard I had already decided to let her win, when we heard the sound of the front door being opened, followed by the relieved voice of Malinge.

'Memsaab come! Memsaab here!'

'Thank you,' I called with a warning coolness. 'Get dinner ready to serve in ten minutes.'

Then Mary burst into the living room. 'I'm so sorry!' she cried. 'Oh, David, I am sorry to be late. I hope I've not worried you.'

There was a wild look in her eyes and a nervous agitation in her every fluttering movement as she smoothed her skirt and pushed back her untidy hair and pulled out a hanky, which she wiped across her flushed and dusty face. Then she rushed across the room and scooped up Clara. Whatever has happened? I wondered, as I watched Mary whispering apologies and endearments into Clara's tangled hair and holding out a hand for Eve, who of course had run to her mother's side. For a moment my wife looked fierce and passionate as she clung to her two children.

I assumed it was a case of frayed nerves. Mary certainly wouldn't be the first woman to crack under the pressure of recent events, in fact several of the wives had already packed their bags and returned home. I wouldn't have been surprised and certainly wouldn't have blamed her if she was on edge. The possibility of a sudden, violent incident hovered at the back of everyone's mind.

'Calm down, Mary,' I said finally, trying for a note of sympathy but at the same time wanting to quell the hysteria in our living room. There was more than enough irrational behaviour out there amongst the white settlers. 'What kept you? Has something upset you?'

'There was an incident in the town centre…' she said breathlessly. Then she seemed to come to her senses because she put Clara down and said much more quietly, 'I'm sorry. I'm fine. Something held me up, that's all.'

'What?' I asked.

'I'll tell you later, David' she said with a meaningful glance at Eve and Clara. Well done, Mary, I remember thinking. You may have had a bit of a shock but you still have enough self-control not to alarm the girls.

'How about a drink?' I said. 'Whisky and soda?'

'Please. I'll just go and tell Malinge to serve dinner as soon as it's ready. You must all be hungry.'

When she came back she was much more composed and sent me a look which I interpreted as an apology. Then she came across and rested a hand on my shoulder. I placed my own hand on top of hers.

'Everything will be all right,' I said.

Those damn words again. So easy to say at the time. Impossible to retrieve now.

Over a dinner of fried chicken and rice, and slices of fresh pineapple for pudding, we chatted about anything other than what had happened to Mary, which would have to wait until later. Judging by her quiet composure, I guessed that it hadn't been anything too serious. Red circles still glowed on her cheeks, as if she had been standing too long in the sun, and occasionally she seemed distracted and asked me to repeat something I'd just said, but otherwise she seemed fine.

'By the way, Mary, I suggested to Harry that we all get together for lunch at the Limuru Club a week on Saturday.' I had been looking forward to telling her this news.

Mary looked confused for a moment then took me by surprise by saying, 'I'd rather not go, if you don't mind, David.'

'Why ever not?'

'Do I really have to spell it out?' she asked, fierce again, telling me without words that this was something linked to whatever had happened during the afternoon. I was again concerned.

'OK, we'll discuss it later.'

'I won't go.'

And instead of hearing the finality in her voice and the warning to leave it, I bumbled on, unwilling to let go of something I was very much looking forward to.

'I know what you're thinking but the club's less than five miles outside Nairobi on the main road. It will be absolutely fine.'

'You don't know what I'm thinking.' Another furious look.

Let it go, I told myself.

Clara gave a huge sigh and lay her head on the table beside her plate of unfinished curry.

'It's OK, sweetheart,' Mary said, stroking her dark hair and looking daggers at me. 'I'm sorry. Mummy and Daddy are talking about things that don't interest you. Eat a bit more curry and you can have ice cream with your pineapple for pudding.'

Clara knew she was being bribed. She looked at her mother with childish disdain.

It was much later, when the girls were in bed and we were sitting quietly on the veranda, each with a whisky and soda at our side, that I broached the subject again.

'Tell me what happened this afternoon.'

'I was trying to forget it.'

'I'd rather know,' I replied.

'Of course. I'm sorry to have been overdramatic. There was a serious incident in town. Apparently – because I only heard the details afterwards – three Kikuyu tribesmen had planned to rob the printing press run by the Pakistani family who own this bungalow.'

I nodded, trying not to show my mounting alarm.

'A couple of their employees were looking out of the window when they noticed three natives hanging around outside the premises. When the men were still there half an hour later, the employees went outside and challenged them. The Kikuyu were ready for them. They had pangas and they used them. It turned very nasty, David. When other employees heard the noise and saw that two of their own were on the ground, bleeding heavily, they called the Nairobi police and they arrived fairly quickly and stopped the fighting… but by the time they got there one of the men was already dead. The police shot one of the Kikuyu but the others were too quick and got away.'

'Poor Mary… I'm sorry, I had no idea it was so serious. What a horrible thing for you to witness.'

'I didn't see it. I just happened to walk past after it had happened. The police asked all of us who were anywhere near for statements. I happened to be one of the people who saw the end of it. I stayed behind and told the police what I had seen – which in fact was very little because it was all over when I got there. That's what made me late.'

I reached across to take her hand. 'I'm so sorry. When you were late home I just assumed it was something trivial or perhaps that you'd met someone…'

Mary turned her head and I saw that her cheeks were flushed. For a few moments she couldn't continue.

'Take your time,' I told her gently.

'Sorry. Just a bit stunned still. You know, the silly thing is that I was worrying more about being late and upsetting you and the girls than the fact that an innocent man had been killed by the Kikuyu right in the middle of town.'

'We don't know what's going on behind the scenes. We don't know who is with us and who isn't. The loyalists are the same colour as the rebels.'

'I suppose this is how things will be from now on,' she said soberly.

'No, not necessarily,' I replied. 'This sounds more like a case of planned robbery than terrorism. It could have happened anywhere at any time. Don't read too much into it. You're not hurt and that's all that matters.' I held both her hands in mine.

She gave me a strange look then. I had calmed and soothed her, yet instead of looking relieved, she looked almost mischievous and, dare I say it, triumphant. You know, after a big flare-up and its aftermath, there is usually a feeling like... well, like a popped balloon. A good sort of tiredness and a sense of relief. But Mary was still bright-eyed and alert. That night she must have had trouble sleeping because I was aware that she got up several times. I heard her footsteps in the veranda, pacing up and down. She must have been replaying what happened.

As I lay in bed, I went over and over her story, imagining the fight, trying to put myself in her shoes. I still couldn't work out what had delayed her so much even if she did have to give a statement, but I decided to let it go. There was no point in going over it all again.

The following day the *Evening Standard* described the incident as 'a storm in a tea-cup', completely in tune with my own thoughts, but history proved us both wrong. It was a spark, but the ground was already tinder-dry.

Perhaps that explained Mary's mood. Intuitively she had got it right and was already one step ahead of me.

Chapter 36

Nairobi 1953
Mary

Time plays tricks, I know, but that afternoon it was cruelly maverick. I remember opening my eyes, dazed and dreamy, and wondering where on earth I was. One arm was numb where I had been lying on it, like someone else's body part, until I rubbed some tingling life back into it. Above me the sky seemed lower, a purple dark with streamers of pink clouds, and the noise of the crickets was intrusive, insistent. Through the narrow wooden railings of the veranda I saw the expanse of grass as neat green slices, and beyond the stripes the outline of trees black against the remaining light. The man beside me slept on.

I looked at Harry's peaceful face and knew that I had found the person who steps into your life once and once only. Too late. I traced his brows and forehead with my finger until he too opened his eyes. I smiled at the play of emotions that passed over his face, as they must have done, unobserved, over mine – confusion, remembering, and finally tenderness as he reached up to kiss me.

The air was cool and the sky quickly darkening.

'What time is it?' I asked him. We were dragging ourselves back into the present, pulling out from under us various crushed items of clothing, me patting my wild hair into some semblance of order, him pushing arms into the shirt we had both been lying on and fastening his trousers with his belt.

'It's after six,' he replied, knowing exactly what that meant.

'Oh no…'

'Don't panic, my love. We'll think of something. Why are you wearing only one sandal?'

'The other one fell into the grass. Harry, I should have been home hours ago. They'll think something has happened to me. Oh heavens…'

He put his arm around my shoulders, twisted me round to face him, and put a finger over my silly chattering mouth. Then he kissed my eyelids gently and tenderly until I was smiling. Damn them all, I thought for one crazy, selfish minute. Just give me my freedom.

'I can be very inventive when I need to be. Part of the job description. I'm used to covering my tracks, remember. Trust me, Mary. I'm not going to be the one to land you in trouble. I'll think of something. It won't be difficult to come up with a story. We're living in a state of emergency, for God's sake, and something unexpected happens almost every day. It's not like we're arriving back late in some sleepy English village where eyes behind net curtains check the exact time. Come on. Let me get you home.'

'I'm never away for more than an hour or two,' I said, still not reassured. 'Never. Especially since the emergency. It's too risky. I know that and David knows that. I just wouldn't be away this long without letting them know.' Then I remembered the arrangements I had made for the girls. 'Oh no! Jennie will have brought Eve and Clara home and will have found no one there except Malinge to let them in! They'll think I'm absolutely irresponsible. I'm always there if they have been out.'

'Mary, dearest… please… be quiet… let me think.'

We were walking briskly towards the car, Harry's keys already in his hands. But before opening the door he turned to me and said,

'I want you to know, Mary, that for me this is not something lightly undertaken. I love you. I think I fell in love with you the day you arrived in Africa.'

'I know that, or I wouldn't be here,' I said, kissing him. 'Now please get me home.'

How unlike our furtive arrival was our exit. Harry revved hard on the gravel path, but the tyres refused to grip. The spinning wheels sent spurts of stones and dust behind us until finally Harry changed gear, pulling the car sideways and jolting it forwards. He turned on to the road. Harry was a brilliant driver so I was not afraid as he put his foot flat on the pedal. Travelling up the escarpment away from the Rift Valley the roads were usually quiet, and that day, like other days, ours was the only car moving in the silence before dusk. We were quiet too, lost in our own thoughts, but physically not losing touch for one moment. Harry's arm was around my shoulder as he drove, or his hand rested gently on my thigh.

'Nothing can drive us apart now, can it?' I asked at one point, more of myself than of Harry.

'If you can make puns like that at a time like this, I look forward to being with you in more relaxed circumstances,' he quipped.

It was the only time we laughed.

I gripped the edges of the car bench like I hang on to my arm-rests each time I fly in order to keep the plane in the air by will power alone. If you try and try hard enough you can make things work out the way you want. The plane won't crash if you grip the seat and if I held the edge of my car seat hard enough my life wouldn't come crashing down around me. I felt physically sick with worry. My heart was racing, my hands were clammy and kept sticking to the gluey plastic of the seat. Stop thinking, stop imagining, I told myself, as image after image of David pacing up and down the sitting room flashed in front of my eyes. What would Eve and Clara be doing? Were they upset because their mother had not come home? At times like that I would normally offer up frantic prayers to the heavens but I knew God would not be sympathetic.

As we raced back down the escarpment towards Nairobi, I dreamt up excuse after excuse and tried them out on an imaginary David, as though rehearsing my part in a play. Or I was in a movie, acting out my arrival at the bungalow again and again until my lines, mouthed silently, seemed convincing and right. I could wrap a hanky round my ankle and say I had fallen off the pavement and it had taken ages to hobble home. I had bumped into a friend who was in a terrible state about the Mau Mau so I had gone home with her until she had calmed down. But who could I ask to provide me with an alibi for that one? I had been for a long walk and simply forgotten about the time. On and on went the rambling plots, which were too corny to convince anyone, while Harry drove very fast along the winding, climbing road that takes you away from the plains of the Great Rift Valley.

On the way, we passed a Masaii warrior holding up his spear in the usual way to ask for a lift. Normally we would have stopped, but not that time. I was once travelling back from Mombassa with David on the murram road, which is half the distance of the tarmac road but, as we soon discovered, much more bumpy and stony. We were reversing down a side track, a wrong turning, when two tall Masaii stepped out from nowhere and blocked our way with their spears. My immediate thought was that they were going to kill us but they only wanted a lift. So off we went again, dust billowing out behind us, two warriors sitting stony-faced on the back seat with spears between their legs, and me still wondering if we would reach our destination alive. In the end they just asked to get out about halfway back. Thus I was introduced to one of many native customs.

There comes a point on the main road when suddenly you round a bend and there is Nairobi spread out below you, and you look down as if you are on top of the world. But that day, as we reached the heights, the traffic increased and the road into the city seemed unusually busy and congested. It was nothing to do with the rush hour because those leaving the city after work were travelling in the opposite direction. Keep going, I prayed. Please let us keep going. But soon we were in a tailback stretching a couple of miles out of the city. People were leaning on their horns. Drivers were out of their cars, Kenyan style, doors left open, shielding their eyes from the setting sun to peer ahead and see what was wrong, or just taking time to lean on the car and light a cigarette. Harry inched forwards, then stopped. Forwards a few feet then stopped again.

'Damn,' he said. 'Now what's happened? This road is never blocked.'

'Maybe an accident,' I suggested.

'Just our luck.'

Tears came easily and slipped down my cheeks while I willed the traffic to slide forwards, to magically clear, so that we could race home. I was in my airplane seat again making the same futile, exhausting, nerve-wracking effort to spur us on – to no avail.

It must have taken an hour for us to inch our way into Delamere Avenue, where finally we saw the police jeeps and swarms of uniformed men ahead of us outside the publishing offices owned by the Pakistani family from whom we rented our bungalow. As we drew level with the building, we saw, behind the cordoned-off area, the body of a native on the ground in a pool of blood that was already the colour of rust. Other cars inched past one by one, everyone rubber-necking, but Harry stopped, called sharply across to one of the policemen, and waved his identity card.

'Intelligence,' he said briskly. 'What's going on?'

'Sir. There has been a fight. An attack by Kikuyu tribesmen on some of the employees of the publishing company.'

'What happened?'

'Some Kikuyu were spotted hanging around outside, Sir. When

the employees went to investigate, they were attacked. Motive not clear yet.'

'Perhaps another revenge attack for a refusal to join the Mau Mau,' Harry said to himself. 'How many wounded and killed?'

'One fatality over there. Two badly injured taken to hospital. Two tribes involved.'

'I see. But why all the traffic? It's taken us an hour to drive the last couple of miles.'

'Routine enquiries, Sir. We had to stop every car to ask for witnesses. Now I'll have to ask you to move on please, Sir.'

Harry pressed the accelerator and, for the first time since we had driven away from the deserted house, he smiled. Then he grabbed my hand and pressed it to his lips.

'Mary, someone up there is on our side.'

Chapter 37

NAIROBI 1953
DAVID

As things turned out, our outing to the Limuru Club proved the last time we went out together as a family. The Mau Mau situation deteriorated rapidly during the weeks that followed and we all had to batten down the hatches – officers, men, wives, families and children. Mary and the girls became hostages in their own home, held not by terrorists but by the fear of them. I was out on patrol, involved in a guerrilla war that was very different from anything I had experienced before. I was not prepared.

But I'm getting ahead of myself. Perhaps it wasn't the most sensible plan – to drive out of Nairobi with my family – but to be honest it was something people still did and any doubts I voice now come with the wisdom of hindsight, overwritten by subsequent experience.

Just before we left, I was disquieted to catch Eve teasing Clara in a stupid, thoughtless way and it made me realise how the Mau Mau business was seeping into the fabric of my family. I had to deal with Eve firmly. Mary had dressed her in a pink dress with a matching bow in her pale hair. She looked like one of those Pears Soap adverts, the perfect little girl, her eyes blue and innocent, but knowing how deceptive appearances can be, especially with that one, I'm afraid I tuned in to what she was saying.

'Well you just mustn't play with him anymore.'

'Why?'

''Cause he's black and we mustn't play with black people.'

Clara gazed up at Eve, her huge eyes expressing a complete rejection of her sister's words.

'I already told you. Lots of times. And you take no notice.'

Clara continued her soft humming.

'Listen to me, Clara. Stop humming. Black people are dangerous.'

'Why?'

'Because that little boy Michael was killed by his black servant, that's why!'

'Don't be silly. Malinge won't hurt us.'

That little girl surprised me in those days with her gentle confidence. Only a few months before she had wept readily when Eve provoked and teased her, but now she was changed. She had grown up about six years in six months, an old head on young shoulders, perhaps too wise for her own good.

'You don't understand, Clara. Listen, I know that the black people in the mountains are angry with the white people and they hate us and they want the servants to run away from their families. They will give the servants knives and guns. Malinge might go. Just you wait and see.' Eve's eyes blazed. She could certainly play the drama queen.

'Malinge won't ever hurt us,' Clara said with soft assurance.

'Well, other black men might,' Eve said, riled that Clara was not rising to her bait.

I decided it was time to intervene. 'Eve! That will do,' I said sharply. 'You are talking nonsense.' I turned Eve round to face me and Clara looked up too. 'Now, listen carefully to me, you two. Only some of the black men are behaving badly. They are a long way from here, right up in the mountains, and they are not going to come here and hurt you or Clara or any of us. Eve, I don't want to hear any more of that silly talk, do you understand?'

I took her by the shoulders and she nodded, but if looks could kill, I would have been a gonner. Clara, in contrast, put her hand in mine. 'You will look after us, won't you, Daddy.' A statement, not a question.

'Of course I will,' I replied. A child's words can melt a man's heart. I vowed that nothing, nothing would happen to either of them.

On our way out of Nairobi the mood in the car was distinctly odd. Eve was sulking after being told off in front of her sister, Clara was in her own world, and Mary was strangely quiet and fiddled with the strand of hair that sometimes came loose and fell over her pretty face. For most of the journey she turned her head away from me, staring out of the window, or pretending to. I noticed that her blue eyes were rimmed with red as if she had been crying. She breathed almost inaudible small sighs. Ever since she had been caught up in the fracas outside the publishing offices in Nairobi she had been distracted and on edge.

We met up with Marjorie and Harry at the bar and had a sherry before lunch, and then it was my turn to feel odd. I experienced something unusual for me – the sense of looking on rather than participating – a bizarre coincidence given the ensuing conversation between Mary and Marjorie. Honestly, I might as well have left a cardboard cut-out of myself propped up at the bar, so uninvolved was I in the conversation. I felt excluded. Although we deliberately talked about other things, the political situation was ever-present, like an uninvited guest. One cardboard cut-out and one unwanted guest. I suppose it was doomed to failure. As usual, Harry and Marjorie behaved like the two independent individuals they were. It's funny but I have never thought of them as a married couple. I knew very little about their relationship, but then why should I? Always stayed clear of personal stuff with Harry, and anyone else for that matter. In public they never showed the slightest sign of intimacy, not that that means anything of course. In those days it wasn't done to paw one another in public. As far as I could tell their marriage was as good as, or better than, most of the other couples out there.

That day, for some reason, Harry and I found it difficult to engage with each other and there were lots of awkward silences. Not surprising, I remember thinking. Troubled times. He must have had a lot on his mind.

'So what are you painting at the moment?' Mary was asking Marjorie.

'Tribesmen,' Marjorie replied cheerfully.

'In tribal costume?'

'No, no. Heads. Staring out of the canvas. I want to get as close to a camera portrait as possible.'

'Oh,' said Mary, bless her, probably racking her brain for something wise to say.

'I'm interested in the stance of the observer compared with the participant. Who is watching whom. We Europeans paint the Africans as specimens, looking straight at them but missing their point of view. I want to get across the idea that they are looking at us. We are the outsiders, after all.'

'I see,' Mary responded politely. Not that it mattered what she said, because Marjorie was content to talk to herself if necessary. She did a lot of thinking out loud.

I felt I should contribute something. 'Why specimens? They live alongside us out here. Like our servants and the African soldiers,' I said.

'They are the exceptions. The minority,' she replied. 'At best they tolerate us, but they remain themselves. We try to absorb them into our culture but it's pointless. Don't think you understand them, David, because you don't.'

I was getting lost and a bit hot under the collar at her outspokenness. 'So the paintings are…' I prompted.

'Africans staring at the painter. Unadorned. Undiluted. I want to capture an expression which is not contaminated, if you see what I mean. They are doing the observing.'

'Yes, I do understand what you are saying,' Mary commented. 'That's quite a challenge, isn't it?'

'Oh, but a challenge is what I like,' Marjorie replied. 'I'm not interested in representing natives with rings in their ears. All that tourist rubbish. I want to capture them stripped of all pretence. Especially now that they are starting to show their true colours, if you'll excuse the pun.'

Harry said nothing during this exchange. Perhaps he knew his wife's views and ideas perfectly well already.

'I think lunch is being served,' I said, taking Mary's arm and giving her a look which she would easily interpret. Enough of this intellectual talk. She knew me through and through and sometimes teased me for being her 'action man'.

'I'll go and gather up the girls,' Mary replied. 'They're over in the corner playing with the Finch children. Do you know Kate Finch?' she asked Marjorie, neatly turning the conversation away from art.

'No. There are those with children, and those without,' Marjorie said bluntly. 'The two don't mix.'

'I suppose not,' Mary replied, and off she went to fetch Eve and Clara, leaving Harry, Marjorie and myself to wander across to the table that had been reserved for us.

Over lunch the conversation limped along with many a long silence. Harry and I attempted our usual banter about cricket but it was like dropping stones into water. Each one sank without trace. Usually Mary engaged so easily with Harry, laughing at his silly jokes and listening eagerly when his conversation became serious, but that day she gave Marjorie her full attention, continuing to offer her openings to talk about her painting and doing a jolly good job of responding with interest. I had never seen Harry in such a detached mood, as if he were preoccupied with something entirely different and was there only in body. For once he made no effort to engage Mary. They hardly exchanged a word. He and I got up soon after the meal and went for a smoke and a brandy with the other men.

As soon as the door closed behind us, there was only one topic of conversation, and we men quickly got down to it, passionate and animated, leaving the women to their children and their coffee.

Chapter 38

NAIROBI 1953
MARY

You might think that a close shave like that – being caught up in an incident right in the centre of Nairobi – would have stopped us in our tracks, but if anything our luck that day in having a readymade alibi only spurred us on to greater boldness and cunning in the months that followed. Lies came easily to my lips. I told David that with the Mau Mau situation growing ever more serious, I had to make lots of extra trips into Nairobi to stock up on household supplies and medicines in case we became prisoners in our own homes, a situation which looked increasingly likely. I told him I went to a regular support group for colonial and forces wives, knowing he would show no interest in the details. I told him I sometimes visited Marjorie to see how her painting was coming along. Fortunately he was so busy and puffed up with a sense of his own importance (no, that's not fair – he was simply taking a genuine pleasure in being involved in active duty) that he did not notice my increasing absences, and Malinge believed my stories readily, more than happy to accept my instructions to keep a close eye on the girls instead of dusting the furniture, because his greatest pleasure was to spend time with them. Especially Clara, whom he adored. Household chores became neglected but of course I turned a blind eye to his taking advantage of me since I was already taking advantage of him.

Looking back, I am amazed that I got away with so many excuses and so many lies. In the month after what I call our Veranda Scene, I think Harry and I became familiar with at least a dozen deserted colonial houses around Lake Naivasha and Lake Elementeita, which we easily broke into because their owners had moved out in such a rush. On warm afternoons and in soft darkening evenings we made love in lush grounds. I lay in long grass that crackled with grasshoppers, felt whispering tall stems blowing across my bare legs and curled my bare toes into grass as soft as velvet. Petals of frangipani fell like confetti on our naked bodies. I persuaded myself that I needed nothing more. For the first time in my life, I felt that I belonged. This is my landscape, I would whisper. This is what I am made of. This is love.

If it rained – which it sometimes did, as if a tap were turned fill on and then off again – we ran inside and slipped between the crisp white sheets of a stranger's perfectly made-up bed. We took cigarettes from a carved wooden box made by a native and sold at the roadside, and, sparking the flame of a gold lighter, we vied with each other to make the most perfect smoke ring inside the mosquito tent that hung over the bed. Afterwards, our bodies soaked with sweat, we stepped into a marble-lined shower and played under the rain of perfumed water. Harry massaged rose and lavender oils into my shoulders and fingered his way down the vertebrae of my spine, pushing his thumbs into the spaces that burned with the red of pain and the purple of pleasure. We dried each other with thick, soft towels that had been laundered and folded and laid out by a servant long gone. Sometimes I slipped on a silk dress or a linen tea frock that I found in the wardrobe and shimmied along the catwalk in front of my captive and adoring audience, until he grabbed me with a rugby tackle and pulled me on to the bed and devoured me all over again.

One of our fantasies was to choose which of our many borrowed houses we would eventually move into when we were free to run away together. The lodge right on the shores of Lake Naivasha, with its sloping lawns and heavy colonial furniture? The red brick building named Element House with its internal courtyard and shady terraces? The grand mock-Elizabethan manor on Hippo Point with its garden of old English roses?

Lost in our own world, we walked hand in hand along the shores of Lake Naivasha, where sometimes we spotted giraffe standing among the yellow-barked acacia trees surrounding the lake, stretching their necks to reach a branch of leaves they would tear off and chew in rubber mouths. Monkeys were our faraway companions, calling and chattering to one another from the tree tops. A hippo maybe opened an eye but otherwise did not interrupt his day-long snooze in the shallows for the sake of two humans with their arms around each other. On one level perhaps we knew full well that our talk of living together was nothing more than a fairy story, but then I was used to telling my girls tales with happy endings. Cinderella finally married her prince. Yet in spinning our sugar-candy stories we always omitted the middle bit about David and Marjorie. Nor did I talk to Harry about what would happen to Clara and Eve. We were hopelessly in love but on some level were perfectly aware that we walked a tightrope between fantasy and reality.

Like an avalanche that has started its terrible fall down the steep side of a mountain, gathering momentum as it rumbled on, there was no stopping us. Today, when I think back to the crazy risks we took to snatch time together, I gasp with amazement and disbelief at our audacity and recklessness. No one caught us, and so we carried on.

There was only one excruciating moment when we came close to giving everything away and that was when David came up with the truly appalling idea that we would have lunch with Marjorie and Harry in the Limuru Club. Heaven only knows how it came about because Harry would never have suggested it. Perhaps it was an arrangement he made with Marjorie. Anyway, my heart sank like the proverbial stone when he announced the outing and I became a nervous wreck. I told David I did not want to go, made up all manner of excuses, but he insisted because, he said, it might be the last chance for the four of us to get together socially before the Mau Mau situation took a turn for the worse and we women found ourselves confined to our homes. I just knew that being with Harry in public would be almost impossible. I'm not that good an actress and could not carry it off. Not with David and Marjorie looking on. I might faint. I could see myself hiding in the ladies' room and refusing to come out. The heart on my sleeve was so large and blood-red that everyone in the room would see its frantic beating the moment my eyes met his.

On the way there, I was ready to open the car door and fling myself out on to the road. A broken bone or two would be preferable to the ordeal that lay ahead. At the entrance of the club, I discovered two heavy rocks had somehow attached themselves to my legs, so that it took a lot of effort and finally an impatient shove from David to get me up the damn steps.

They were at the bar. Harry was the first to turn as we walked across the room. Our eyes met for just one second because any longer and we would not have been able to look away. But eyes can express longing and warning in one fleeting glance. They can say 'This will be hard' and 'We have to behave like friends' and 'I adore you. I want you. I love you.' Harry took my hand, as he always did. In my imagination I brought it to my lips and smothered his freckled fingers with kisses. My face was on fire. He brushed against me, deliberately, taking advantage of Marjorie turning from the bar to greet David.

The way I finally coped – and it was some effort, with my heart playing ping-pong and my betraying eyes constantly slipping sideways to steal a look at Harry – was to give Marjorie my full attention. I was such a fake, expressing interest in her painting when I barely heard what she had to say to me. I used her and took advantage of her, this woman whose passion for her work was genuine and who seemed a bit surprised that for once no one cut her off mid-sentence. She was used to seeing eyes glaze over and the topic of conversation abruptly changed. At the crowded bar, Harry seized every opportunity to brush against me. His secret signals sent shivers up my spine while his wife talked on about the impact of the painter's perspective and I nodded my head and said 'Yes' in the right places, praying all the while that my own passion for her husband would remain unobserved.

We got away with it, Harry and I, but to anyone who knew him well his manner must have seemed unusually reserved, while I was either completely silent or chattered like a nervous adolescent. But then we were living in unusual times, with terrorism a constant threat, and we all understood that it affected different people in different ways. Harry would certainly have been excused for not exuding his usual charm because we could assume that he was party to information that might be worrying him. With the exception of the bulletproof Marjorie and a few others, probably most people had retreated over the past weeks to a more private and protected personal space where fear kept them company. I'm sure I was not the only one to draw an imaginary circle around my body, daring others to cross the line at their peril. News of another attack much closer to Nairobi was on everybody's lips but we all swallowed hard to keep panic from dribbling out. To a lesser or greater extent, all of us were marionettes who danced to the music of watchfulness. We looked more often over our shoulders. People who were models of politeness suddenly turned twitchy and rude. For Harry and me it was a blessing. Tension, as tangible as the cigarette smoke wafting from group to group, excused just about anything.

Who would notice a man and a woman behaving oddly against such a backcloth?

Chapter 39

Nairobi 1953
David

It was November. Mary and the girls were confined to the house under strict orders to remain there. There had been more vicious attacks and then nothing for a number of weeks, and in the lull we began to breathe more easily. I hoped that Harry was wrong when he said this space was a teasing game played by the Kikuyu, who waited and watched. Harry said that there was more to come. My opinion was that perhaps we were approaching the end of a short-lived and brutal flare-up because the Kikuyu had neither the ability nor the resources to mount anything more prolonged. If there were further skirmishes, they would be dealt with promptly and efficiently. We were all on red alert. Every soldier in Nairobi was primed and ready to act if necessary. While out on patrol on a still, starry night I even dared imagine that maybe soon Nairobi would return to its sultry, tranquil ways, with Harry and me back on the cricket pitch and Mary and the girls released from their locked cage. My song birds would fly and sing again.

It was at around this time of waiting that we heard that an old mate and colleague of mine, Wavell, was coming out to join us. Harry, of course, was one of the first to hear. Although I didn't see much of him now that we were both so fully occupied – one gathering information and the other using it to work with the men on the ground – we still occasionally met up.

'Wavell!' I exclaimed as we snatched a quick coffee before I set out to check up on one of the patrols in the city centre. 'Wasn't he sent home on medical grounds?'

'You're right, he was,' Harry replied. 'The poor bugger went back to a civi job training national service sergeants.'

'What a waste. Major is he now? He's only thirty-eight and he's been condemned to shuffling papers at a desk and standing in the classroom.'

'Well, let's just say I heard he didn't hesitate when they asked him to come back out here. He'll be stationed with the Black Watch up in the Aberdare Mountains. Thank God they've sent us someone with relevant skills because from what I've gathered, the poor buggers up there spend their days playing hide-and-seek and looking under the bloody bushes for Mau Mau footprints.'

'Come off it…' Anger rose like bile. I was one of those he was condemning.

'Sorry, old man, I didn't mean you. I know you do a good job. Word gets back to me. But some of the training is a bit pointless, isn't it?'

'For God's sake, Harry, we're doing our best, dealing with the unknown,' I snapped. 'This business is a different kind of conflict altogether and none of us have any experience with it. We're having to learn the rules as we go along. You try training men to deal with an enemy as slippery and savage as the Kikuyu in territory that's almost impenetrable. It's an incredibly frustrating way to fight.'

'Sorry. That was out of line. Of course it must be difficult.'

'It's damn near impossible. We have no idea where the Kikuyu are grouped nor how they move about the mountains like black ghosts.'

'I know. That's why I'm pleased we've got Wavell to take command.'

'Got hurt, didn't he?' I asked, grudgingly letting the topic go.

'He lost a hand in an ambush in India in 1943, the same kind of ambush he'll be preparing the men for out here. He's a very brave chap. Of course, he's his father's son.'

'Field Marshall Wavell?'

'The same. Commander in Chief of the Western Desert Force in the Libyan desert. First commander of the 8th Army.'

'Well, Wavell will be made very welcome,' I said.

I think many of us were reassured by the news of Wavell's return. Some of my men were feeling a bit twitchy, especially the young ones, because we were stuck in limbo, neither working as a peace-keeping force nor fully in action. Wavell would sort things out. Either the Mau Mau would retreat or we would push forward to hunt them out and bring them down. He had a reputation as one of the best when it came to knowledge about observation patrols and guerrilla warfare. He knew how to sniff out an enemy who slipped as silently as a snake along the ground and through the undergrowth. I can tell you the Mau Mau were a damn sight harder to find than the Germans or the Italians were in the desert. Up in the Aberdare Mountains there were no open spaces where you might just come upon a platoon unawares, and you were always pushing through the darkest undergrowth, tripping on roots, wading through muddy scrub land, cutting yourself on thorns and razor-edged leaves. Up in the mountains the sunlight was completely cut off. Or you'd be dazzled by a rare ray of light, which left you seeing green and pink dancing spots once the darkness came again. Sometimes you could hardly see more than a few feet ahead. And rain dripped steadily from the plate-sized leaves until you were cold and soaked.

Looking back, I think I had a harder time of it in Kenya once the stakes were raised than in Libya during the war. We were searching for an elusive enemy in an impossible terrain and to be honest we didn't know where the hell the Mau Mau were. They were cunning and invisible and the odds were stacked against us because they knew their land, every inch of it, while we were the outsiders, often searching in the wrong places and following the false trails they laid for us. In the desert things were clear-cut. We had regular information and we were well prepared. Every day, sometimes twice a day, there would be a conference involving the top six men, who would ask: What is Rommel doing? What are his tactics? How do we respond? And so as we advanced, we knew exactly when to lead our men forward and when to bring them to a standstill because we had inside information. An intelligence unit based at Siwa, about two hundred miles inside Libya, relayed everything they knew. Marvellous. They dropped behind the enemy lines and sent us dispatches. Tobruk was typical. We knew the exact moment at which to set out to strengthen our position there, and that was because we had the correct information. We managed to block enemy supplies, cutting off his lines completely and leaving Rommel with nothing. The intelligence units were one step ahead of them all the time, and even though the Italians and Germans used slightly different tactics, broadly speaking we were fighting a known enemy. A predictable enemy.

But the Mau Mau were an altogether different kettle of fish. Although we had the intelligence corps working with us, they produced very little useful information. It was like walking blindfold through a maze. Like fighting shadows. You know, it reminds me of the al-Qaeda terrorism network, dispersed, spread out and hiding God only knows where. Heaven help our boys in Iraq and Afghanistan. How do those poor soldiers track down terrorist units that could be hiding in wait anywhere in those mountains? How long have they been looking for Bin Laden? And now the bombs on London tubes and buses. Terrible. What an ugly world we live in.

Chapter 40

Edinburgh 2005
Eve

My father has stopped talking and is away in his own world, whether in Kenya or Iraq I am not sure, but I judge it time to make a coffee and tell him about Clara's phone call. I have been waiting for an opportunity.

'Time for a break?' I ask.

'What? Oh, I was miles away! Yes, I need a coffee.'

Soon I am back, crossing the landing back to my study bearing his steaming mug.

'We need to go to the library,' he announces. What, again! We must be their most frequent visitors. My father is getting through, or starting and abandoning, five books every few days.

'I'm out of bread. Why can't they make bread that lasts? Those rolls go stale in a day. Oh, and I want a shower like the one I had in hospital. That woman came and fitted a medieval seat in my bath.'

'I know. I saw it,' I smile. It is a bit basic and very ugly.

'I'm not sitting on that. I want a shower.'

A few weeks ago my father became acutely ill with a chest infection. I could hear how bad his chest was and from the heat of his forehead I could tell he was running a very high temperature. However, my father is a stranger to illness, having never even suffered from the common cold, and so he did not/would not recognise it as serious even when it was about to kill him. 'Don't you call out the doctor,' he ordered. 'Don't you call.' I disobeyed.

'You're really quite poorly,' our GP told him, having established that his temperature was 105 degrees and he could not stand unaided. 'I think you need to go to hospital so they can give you fluids and antibiotics.'

'Not going to hospital,' my grey-faced, wheezing, sweating father replied while our GP – who knows us very well – sent a discrete signal to me over his lolling head.

'OK. Well, let's see if you can get up and walk,' said the GP. Of course my father couldn't even stand and so soon, complaining loudly that it was all a fuss about nothing between rasping breaths, he was in the ambulance and on his way. During his ten-day stay he discovered great delight not just in telling his stories to the young nurses but in the walk-in shower.

'OK,' I reply. 'We can get the bath taken out and fit a shower.' I am amazed that he is willing to put up with the upheaval and the expense. My father can still surprise me. Tactfully I steer the conversation back to what I need to say.

'Clara phoned last night,' I begin.

'And how is your sister?'

'Worried.'

'What about? Which son now? Or is it that damn ex-husband of hers not paying his dues again?'

'All of the above,' I say. We share a despair which verges on hysteria when it comes to my sister, though we love her dearly and wish she could find happiness. First she married an everlasting bachelor architect, seduced by his fabulous Chiswick abode. Nest-making has always been important to the pair of us, perhaps the result of childhoods spent in buff-painted army quarters. Then, when the pig left her for a younger model, she moved into a poky semi; one son retreated to the attic, where he remains holed up at the age of twenty-five, while the other hovered between imminent arrest, rock-stardom and a degree in music. And she's got herself another ghastly man with another ghastly big house in West London. Terrible taste in men, my sister! And so wise and competent and clear-sighted in every other way.

'She ought to take Oliver to court. How much does he owe her now?'

'Thousands and thousands,' I reply. 'But she can't face any more court after more or less living in one during the divorce. Clara says no more lawyers because they cost £200 an hour, even on the phone.'

'He damn well should be made to pay up,' my father says, predictably. 'I just don't understand it.'

'I'm afraid I do. Just about every third woman in the country is in the same boat. The Child Support Agency is a total shambles. Even the government admits it's a farce.'

'She asked me to lend her money again last week, you know,' my father admits, thinking he has dropped a clanger, but I know this too. Clara and I are always open with each other.

'And what did you say?'

'I don't see why I should be paying her son's university fees!' my father says huffily. 'But I told her I'd send her something.'

'That's good of you,' I say. It isn't the first time such a request has come his way.

'What else did your sister have to say?' She is always 'your sister', not Clara, as if that label somehow diminishes her.

'She was telling me about the London bombs…'

'Oh, of course. I'd forgotten about that. She wasn't caught up in it, was she?' Of course he hasn't forgotten, but he files the present in a small well-concealed drawer in the cabinet of his mind, while the past is in a much more accessible place. He told me recently that when he goes to bed – very early because he gets cold sitting in his lounge, where he refuses to put on any heating – and lies under the electric blanket, he always begins thinking about his very earliest memory, when he is about two years old with his mother in Liverpool, and continues on from there through his childhood, event by event, through his adolescence, into the war years. Is this how old people cope with sleepless nights? I don't think I have a continuous film of my life like that. Just snapshots. Maybe the movie comes when you grow older.

'No, she wasn't caught up in it,' I say, picking up the thread, 'but it's left her feeling vulnerable and frightened. She has to force herself to get on the tube to work every morning and she says she sits there tense, looking around her, looking at anyone who might be Muslim or who has a rucksack or who looks shifty, and then despising herself for being racist and a snob. She says she knows it's crazy looking for potential terrorists but she can't help it, and all her friends are doing exactly the same thing.'

'Of course she can't help it. It's natural after what happened.'

'She says everyone is on edge. At work, she was talking to one of the partners and he said, "Oh, you've got entirely the wrong attitude. You have to carry on as if nothing has happened or they have won." She replied, "I'm sorry, but I can't do that." Most of the people she knows feel like her rather than the guy in the office. Some are getting on buses, hoping that they might be safer, and one friend is cycling into the city, risking life and limb in a different way. Poor Clara. She has enough on her plate without worrying about terrorists. She's concerned about Daniel travelling by tube to work at Heathrow every day. Billy's safe enough down in Sussex, I suppose, but who knows? We can't guess what will happen next.'

'Nor could we in Nairobi,' my father says. 'That's what I was saying. Fighting an invisible enemy was demoralising, much worse than the first or second world wars. Like fighting ghosts.'

'Of course. I hadn't made the connection between the kind of enemy you were fighting in Nairobi and the terrorists now.'

'Well… it wasn't quite on the same scale… but you could predict nothing.'

'What happened after Wavell came out?' I ask.

'It was terrible,' my father replies. 'It was the beginning of…'

'Hang on,' I say, leaping back into my chair and lifting my fingers over the keyboard because I must not miss the seamless link between the parts of the story my father tells me in casual conversation and the parts he dictates as I type.

'On you go. Wavell had just come out…'

Chapter 41

Nairobi 1953
David

It was Christmas Eve.

Wavell was dead.

Killed by the Mau Mau during his first hours of active service.

Did they lie in wait for him – him alone – or was it just another random act of violence?

We never found out.

That was the turning point.

The first response from many of the men, including my own soldiers, was ugly talk of revenge, but it was their way of letting go of difficult emotions. They knew what lay ahead now and they also knew that it wasn't individual acts of retaliation. The night Wavell was killed, I sat up late with my lads, talking to them quietly and calmly about the challenges we would now face, but also, I hope, reassuring them that we were the most sophisticated and best trained soldiers in the world and could handle this. I was comfortable in that role, even breaking bad news, and knew I had the men's full support and cooperation. It showed on their faces and in the way they fell quiet the minute I walked into the room. They told me things other soldiers would not reveal to their commanding officers. I made myself available to them. I came from the same kind of background and I believe they respected that.

By myself, I pondered on the fact that Nairobi was now a dangerous place and had become the stage for what might be a bloody battle. The time had come for us all to be vigilant, to watch and wait. A rota was set up so that the nightly armed patrol was shared amongst everyone because we had very few fighting troops out there. Each officer and every soldier took a turn. Every third night one of my men would accompany me as we drove the streets of Nairobi and its surrounds with only a gun standing between survival and death. It was us against the Mau Mau.

On the evenings when I was not on patrol, my job was to read all the incoming messages and then, leaving my sergeant in charge, personally take them round; A Branch if it was a routine matter, G Branch if there was a need to involve the military. In the army, rules and routines like these are always in place; our job was to carry them out. After I had handed the messages to the G Branch major he would decide if he needed to consult with other officers. Get the general himself out of bed if necessary. As I drove from depot to depot, I felt an unsettling sense of deja vu, of memories of being a Signals sergeant in the 8th Army delivering messages in my jeep in the desert.

Having done the rounds and delivered the memos and messages, at about 2 a.m. I would set off to check the sentry posts situated in the main danger zones, to make sure that the men were alert and on guard, and that nothing untoward had happened. I remember one evening I set off to check up on the men at Government House, where defences had been erected around the perimeter so that there was only one entry, with a single sentry box where the men on duty checked everyone's identity. What did I find? The two soldiers inside the hut were asleep. The two outside were dozing, one with his head resting on the striped barrier. I yelled 'Duty Officer!' at the top of my voice. It was a stupid thing to do because if they had reacted as they had been trained to do, they would have shot me. Instead they jumped to attention, shouting 'Sir!', while a window above my head was pushed open and a flutey female voice called out, 'Do you mind making less noise down there? I'd like to sleep.' The governor's wife! I decided not to reply and the window slammed down.

This checking up on sentries would take me several hours and then I would set off for the more isolated spots around Nairobi, where we had set up more guards. If anything was going to happen to me, it would be then, on some dark and isolated stretch of road in the hills between one watch-out and another. Nothing could save you up there. You were alone.

Each week centred around the nights when I was on patrol. We were a mixed bag of about a dozen officers from various branches – Ordinance, REME, Service Corps and so on – each one well trained and competent. We prowled the perimeters of Nairobi and as I peered into the dark corners of the city, I told myself that these were preventative measures and that the chance of open combat with a group of Mau Mau warriors was slight. That's what I said to myself. Prepare for the worst, but don't expect it. That was what we had been told in training. My reactions in those days were very quick, and if I had heard so much as a footstep behind me, my hand would have been on my gun. There was no point in anticipating an attack. If you spent your time dwelling on theoretical risks you would be paralysed with fear and useless if you did have to react suddenly. I was known to be a steady chap, not easily ruffled.

As the sun rose I would be heading back to Headquarters to be relieved by the next man. We did twelve-hour shifts, 8 a.m. to 8 p.m. or 8 p.m. to 8 a.m., and no, I didn't take the next day off. I went home, had a shower, breakfasted with Mary, and went straight back to my office. In the afternoon, I'd be playing cricket. Some things didn't change.

Chapter 42

Nairobi 1954
David

From a selfish point of view, I didn't want Mary out there with me. Once a state of emergency had been declared, Nairobi was no place for a woman like her and two little girls. I had a job to do and I wanted to give it my full attention. My gut feeling was that she should pack her bags and leave. I didn't need the extra worry.

A group of us – officers with families still out here – met regularly after committee meetings and briefings in Headquarters to discuss the more personal side of the situation. Only one thing was on our minds: how could we best ensure the safety of our families in a volatile and unpredictable situation? After endless talk, we came up with a couple of practical suggestions, but it felt like putting a plaster over a gaping wound. We agreed, all of us, that our wives and children would, from now on, remain at home behind locked doors whenever we were out, whether at Headquarters or on patrol. And we agreed that all the wives would be given instruction in using arms. Neither decision was popular, especially among the younger, more feisty wives, but we insisted. It was that or return to England. So there we were, women and children confined to their homes much of the time, and the women armed in case there was an attack and they had to open fire.

I really wasn't happy. Harry attended these meetings to keep abreast of what was going on, rather than from any personal anxiety over Marjorie.

'Would you mind hanging on a minute?' I said quietly one afternoon as the others went on their way.

'Certainly,' he said, continuing to read some memos until we were alone.

'These precautions are all very well but the truth is that the women and children shouldn't still be out here,' I dived straight in. 'What do you think?'

'That may be too simplistic, David. It's easy to generalise,' he replied. 'Maybe I'm not the one to ask because Marjorie decided to stay early on and won't budge now. She says she accepts the consequences.'

'Mary said the same but her behaviour makes me think she regrets her choice. She's on edge all the time. She says she's fine, but she isn't. Is Marjorie really OK?'

'Same as ever. Nerves of steel.'

'Mary seems miles away. Once or twice I've come home to find her pacing up and down the veranda. She says she's just thinking if I ask her what's wrong.'

'Well, you can't expect her to behave as if she were on holiday, can you?'

'Obviously not,' I snapped, 'but if she's going to sit out the emergency, she's going to have to relax or her nerves will be in shreds. I don't need that.'

'It must be very difficult for her,' Harry said. A bland comment if ever there was one. He was normally so astute.

'Of course it's difficult.'

'She is an exceptional woman, David. Such a complex mixture of strength and fragility.'

My anger flared up. I felt patronised and insulted. Harry was talking about my wife as if he knew her better than I did.

'You don't have to tell me that,' I snapped.

'Sorry,' he said. 'Tactless of me.'

I said nothing, letting my silence speak for itself.

'So what's the agenda for the rest of the day?' Harry asked. It was an adroit change of topic but nothing could hide the flush on his face or the fact that he could not meet my eyes. He knew that he had overstepped the mark.

'I'm off to give Sergeant Farrow some moral support, poor chap,' I replied, thankful to hide my annoyance under business as usual. 'I have often wondered what a first-class infantry soldier like Fallow is doing in a classroom. Sterling stuff, one hundred per cent loyal, absolutely trustworthy. But his maths is woeful, so I've been tutoring him. Last week I crept in to the examining room, stood where I could see what he was doing, and shuddered as he made one appalling mistake after another. He failed of course and he's been demoted.'

'Poor sod. Bloody army rules. Can't you step in?'

'Well... I went to his CO and told him, "This man Farrow is a first-class soldier. Can't add up, that's all. He doesn't deserve demotion." "You don't have to tell me," the CO said, "but there is nothing I can do. My hands are tied. It's the system."'

'Damn the system,' Harry said, quick as lightning.

'Exactly. Look, I can tell you because I know you'll keep it to yourself, but I'm about to do my best to get round the bloody system if that's what it takes to get justice. I'm going above the CO's head.'

'Good for you,' Harry said. 'Couldn't agree more.'

And with that, we managed to part on good terms.

On my bed that night, unable to sleep, I thought about Harry's words, not about Farrow but about Mary. 'Strong and fragile.' How right he was, but why did he comment on her in such a personal, almost intimate way? It was completely out of character – for him as for any other colleague. You don't step over the line and express an opinion on someone else's wife. He knew it, too. It shocked me because normally he was absolutely discreet and diplomatic.

I thought too about the signs Mary gave me that she wasn't really coping. I had surprised her in tears one day when I arrived home early. She apologised and said sometimes it got her down being shut in the house with the girls all day. Understandable. But she seemed distracted when we sat together in the evenings. As if she was miles away.

One day, when the two of us were alone and I had just removed my revolver from its case to check it over, she asked, 'And by the way, where am I supposed to keep mine?'

I was taken aback by such a stupid question; even more by her sarcastic tone. I hadn't thought to tell her where to keep her gun because she had been so touchy that day on the firing range.

'At night, under your pillow or in a drawer by your bed where you can grab it, of course,' I replied. 'I hope you haven't been keeping it on full view somewhere!'

Her withering look told me she would not deign to respond.

'And for God's sake don't tell either of those silly little girls where it is.'

'David, you're being patronising. As if I would. And they're not silly. They're being remarkably sensible and helping me by behaving well – most of the time, anyway.'

'But no child is sensible when it comes to a gun,' I reiterated. 'I'm serious, Mary. Hide the gun somewhere during the day and sleep with it under your pillow at night.'

She sighed. Her glance was scathing.

'You are doing so well, my dear,' I said to encourage her. 'Just try to keep a clear head and you will be fine. You have lived through a war. You have worked in dangerous places. I have every confidence in you.' It was normal for her to feel anxious, I told myself. Mary would prove herself to be of sterling stuff if ever she were faced with the worst.

As we walked from the bungalow to the car later that evening to visit friends, for one fleeting moment I saw the pair of us as others might have done, a sturdy military man in full army uniform walking with a straight back and a firm stride beside a delicate, slim woman with light brown curling hair in a dress of red poppies. Which one was cut out to fire a gun? Which one was in most danger?

*

'Poor Mother,' I say, because his words bring back such clear memories for me too. I know I was only a child but with a child's instinct I knew that my mother was unhappy and distracted, although most of the time she managed not to show it. It wasn't fear, because I recognised that she was very strong in her own way. I don't know what it was. Once or twice I caught her weeping in her bedroom. Sometimes, when Clara and I were playing quietly together under the shade of the big tree, she would pace round and round the grounds, completely lost in her own thoughts, wringing her hands as though she were squeezing a cloth that was full of water.

'Anyway, she did take us home not long afterwards, so no harm was done,' I say, trying to placate him. I don't want him getting in a state.

'No harm was done!' he shouts. 'You don't know… you don't know what you are talking about.'

I glance at him and am shocked to see that his face is set in hard lines of anger. He is agitated and I think that telling this story is taking too much out of him. But on he goes.

'Don't interrupt me. I told her she was safe. I told her no harm would come to her. And she believed me. She trusted me. "The door is locked," I would say. "You have a gun and can use it," I would tell her. "No one will come in and hurt you or the girls."'

His hands are balled up, tight fists, and I can hear his breathing hard and fast and wheezy.

'But we did fly home in the end. The army found us a rented house in London, didn't they? And then she seemed to have some kind of nervous reaction, afterwards, which is hardly surprising. I remember the day she came downstairs with her bags packed and told us she had to go to hospital because she wasn't well. Sorry. I've interrupted you again.'

My father is lost in thought for a while, then he says something very odd indeed. 'Of course, you and Clara don't know the worst. We never told you the truth because at the time you were too young and then later it seemed best…'

'Too young for what?'

'What happened to her.'

'What do you mean, "What happened to her"?' What is my father talking about? 'I know she suffered from nerves after Nairobi but nothing actually happened to her.'

'You don't know. We never told you,' he says in such a harsh voice that the years drop away and I am seven and he is a strict disciplinarian in a khaki uniform criss-crossed with a Sam Brown leather strap, someone I dare not contradict or disobey. Someone I both love and fear.

'What?' I ask meekly.

'Words. Words. Futile damn words. Nothing. Nothing I can write about. Best forgotten now. It happened more than fifty years ago, gone now as Mary is gone.'

There are tears in his eyes. He looks away because his daughter must not see him crying. He pushes back his chair, shrugs on his coat, descends the stairs brushing off my attempts to steady him, and walks out of the door. Without another word.

On the Friday of that week my father does not arrive on my doorstep eager to carry on with his story. Nor the following Tuesday. When I mention it, he changes the subject or makes an excuse until I wonder, with sorrow and bewilderment, if our days of writing together are over. He has not finished playing his part but he has already left the stage. Soon I stop asking him because it gives him too much pain.

Why does he not come back to tell me what happened in Nairobi?

Chapter 43

NAIROBI 1954
EVE

Eve, Eve.

Clara is calling from her bed. She can come into my bed now.

Mummy has locked our door from the outside and gone down the corridor to her own room. I push open my shutters very slowly or else they squeak and climb out of my window on to the veranda, warm wood under my feet, and tiptoe round to the other side of the bungalow. When I stand tall under Mummy's bedroom window I can see through the crack in her shutters. First she is a statue, not moving, looking but not looking. Letting all the day thoughts settle down and drift away, like I do at night. My mummy is a statue and watching her keep so still makes me want to wriggle. Then she pushes back her hair and sighs. She heaves and pushes the heavy chest of drawers up against the door and under the door handle so no one can break in. Then she lies on her bed.

Sometimes we all sleep in Mummy's room. Clara and I snuggle into Mummy's bed, which smells of talcum powder, and Mummy lies on top of Daddy's bed until he comes home in the morning. He is cross when he finds us all in the same room. When I was pretending to be asleep I heard him talking to Mummy in his stern voice.

You in one room at this end of the corridor. The girls in their room at the other end. That way, if the worst thing happens, I won't lose all three of you.

And Mummy said, What a stupid thing to say, David. If the Mau Mau break in here we'll all die anyway whichever rooms we are in.

And Daddy said, I can't even think about that so let me imagine what I need to imagine when I'm out there in the dark. Please, Mary. Just do what I ask.

I know where Mummy keeps her revolver – in her bedside drawer under her pretty embroidered handkerchiefs and lace underwear. It's not a very clever place to hide it because I found it the first time I looked because you can feel something hard straightaway when it's only wrapped in soft silky stuff. One day I touched it. I just lifted it out very carefully without disturbing the folds, but best not to play with it, I thought, so I put it back in its secret place. I haven't told Clara about the gun because she is too young and may shoot her fingers off or something silly. Mummy doesn't often sleep after she goes into her room. Clara and I can hear her pacing about, up and down, up and down. Anyway, I can see her through the shutters. She never finds out that I can climb out so easily.

Clara climbs into my bed. Soft, pretty Clara. I love my little sister when she wears only her white vest and pants because she is a cuddly doll with skin like milk chocolate. I wish I had round soft arms and legs instead of my skinny bones. Turn over, I say, and she curls up like the C that starts her name and I curl up behind her. We fit together, me on the outside, she like a lining. What shall we play? Letters or jam cutters? Letters first, Clara says, wriggling a bit until she is comfy. She pulls up her vest and on her bare back, snuggled down together in the dark under the sheet, I trace letters. I start with L because it is easy. T and S are easy too. N is too like M so she has to ask me to make the letter twice. E and F are hard. I do ten letters and Clara gets a mark out of ten, then we both turn round the other way, settle again, and it's her turn to write letters on my back. It's much easier for me because Clara writes the same few letters over and over because she has forgotten the rest. Her fingers make me shiver; I love having my back touched. Jam cutters now, she says, and we turn around again. The real name for the game is pastry cutters but it got shortened. I remember helping Granny make pastry. The dough is a soft, squidgy ball which I pull about and squeeze with my fingers until it is shiny-smooth enough to roll flat, but not too flat or it will break, and then we use a round metal shape with serrated edges to cut out the circles. You go twist, twist, twist with the cutter. You lift out the circle of pastry and put it in the jam tart tin. Soon the sheet of pastry is full of holes, so you roll it up and start again. The trick is to make the holes as close together as possible so you don't have much left over to roll out again because it is never quite as soft the second time. I make my hand into a jam tart cutter and start cutting out the pastry which is Clara's back. Twist, twist, twist. Right, left, right. I start at the top and work my way down, not leaving too much, making the holes close together. She wriggles because it tickles and gives her goose bumps. My turn now. Her sharp little fingers cutting out the pastry give me shivery feelings that run up and down my spine. I never want it to stop. There are other games. Snakes which slither from our shoulders to our bottoms. Pitter Patter like rain drops all over your back.

We grow soft and sleepy playing our games and usually we nod off, not waking even when Daddy comes home early in the morning and unlocks our door and peeps round to make sure we are safe. We are rabbits in a burrow, half-buried, and so comfy we don't move at all. Clara is whispering into the night. Is she asleep or awake? Always she pushes little words out as she drops off to sleep. Maybe she thinks she is talking to herself inside her head and I can't hear her. Mostly she talks nonsense. Stuff she makes up. One night, as she falls asleep, she whispers a story that sounds real. Maybe she is dreaming and talking in her sleep.

Black men are here. Where the servants live. Who are they? Mummy and Daddy are out. Eve is inside. I'm under the swing tree. Round and hidden as a mouse. I'm drawing a dirt picture with my finger of a little girl, like me. Malinge and Niangueso and Tom are shouting at the men to go away, go away, go away, but the men are shouting back. No, shouts Niangueso. No, shouts Malinge. Niangueso is very angry. He runs into the kitchen and gets our carving knife, the long one with the ivory handle that Daddy uses to slice roast chicken on a Sunday. Niangueso is waving the knife in the air. Tom and Malinge hide behind him. They are scared. One of the other men lifts his machete and shouts loudly. Two black men with sharp blades in their hands. Sharp blades can cut you. Blood will drip on the red soil. They move closer together, step by step. Bare feet. The tip of the carving knife touches the machete man's throat like a tongue. The machete is at the side of Niangueso's throat. I imagine a slice of red. Here's our car with Daddy driving and Mummy in the front seat, the wheels crunch the gravel and the men run away through a gap in the fence. On Niangueso's throat there is a teardrop of blood. Did I dream that? I don't think so. It was real.

Who were those men? I ask Malinge later. We sit together under the tree. Wild men, he tells me. Bad men. Want Niangueso, Tom and me to fight with them against white men. They tell us, you go now into the mountains. Take off your clothes like the newborn. Eat the flesh of a new-killed goat. Drink the blood running from its slit throat. We tell him no. Make the pledge, they yell at us, make the pledge. Go, go. Eat goat meat. We tell them no again. We stay loyal to bwana here, good boss, and the men are very angry. They say they kill us.

Don't leave us, Malinge. You are my best friend.

You my friend, Miss Clara.

Clara is humming to herself now like a bumble-bee. I drop off to sleep, like falling off a ledge. My body jerks me awake again. I half-wake, fall off the ledge, wake. Her humming is soothing and nice. Quiet words pop into the humming. A bit of humming and a bit of singing. I am so sleepy I'm not really listening. Clara often sings herself to sleep after we have played the back games. I am too tired...

Hum... hum... I can see through my window the black black night. Hum... hum... The moon shines in the black sky on leaves shaped like boats which blow outside my window. The sailing moon crosses the sea of the sky in the wind. But look. The leaves shake and tremble because a black warrior is climbing up the branches where he can see Eve and me in our beds. Dry rough feet on dry scraped branches. Toes curled to grip. He is deciding – shall I come in or shall I stay here in the tree watching. I know a little boy who was killed. Michael. A black man in a tree outside his house chose to come inside. Black man, please don't come in. Please don't hurt us. Climb back down the tree. Throw down that machete. Don't come in the window. Don't cut my skin. Don't cut my throat. Don't chop off my hands. Don't make me bleed. Hum... hum... I am Clara the shadow sister. I am Clara the little sister. My grey eyes are magic eyes that see black men twisted in the trees in the night. Hanging like black bats. I see things no one else can see. Sleep on your left side, Clara. Turn over on to your left side. Then the knife won't go through your heart. Hum... hum...

Chapter 44

EDINBURGH 2005
EVE

I am grinding a fragile sliver of ice-green glass which, if it does not break, will be one of the slender reeds that grow at the edge of the sea where the figure, my mother, will stand, half-hidden, ready to make her last graceful dive into the water. This piece has totally absorbed my emotions and my energies; I am intrigued by the way it has transformed itself by some creative will of its own, almost without conscious thought from me, from a design on paper to a flat glass panel to a three-dimensional piece as I have overlaid the sea with waves of a dozen different blues and the corner of the sandy beach with rough grass. Each spike of sea grass will be delicate and pointed, slightly paler or darker than the one before, until I have a rainbow of greens. They will be razor sharp so that it hurts when you look at them. Each wave will suggest immeasurable depth and the wind, caught in the white horses I have cut from smoky white glass, will have the colour and texture of fog. The figure will be frozen forever in the second before she dives in and swims away towards freedom. I am saying farewell to my mother in the only way I know how.

That's my doorbell. Damn and damnation. Why can't I be left alone when I am concentrating this hard? I can't bear to be interrupted during these precious hours in the morning when my energy flows fast from my fingers into the glass. If it's my neighbour complaining about my wheelie bin not being exactly aligned behind the wall out of sight of passers by, I will be very rude indeed. In fact, I won't go down. If I worked in an office with my face staring at a screen there would be no doorbell to interrupt me. My workplace just happens to be at home. But as I return to my grinding wheel the bell buzzes again. Longer this time. Down the stairs I run in my filthy old apron, barefoot, my arms dusty to the elbow and my hands black. Shit!

There on my doorstep stands my father. His face is grim. In the whole year that he has been living at the end of the road he has never once arrived like this out of the blue. He waits to be invited to coffee or dinner, no more thinking of turning up unannounced than of walking down the street without his jacket on. I stare at him through the glass in the door while fumbling with the catch, but he gives nothing away. Not a wave. Not a smile. Not even a look of recognition. Whatever is the matter?

'Let's finish the writing,' he says, as usual without so much as a 'How are you' or 'I hope I'm not disturbing you', and already he is pushing past me into the house. I notice that his breathing is rapid and shallow as he slowly climbs the stairs in front of me. He seems to be sucking in air using only the top few inches of his lungs, instead of filling his chest fully. On we go, a strange, slow, silent procession of two people taking the stairs at snail's pace. I judge it best not to interrupt his concentration with chatter and trivia. At the top landing he stops, breathing hard, and surveys the open and half-open doors, unable to choose because he can't remember which one leads to my study.

'In there,' I say, pointing, unable to bear the suspense, his hesitation. 'I'll just go and wash my hands, OK? Coffee?'

'Yes,' he says. Good. That gives me five minutes to compose myself and find the Off switch for Glass Panels and the On switch for Father Writing. I can't make the transition instantly. This is all a bit unexpected and my imagination cannot instantly block out the little daggers and shards in almond green.

When I return he is leaning his elbows on my desk, lost in thought. He looks at me briefly as I place his frothed, sweetened, tongue-scorching coffee and one of his favourite chocolate biscuits on the desk before him. I settle myself at my computer to await my instructions.

'One night I came home from patrol to a scene of appalling chaos and tragedy…'

'Hang on, please. I just need to get your file up. Just a minute.' This is clearly a prepared speech. I bet he has been working on it half the night to get the words just right. He often complains that he does not have a good enough vocabulary. But what on earth is he talking about? He takes a sip of his coffee and offers me the merest sign that it is just right.

'OK,' I say. 'On you go. Do I start where we left off last time?'

No answer.

'I came back home that night to a scene of such heartbreaking tragedy… I never want to witness anything like it again as long as I live…' There are tears in his eyes as he struggles to get the words out. I am afraid for him. Ever watchful that the aged brain might finally blow a fuse, I feel my heart skipping a beat or two until eventually he recovers his equilibrium and is once again the confident storyteller ready to relate his tale. There are no hesitations, no false starts, no unfinished sentences. It is as if the words have been rehearsed so many times they are already open on the page of his mind, so that his only task is to read them. He talks and talks until everything is said.

Chapter 45

Nairobi 1954
David

In the early hours of the morning we received orders to go to a white farmer in the hills, a very experienced British farmer, James Broadrow, whose family had owned and farmed the land for two generations. He was not as far out of Nairobi as the other estates we had been called to and as we drove the few miles, I prayed that it was something minor.

When we arrived, the man was waiting alone outside his farmhouse and was literally wringing his hands. Without a word, he led us round the back of his beautiful house, through his paddock and into a field, hidden from the driveway, where about fifty cows lay slaughtered. Not just slaughtered either. Their bellies were ripped open and their intestines spilled out in pale bloodied coils on to the red soil. Their faces were slashed and their eyes had been gouged out. Some had been hamstrung. As I walked amongst them, I saw that a few were still moving. I have seen my share of gut-wrenching sights in the war and I'm pretty tough, but when I looked into the mute and uncomprehending faces of those big dying animals it was hard not to feel sick to the soul. Of course I shot them, one by one, until every carcass was still. Among the corpses lay two dogs, so brutally hacked to pieces – sliced like bacon – that their suffering must have been unbearable. One of my soldiers vomited into the grass. Another walked away.

'Bastards. Evil bastards,' said Pete Rawford, one of the few white men in my group. The other soldiers were black, from the African Rifles. Most of my soldiers were black. Then to my horror Pete Rawford raised his head and howled up at the skies. 'Death to the whole damn lot of them. Filthy black motherfuckers…'

I grabbed his shoulder and said sharply, 'That's enough, Rawford. You're insulting other loyal soldiers here.'

But my black soldiers did not react. They had far too much dignity and self-control to respond to such a common insult. No doubt they had heard it many times before. One black man was the same as another black man to some of the ignorant colonials. No matter that these good men were fighting for our king and country.

'Sorry, Sir. I've never seen anything as revolting as this.'

'I understand. But that was out of order.'

'Sir.'

'Just check that I've not left any alive and shoot anything that still moves,' I told him, to give him something to do.

I took James Broadrow by the arm and led him back to the house. The man was in shock. I knew that his wife had gone back to England, but I was surprised to find the place completely deserted. There was not a servant in sight. Not a soul left to share this man's agony.

'The servants…?' I asked once he was seated and I had found the whisky and thrust a large tumbler-full into his shaking hands.

'Ran away and joined the Mau Mau. Twenty-four men who have been with me for years. Some of them worked for my father before me. Each and every one a bloody traitor. The native whores have vanished too. God damn them all…'

Jesus, this was bad. I glanced at the two men who had positioned themselves near the sitting room entrance – two more were on guard outside – and we exchanged a brief look of shock and despair. What to say in a situation like this? How to offer comfort? And how would other white families feel once this news got out?

'Listen, I want you to come with us in the jeep back to base, James. Just grab a few night things, no hurry, and we'll take you down to HQ and find somewhere for you to sleep for the night. Then we can make more permanent arrangements. This is no time for decisions, but the sooner we all get out of here the better.'

He offered no resistance. He seemed broken. Within minutes he was back in the sitting room with a small bag and was sleep-walking with us under the brilliant stars of the African sky. In the truck, he said not another word.

I had a brief memo from the CO some days afterwards, when the drama had raced round the grapevine and been reported in all its gory details by the papers, congratulating me on acting calmly and competently in a very distressing situation. Had Broadrow told him? I doubt it because he had been in no state to observe anything. It must have been one of the soldiers. I silently thanked him. Black or white. It gave me a great sense of satisfaction to have their trust.

*

By the time I arrived home at 8 a.m., having written a full report and found Broadrow somewhere to sleep, as well as someone to keep an eye on him and to see to his needs, I was knackered. And shocked, I can tell you. I think it was the sight of the butchered dogs that gave me the creeps. I was looking forward to unwinding and getting some sleep as my car wheels crunched slowly up our gravel drive.

A military police car was parked further up the drive.

A uniformed soldier stood on guard outside my front door. Ramrod straight.

Still raw with what I had just witnessed, I opened my car door and ran.

At that moment all self-control deserted me. This was personal. This was not part of my job.

'What's going on?' I shouted like a madman as I ran into the hall.

'Sir,' said the soldier on duty, saluting and snapping his heels together as he was trained to do. His face remained expressionless. Damn 'Sir,' I thought. Just tell me what's happened.

'Mary!' I shouted. 'Mary, where are you?'

But it was Marjorie, not Mary, who was in the hall coming forwards to meet me with a grim expression and an arm outstretched as if to stop me going any further.

'David...' she said, gripping my arm, trying to hold me back. 'I'm afraid something has happened...'

'I can see something has bloody happened! What? Tell me, Marjorie.' I was shouting. I was completely overwrought. 'Where's Mary? Where are the girls?' I shook off her hand, flung her aside so that I could get along the corridor, and ran again. I was running, running. I was reacting exactly as I had been trained never to react. No cool head now. Just sheer panic.

I see it now so clearly. It was dark except for the small night light on the bedside table, the painted owl whose eyes lit up green, so beloved by the girls. Mary was sitting on the edge of her bed in her flowered cotton dressing-gown, barefoot, motionless, her head hanging down, her hands together in her lap. My first thought was that she looked like a prisoner because on an upright chair next to the bed a young WRAC was watching over her. As I entered, this young uniformed woman leapt to her feet and saluted. Mary looked up then and looked straight into my eyes and with that exchange I knew for a fact that she was not beaten. She was not beaten. Whatever had happened, she was still Mary.

'Leave us alone,' I commanded.

'Sir!' The young policewoman went out, shutting the door behind her.

Then I was on the bed next to my dear wife, my arm around her, just holding her firmly but gently to tell her that I was here now, and that now everything would be all right. For a long time we sat like that, a man telling his wife without words that he was here now. He would take care of her. She was icy-cold, despite the warmth of the sun that was now above the horizon. I lifted her legs on to the bed and tucked the sheet around her and gently moved her back so that she could lean back against her pillows. I touched her cheek. I gently pushed her tangled hair from her face.

'Eve and Clara…?' I was holding my breath.

'They are all right. They are still in their room. They are fine,' she whispered. 'Fiona, the WRAC who was here, unlocked their door and peeped in and they were still asleep.'

'What happened?'

At first she could not speak, but looked up at me in a way that gave me the creeps. Cows' eyes. Wounded bloody cows with brown eyes that pleaded 'Stop this hurting'. Get a grip, I told myself. This is not the same scene. No Mau Mau has been here to slice my women to bloody pieces. 'Take your time, my dear. Has someone frightened you?' And no sooner were the words out of my mouth than I realised what a damn stupid question it was.

Again she nodded.

'Can you tell me, Mary? What happened here?'

'Someone broke in,' she said.

And with those words I felt my body grow cold like hers, a shocking, draining feeling which I did my best to hide. 'Where?'

'Here,' she said. 'In here.'

Stupid, stupid. I was neither thinking nor seeing. Now I noticed that one of the shutters, closed to keep her in darkness, was hanging from its hinges and the window behind it was broken as if a fist had been shoved through it. The glass had been swept up, although now that I looked carefully at the floorboards I could see a few shards and glass dust below the sill. Someone knocked gently on the bedroom door. Mary jumped.

'Leave us alone,' I barked.

Ignoring my command, Marjorie stuck her head round the door. 'I'm going to make some tea,' she said. 'I think you probably both need a hot drink with a shot of something strong in it.' And then she was gone.

'Mary, are you hurt?'

'Yes,' she whispered, and then as if it were her fault she blurted out, 'I'm sorry, David. I'm so sorry to cause all this fuss for you. It's not what you need.'

'Ssh,' I said, stroking her hair. 'It's not your fault. Don't be silly, sweetheart.'

'He broke into my room after I had gone to sleep and…'

'Who?' I interrupted. 'Who?' I was shouting now and Mary was pulling away from me, fear in her eyes. Calm down, I told myself. For God's sake get a grip. This is not helping her.

'I don't know,' Mary was saying.

Of course she would be in shock. I was asking too much too soon. I was behaving appallingly, shouting and jumping up and down. I stayed silent then. I stroked her hand and her hair until she relaxed back against my shoulder.

When Marjorie knocked a second time, ten minutes later, she must have seen a strange sight – two people leaning together, neither saying a word, both staring straight ahead. As if in acknowledgment, she put the tray of tea and biscuits on a table and left, closing the door very quietly behind her.

Half an hour later Mary was asleep, her head heavy and tilted sideways. Poor, exhausted Mary. I managed to extract myself without waking her, and while she lay on the bed I took the opportunity to look at her properly. Of course with her dressing-gown still wrapped around her, I could only see her face and arms and legs, but there were no cuts, no bruises. Yet she said she was hurt. I crept out of the room. Down the corridor, in the sitting room, I faced Marjorie and the woman sergeant. They both looked completely wrung out.

'Thank you both,' I said. 'I am very grateful. Marjorie, please go home now and I'll come round later and talk to you. Mary is asleep. You should get back. I can't thank you enough for what you have done.'

'I'll drive Mrs Frame back, Sir,' the WRAC offered.

'I can drive myself,' Marjorie said frostily as she rose from her chair. 'David, has Mary told you what happened? Don't you think it would be sensible for me to tell you rather than disappearing and leaving you in the dark?'

'I know enough for now, Marjorie, thank you. The rest can wait until we have both had some sleep. Can I phone you later?'

She gave me a quizzical look and said quietly, 'I'm so very very sorry. You two don't deserve this.'

I took both her hands then and held them for a moment in mine. Thank God for this strong woman, this unemotional but confident woman who seemed able to cope with anything. I felt very emotional as I said goodbye, but it would not do to show my feelings to Marjorie, nor to the two soldiers who told me they had been ordered by HQ to remain on patrol at the door and in the grounds of the bungalow for the rest of the day.

'Well done,' I said. 'And thank you.'

For a long, long time I lay on my bed listening to Mary's regular breathing. I was overwound, overwrought. What I had seen at Broadrow's farm had been more than enough for one night, so I suppose my professional armour was already well pierced. It was the sight of those dogs that had broken down my emotional barriers. Not like me at all.

I couldn't sleep because I was guarding Mary, who slept on beside me. I vowed nothing would ever happen to her again. Later, I would make arrangements for her to fly home with the girls. The sooner the better. I blamed only myself for being persuaded to let her stay. I was the head of the family. I should have insisted.

Chapter 46

Nairobi 1954
David

I suppose I must have dozed off beside Mary because I was aware of coming up from great dark depths of sleep and then I realised why. There were scraping noises outside the window. And, just as I was trained to do, without a second's pause for thought, I grabbed my revolver, leapt to one side of the window and tore back the shutter. It lurched off its broken hinges and fell clattering and banging to the floor. Mary woke, screamed and sat bolt upright in bed. Two more little screams came from outside, not the blood-curdling yells of natives but the squeaks and cries of little girls. My little girls. Oh my God. One panic after another. This was no second attack but a scene of muddled domesticity. I called to the girls, put an arm round Mary, picked up the shutter, and ran outside to find Eve and Clara padding barefoot along the veranda and then leaping one after the other into my arms.

'Hello,' I said, keeping my voice even. 'You gave me a fright.'

'Silly,' said Clara. 'Only us. We always wait outside Mummy's window till she wakes up.'

'What was that crash?' asked Eve. 'And why are there soldiers in our garden? I said hello to one and asked him what he was doing and he said he was just keeping an eye on the place and I said that was nice of him.'

My certainty that they knew nothing, had seen nothing, was the only salvageable part of that frightful night, and so it would remain.

'Eve, could you be a very big girl and put the kettle on and make a pot of tea for Mummy?'

Eve was pleased. Making hot drinks was something she had only recently been promoted to doing.

'Where's Malinge?' Clara asked.

'Malinge and the others are having a day off,' I improvised. One of the soldiers had informed me that all three servants had been taken away in handcuffs and were at the police station being questioned. Given the number of servants who had defected, and the hatred felt towards them, they would be given a very hard time. I prayed that they were not roughed up.

'OK,' Eve said. 'Clara, come with me. You can put the biscuits on a plate.'

Off they went, little backs straight, proud to be given a grown-up task to do. Which gave me at least ten minutes to think about how to talk to Mary.

I played it all again. The girls are fine; my girls are not hurt or frightened. Mary said she was hurt but I saw no signs of injury; maybe she was bruised somehow. All in all, it could be much worse. Such were my naive ramblings as I went back inside the bungalow and returned to our bedroom. It never occurred to me then that what had happened in the course of that night, which in those sunny morning hours I dismissed so lightly, would change the course of our lives forever. And those of several other people.

When I returned, Mary was up and splashing cold water over her face at the washstand.

I put a hand on her shoulder and turned her round to face me. The damp flannel dripped on to the wooden floorboards. 'Just two things for now,' I told her gently but firmly. 'One, I don't want you to tell Eve or Clara about last night. It will only frighten them. By some miracle, they seem to have slept through it all. Two…'

'I agree,' Mary interrupted. 'Last night… well, it all happened so quickly and there was no noise at all… and yes… it's lucky their room is at the other end of the corridor.'

'Two,' I continued, 'I am going to arrange for you and the girls to fly home. You will have to stay for an enquiry but I will ask that your evidence is given in private, and as soon as that's over you will be on your way. I should have insisted you went months ago. I blame myself.'

For a moment Mary said nothing. I think she knew that there was no opposing me this time. Once my mind is made up, I don't change it.

'When the girls have brought you some tea, which will no doubt be as cold as it usually is, I'll send them off to play in their room so that we can talk.'

She finished wiping her face, folded the flannel in half and half again and placed it on the side of the basin. I was watching her closely for some further reaction as she took her hairbrush from her dressing table and slowly pulled it through her knotted hair, but she seemed very calm. Her face was blank. Perhaps this was her way of coping with whatever had happened.

After the girls had come in with the tea, Eve carrying the tray and walking like a little geisha in crumpled pyjamas accompanied by Clara who pointed out the assortment of biscuits, and after the cuddles and the chatter, somehow I got rid of them by bribing them with a trip to the market stalls if they would go and do a jigsaw in their room for an hour while Mummy and I talked. But first Clara ate the biscuits and Eve insisted we play I Spy. It's amazing what you can do without any mental involvement. I played I Spy while my mind was absolutely elsewhere, asking all sorts of questions that I wanted Mary to answer. Mary slipped away to the bathroom and dressed.

Everything seemed so ordinary and normal until I glanced out of the window and saw one of the soldiers walking around the perimeter of the grounds. Stupid, stupid. It was not normal. It was almost midday and I still did not know what had happened.

Finally Mary and I were alone. We sat in the two armchairs on either side of the coffee table while a warm breeze blew through the jagged hole in the window and lifted the corners of the tablecloth and blew waves across the rumpled sheets. I glanced at Mary, and she glanced at me, and neither of us could begin. I held on to the hope that I was dealing with something that had been blown out of proportion by the night and my absence.

'I think you had better tell me now. What happened last night?' I finally blurted out because she remained stonily silent and I could not sit through any more suspense. I had been up all night and I was exhausted. I got out of my chair and paced up and down the room.

She sighed. A long pause. 'Someone... a man broke into the bedroom while I was asleep.'

'Oh Mary...'

'It was...'

'You must have been absolutely terrified...'

'I was. I panicked'

'And he left when he realised there was someone here? Did he go back out of the window...'

'No. He didn't go.'

'What?'

'He saw that I was in bed. He didn't leave.'

'What did he do? For God's sake...'

She was silent.

'Was he black?' It was a stupid question, blurted out before I had half the facts. But the images of the night were crowding in again. James Broadrow. Cows with their bellies slit open. Dogs without eyes or legs, still breathing... flashbacks of an attack of black on white.

'I don't know.'

'Mary, you must know what colour he was.'

She remained very quiet and composed, and stared out of the window as if something out there engrossed her attention. She was both miles away and very much present in her stillness. Finally she spoke.

'David, please sit down and stop interrupting. I can't talk with you pacing up and down. At this stage does it honestly matter what colour he was?'

'Yes, it does.'

'David, either be quiet and let me talk or go away,' she snapped with a spark I recognised as truly her own, and it jolted me into seeing what a fool I was being.

'It was in the early hours of the morning. I was fast asleep. The noise of the glass breaking must have woken me and for a few moments I just lay there until my eyes grew used to the darkness and then I saw the shape of someone in the room, in the corner by the window. Perhaps I thought it was you. It was very dark and I was not really awake. I remember thinking, This is not real. This must be a bad dream. Then... then he moved towards the bed and before I could get away he put his hand over my mouth and held it there. The whole time he was in the room he had his hand over my mouth. It was over very quickly, very quickly, and he left the way he had come.'

I could see it now, the black unwashed hand, a black stinking hand held over Mary's soft mouth and the image made me sick to the stomach. 'Did you see him?' I asked.

'I haven't finished, David,' she said, ignoring my question. 'Afterwards I think I just lay on my bed, too shocked to move. Then I got up and took a long hot shower. I stood under the water until my skin was red trying to wash away the insult. Then I phoned Marjorie and she came straight over, and she phoned the military police. I remember I was shivering so much I couldn't speak. She was wonderful. Our three servants were arrested and taken away, though I swear it was none of them. David, you must sort that out as soon as possible. The thought of Malinge being put through… Then the soldiers arrived and the policewoman. And then you came home.'

Still something was unsaid, and I shied away from it. Partly I was obsessed with establishing the colour of the man. I wanted to know for a fact that he was black because there was no alternative. The only possible, plausible explanation was that Mary had been the latest victim of yet another Mau Mau attack. So it had happened after all. In my own back yard.

Sometimes you choose to focus on something off to one side of the main event because you are trying to avoid the blinding truth. Mary was watching me, knowing that in the end I would have to ask about the missing piece. The part she had not told me.

'He hurt you?'

She told me what had happened. My denial was instant. It was her imagination. Her distress. I was stunned, speechless. I remember thinking, I can't deal with this. If she had been hurt, yes, wounded, yes, even mutilated, yes, I would take care of her and love her for the rest of her life. But not this. The worst act of filth and depravity. I remember the kneejerk thing I said then was, 'Have you had a bath?' and she looked at me with such a scathing look because of course she had already told me that the first thing she did was to stand under a red hot shower.

'I'm going to call the doctor. You need to be… attended to.'

'No,' she said firmly. 'No, David. There's no need. It was over so quickly and I sort of blanked it out as if it wasn't happening and I'm not hurt.'

'You need a doctor, Mary.' It was all I could think of. Getting her mended somehow so that the damage would be undone. A doctor could clean her out and purge her.

'Listen, David. No one knows except Marjorie. As soon as she arrived, before she made any telephone calls, I made her swear not to tell the police or anyone else, only that a man broke in, probably with the intention of stealing something and that somehow I managed to frighten him away. Marjorie understands what would happen if this got out. She knows what it's like to live in a goldfish bowl. Listen, as far as the world is concerned, a man broke in to my room through a window and was frightened off again. Nothing happened.'

'So only Marjorie knows. And Harry will know.'

'No,' Mary looked away, her face flushed at the thought of anyone else being party to this. 'I asked her, begged her, not to tell Harry.'

'She's bound to tell him. He's her husband.'

'Sometimes we women are good at sticking together. Marjorie promised not to tell Harry and I believe her.'

I realised I had been holding my breath like a man drowning. Now I reached the surface and breathed out.

'It's OK,' Mary said with bitterness. 'Your reputation is safe, David. Our marriage, on the outside at least, will carry on as before. If you want that.'

I didn't answer immediately. 'I need some time.' It was a callous thing to say, I know, but I felt that strongly about it. I might not be able to come to terms with this.

Mary was like a beautiful bruised flower crushed underfoot. That's what I should have thought. I should have taken her in my arms. But the sounds that travelled like tickertape across my mind were 'shop-soiled' and 'dirty' and 'spoiled'. Could I love a woman who had been... I can't say that word. I never will.

Chapter 47

NAIROBI 1954
MARY

I woke late and blurred with dreams. The sun was streaming through the vertical gap where my two wooden shutters – one repaired promptly and hung back on its hinges – did not quite meet, painting my sheet with a single blinding stripe of gold. I lay under my flag of white and yellow, wondering which country I belonged to. Does the country of love have its own flag? For a few moments I chose not to move but to follow the line of light from the window, across the floorboards, up and over the bed, and onwards up the wall, wondering which theory of geometry could explain how its perfect straightness was pushed sideways by my bed in two places. Whatever – this searchlight had shone across my pillow and over my eyelids, rousing me from deep sleep.

Muffled little snorts of laughter and whispers reached me from outside. Eve and Clara, I bet, were crouched down below my window waiting for me to wake or, more likely, were whispering in stage-loud voices and laughing at the merest excuse and banging their backs repeatedly against the panels of wood, trying their hardest to shake me from slumber. Poor loves, they were captives now where before they were wild and free. The boundary of their play world had shrunk to the confines of the veranda, sometimes stretching to the garden if their guards, Malinge and I, accompanied them. Their position in my own world had shifted too. They had been pushed from centre stage, where they basked all their short years in the spotlight of my constant love, to a place in the wings where I watched them watching me, knowing, in the way children know, that often my thoughts were elsewhere and that some other figure had usurped their place. They were waiting to return.

I threw back the covers, breaking the line of light into zigzags, and stretched my arms above my head before swinging my brown, bare legs to the floor. David must have left hours ago. His bed next to mine was its usual rumpled mess, with his pillow holding the shape of his sleeping head. Why do men never make their beds? I padded across to the window and gingerly, inch by inch, opened the shutters, hoping to catch a glimpse of my spying daughters before they saw me, but wood creaks and the noise I made was their signal to turn their dear, unbrushed heads to squeal at me.

'Mummy, you're late!'

And from Clara, 'Mummy, we've been waiting ages and ages for you to wake up. It's boring sitting here and I've got cramp in my legs and Eve won't tell me the next chapter of the jam tart story…'

'Because I haven't decided what happens next, silly…'

'Come on, climb in, you little monkeys,' I said, knowing my lines by heart. Up they came, clambering adroitly on to the window sill, wearing, as usual, only their vests and pants, to jump all over me, a bundle of little girls with sun-sweet hair and soft warm flesh which smelt of baby powder and damp flowers. I sat braced on the floor beneath my window, back against the wall, legs out in front to keep my balance, while the girls squirmed their way into my arms, crawling and wriggling to fuse with me. Clara's arms were round my neck in a hug that nearly throttled me. Eve's arm was around my waist. I rocked them in my arms until naughty Eve braced her bare toes against the floorboards to give her enough leverage to push us all over. A family of snakes off the Ludo board, we wound up writhing around on the floor and laughing until we could hardly breathe.

Suddenly I felt sick. Being flat on the floor with two weights on top of me had turned my stomach inside out, but I didn't want to interrupt our play so I swallowed hard and thought nothing of it. But the feeling of sickness increased until I had no option but to push the girls away and sit up. I was dizzy too and had to put my head in my hands. For a few moments, the girls thought I was still playing and, sitting up too, started the rocking all over again. While they were flushed with fun, having their Mummy to themselves for once, I was swallowing waves of nausea .

'Oh, just a moment,' I cried, trying to smile and not show my distress. 'Let me up, you two. I'm getting giddy with all that rocking.' Then I simply had to jump up and run to the bathroom, where I threw up into the sink. I rinsed my mouth with water. A flannel held under the cold tap and rubbed hard on my skin calmed me but the reflection of my face in the mirror was grey. Whatever did we eat last night?

'What's the matter, Mummy?'

Eve and Clara were outside the bathroom door, listening. Damn, they heard it all – not that vomiting noises are exactly easy to disguise. I wiped my face again and emerged. Two worried faces stared up at me.

'It's nothing,' I told them. 'I must have eaten something that disagreed with me. A bit sick, that's all.' Suddenly I wanted a piece of dry, almost burnt toast. 'Come on. I need some breakfast. How about you?'

'Pancakes?' Clara asked.

'No. Toast,' I said firmly, quickly banishing all images of pancakes, sugar, sickly maple syrup, and anything else except dry, crackly toast.

In the kitchen I started to put on coffee, then realised I didn't want any. The aroma from the jar made me queasy. I put two slices of bread into the toaster and got the butter from the fridge. My need for toast, burnt toast, was urgent.

'I'll make you pancakes another day but it's too late this morning,' I said, using the first excuse that popped into my head. 'But you can have anything you like on your toast. How about that?'

'Honey,' said Clara.

'Mashed banana,' said Eve.

'Fine,' I said, and though the honey was manageable, nice enough to lick up a spoonful myself, I found myself retching again as I mashed banana to a slimy pulp. Heavens, I was not myself.

We carried our plates outside and there, sitting on the bare boards with our backs against the old cushions, we chatted and planned the day ahead. Clara sat squashed right up next to me and, reaching up to pat my face, left fingerprints of sticky honey on my skin. Eve couldn't sit still for more than a few seconds. She soon detached herself from my arm to play a solitary game of hopscotch up and down the bouncy boards while eating toast and squashed banana – up and down, bounce bounce – until I had to look away. At last my stack of dry toast settled my tummy and I started to feel fine. I decided nothing was amiss. I'd just had a bit of a bumpy start to my day.

'Mummy, can we please go to the market stalls after lunch? I'm fed up with playing in the house and garden. I'm all fidgety. Please,' Eve asked.

'No, darling,' I said. 'You know we can't go into town just now.'

'Please.'

'It's not a question of please. It's nothing to do with me not letting you. Nairobi is not a safe place at the moment, so we all have to stay here.'

'But you go there,' she said accusingly.

'I'm grown up and can look after myself,' I replied.

'But somebody might stick a knife in you…' she said with childish drama.

'Or a panga,' Clara added, rolling her beautiful grey eyes at me like a silent movie star. That's who she reminds me of. Greta Garbo. With a lacy veil over her beautiful round face, she could be her double.

'Don't be silly,' I told them a bit too sharply. 'I'm quite safe running round the shops in the daytime.'

'Then why aren't we?'

'Because if anything happened… if there was any trouble… I would have to take care of you two as well as myself, and that's three people to worry about. Three people to get to somewhere safe.'

'Anyway, you stay away for hours and hours,' Eve said with a sly look at me.

'Not often. Only if I have lots of errands.'

'Well, we've been writing down how many hours you stay away, haven't we, Clara? I've made a page with the days at the top and the numbers underneath.'

I gasped inwardly. The wretch! The naughty, spying little demon!

'Yes. You never used to go away so much. Why do you?' Clara added.

'Because we are living in difficult times and I have to meet people and get to the shops while I can.'

'It doesn't take four hours to meet people,' Eve said wickedly.

The pest. The rotten little spy. And if she mentioned any of this to David… 'Look, you don't understand because you are too young, but I have things to do that I didn't have to do before because we are living in an emergency. You understand that, don't you? Meetings do jolly well take four hours because we have to discuss what to do if any natives try to break into one of the houses…'

'Will bad natives break into our house?' Clara asked, inevitably.

'No,' I replied. 'No, of course not.' This was getting tricky.

'But if they do…' she persisted.

I sighed. I could see this coming a mile off when I mentioned break-ins, so it was my own fault. 'We are only making preparations. Just in case.'

'Well, I'm still bored and my legs are still fidgety and I want to go somewhere.' To my relief Eve changed the subject.

'Darling, I'll tell you what. How about going for a drive to see the flamingos this afternoon? Would you like that? I'm sure we could do that, and if Daddy is cross, well, don't worry because I'll just say it was all my fault.'

'Yes!' they both shouted, and for a while they left me in peace to doze and dream while they chased each other round and round the veranda.

The next morning I was up early as a sudden wave of nausea had me running to the bathroom in a performance which was a repeat of the day before. I muffled my whole head in a towel and tried to be sick quietly so that the children and servants didn't hear but my stomach heaved over and over until I was a limp rag on the cold tiled floor. And here were the girls, right on cue, padding down the corridor, little bare feet running on floorboards, calling out to me. I kicked the door shut in their faces and reached up to push home the latch. I lay there, ignoring their anxious voices, until I found the strength to clean my teeth and swill my mouth and walk out into another day pretending that everything was all right.

Chapter 48

NAIROBI 1954
MARY

Neither husband nor lover had noticed the slight thickening of my waist, nor did they know that there was a tenderness in my breasts if I was touched. I'll rephrase that. Nor did Harry notice that my breasts were tender when he stroked them. The morning sickness had worn off somewhat and only Eve and Clara observed without comment my breakfast ritual of burnt toast and pickles. I was not a novice. This was not my first pregnancy so I knew what to expect and could react to the momentous changes inside me while remaining outwardly calm. And yet... this beginning of a new life filled me with breathtaking wonder and joy as I paced the grounds of our bungalow and walked the broad, palm-lined avenues of Nairobi carrying my precious secret. Wonder, yes, but also unutterable sadness and a loss experienced before the event because this time, perhaps, I was only the vessel that carried the beloved child, my purpose to take her to dry land and leave her.

Today, finally, I was on my way to see Harry for the last time, although I had not told him this. I had told him nothing. So infatuated was I by that charismatic man, so imprinted on that one human being that, like the baby chicks that follow their mother duck, I must go where he went. So I approached him with stealth, otherwise with sugar words and honey plans he would spin me a tale of such convincing sweetness that I would fall immediately under his spell again. I would believe him when he told me that we were free spirits only a suitcase and a plane ticket away from starting a new life together. I would nod when he described a couple hand in hand in some far-flung part of the world with their past dumped like left luggage, in Africa, a thousand miles away. I imagined him saying, 'Come away with me. Anywhere. I can leave the army. I can earn my living wherever I want to. What is stopping us from being together?'

So I travelled with an ice pack on my heart and talked to myself under my breath as I went, like a madwoman, rehearsing my options, which were unlikely, unsatisfactory, downright insane... or heartbreaking:

1. Confess to nothing, tell him that the child is David's, and carry on as before. But I was a poor liar and the child might have freckles and be an indifferent batsman.

2. Tell David the truth. He will offer to bring up the child as his own, and we will carry on as before. Who was I kidding? With David's pride and principles? And repugnance of all things sexual?

3. Tell David the truth. He will refuse to bring up the child as his own. I will return to England for the birth and then the adoption, which David will insist is part of the contract. Then I will return here, where we will carry on as before.

4. Tell David the truth. He will refuse to bring up Harry's child. He will divorce me through the army courts on the grounds of adultery and gain custody of Eve and Clara. We will not carry on as before. I will return to England to have the baby and live as a divorced woman with an illegitimate child, stigmatised by society, alone, without my girls.

5. Run away with Harry. Take the girls too.

No, cross that out. My pencil slipped.

All the drama had shrunk to a simple one-liner which read:

You must choose between your lover and your children because you cannot have both. That is the sword that hangs over your head. It will be David's weapon of choice because he will not give up Eve and Clara without a bloody fight.

I couldn't choose.

I had to choose.

I couldn't.

I could.

As I paced the streets, stepping in and out of the shade cast by the jacaranda trees smothered with their flowers of pink and vermillion and cream and yellow, oblivious of people who passed me or bumped into me because I was not looking where I was going, pieces of a plan seemed to fall out of the thin hot air and I caught them and fitted them together with trembling hands. I walked and walked. Tears slid down my cheeks and fell on the dusty pavements, a Hansel trail of water that might lead me out of danger. A crazy, desperate scenario was offered to me like a gift from the gods. Where it came from I had no idea. It was bold and there was a chance I would not carry it off, but it gave each person in my sorry tale the chance to save face. And that, it seemed, was what was demanded of me.

*

'I was getting worried about you,' Harry said, jumping up from the table where he sat with an empty glass, his book closed, not even trying to look casually absorbed. 'You are late...'

'I'm so sorry, dearest, I am so sorry,' I said. My final truthful words, because from then on I was a fly in a cobweb of lies and deceit. 'I was delayed because Eve fell and grazed her knee...'

'Is she...'

'She's fine,' I interrupted. 'I had to make a bit of a fuss of her, that's all, before I could get away. I'm so sorry. Come on. Let's go.'

He rested a warm hand on my back and helped me into the passenger seat, not wasting a moment on recriminations. Once on the road out of Nairobi I leaned against him while his arm enclosed me. Our silence was sweet and nourishing, but I could not be lulled.

Harry headed for the Great Rift Valley, a massive fracture line that formed in the prehistoric Kenyan landscape, cracking the great plains and savannas in two. I have heard that this fissure is so deep and so sharply defined that it can be seen from space. Landscape as political metaphor – so obvious that someone should scrawl Black on one side and White on the other, while bodies of both colours tumble into the void. The bottomless chasm was an expression of other people's suffering but it was also my own intimate representation of the future. This was what I must do: I must cut down and undermine the foundations of our love. Love packed tight like soil is hard to break and crumble. I used a trowel, a spade, a pickaxe, but the ground resisted until I set to on my knees with my bare hands and scrabbled and dug until the skin under my nails was bleeding and my arms were torn and scratched. I sealed the wounded rough edges of land with wet slaps of cement so that they could not be repaired.

The man I loved with all my heart knew nothing of the scenes I had prepared and painted as he drove us towards our ending.

FOLKESTONE
2003

Chapter 49

FOLKESTONE 2003
MARY

Dearest Ann

This letter will come as a surprise and a shock. Sorry is a totally inadequate word so I will not insult you by writing it. Please believe me when I say that I have written you a thousand words a thousand times, in my head and on paper, and still I could not send them. It is cowardly of me to wait until now when I am old and ill. I have left instructions in my will that this letter be sent to you, unopened. By the time you read it, I will no longer be alive.

The very least I can do now – so late – is to tell you about your past.

Let me start at the beginning. I married when I was very young and I truly thought that I was in love. Perhaps I was. Then the war intervened, as it did for most people of my generation, and I had to grow up fast. For six years I did not see my husband because he was in the 8th Army in the Libyan desert while I was in Edinburgh with the Red Cross, and at the end of the war halfway across the world in Singapore and then Australia. When you watch young men grit their teeth through the most appalling pain and injuries, and hear them joke when their hearts are breaking, and put on a brave face when they have lost their sight or their limbs, you grow up very fast. You appreciate that while the world is a cruel and brutal place, there are many individuals in that world who are incredibly generous and courageous. They are the ones who give you the determination to carry on.

After the Red Cross years, a period in my life when I felt useful and fulfilled, I was reunited with my husband. It was never the same. I wonder how many women, like me, met up with a man who had changed into a stranger, separated from them by six years of intense experience shared with colleagues and friends. How many women found the transition to domesticity insulting and demeaning? We were sent back to our hoovering and cooking as if we had never played an active, vital part in the war – centre stage, not waiting in the wings. We worked in the ammunitions factories and as ambulance drivers and in the WAAC. We did men's jobs, and we did them well.

For me, the transition from active service to peacetime was made more extreme because we moved in with my parents in their house in a tiny village in Dorset. We had no money to buy a house of our own. There I felt stifled. There was no air. Two women in one kitchen. Gossip over the shop counter and the deadening routine of a life written very small. I longed to fly. Then I gave birth to my first child, Eve, and I had something to live for again. Two and a half years later I had Clara. My two beautiful daughters. I adored and cherished them.

Feeling the same post-war ennui and restlessness as I did, my husband applied to join the army – after all, his war years had been vivid and meaningful too – and he was accepted. That's all you need to know of my life when I was in my twenties. After four dismal years in Dorset, I boarded a steamer ship with the two little girls and crossed the ocean to Africa. David had gone out before me. It was to be a new start. A new life.

Bear with me, dear Ann. This is all preliminary stuff which you need to know in order to understand the rest. The next step in my life is significant. When I got off the train from Mombassa en route to Nairobi, stupid and dull with exhaustion from the long journey, there on the platform was a man who, though I did not know it then, would change my life more than any voyage across an ocean. His name is Harry Frame and of course you know him. He is your father, or at least the man you have always called your father. We fell in love. Please believe me when I say that we loved each other truly and completely and if we had not already committed ourselves to others, I would not be writing this letter now. We would have run away together. Remember this was fifty years ago. A divorced woman was an outcast. A woman who had an affair and an illegitimate child was a pariah. Have you read *The Scarlet Letter*? Well, things hadn't changed all that much for women. It was all very different then.

Harry gave me everything. Friendship, love, laughter, passion. He is the man I should have met ten years earlier, but unfortunately we cannot rewrite our lives like that. For six months in Nairobi I found with him the most complete happiness I have ever known. I can recall every moment of it still, so vivid and real were those months with him. And then we grew careless and I became pregnant with his child.

Ann, try to imagine the context. We were living in a tight-knit, sniffy, ultra-conservative enclave of army officers and white colonials while the Mau Mau, despairing of ever re-establishing their way of living on their own land, rose up and organised themselves into a terrorist movement. White people were being attacked and killed by black. The government reacted by killing the Kikuyu in their thousands and rounding the rest up in detention camps. When I met Harry, all this had just started. Somehow, though, we remained apart from it and it did not really touch us.

I can imagine you reading this, beginning to see where I am leading. I imagine your eyes wide with astonishment and horror. Bear with me, please. Let me finish.

Until I knew that I was carrying Harry's child, I basked selfishly in the warmth of his love and in this moonstruck state I managed not to think about the consequences of my actions, nor the feelings of my husband and Marjorie, nor even to connect with the bloody upheaval between black and white that was erupting all around me. I floated along in my bubble. It shames me now to remember how self-absorbed I was, and the only excuse I can offer is that the love we felt for each other was stronger and more absorbing than anything I had previously experienced. I thought about him night and day. The spaces between being with him hardly existed except in expectation.

But with his child growing in my belly, I became as protective as a lioness on the Serengeti Plains. Don't think that I stopped loving him. Not for one moment did my feelings for Harry change. But now I was responsible for our child. I knew that if I told Harry that I was pregnant, he would persuade me to leave my husband and go away with him. And that way lay disaster. Selfish though I was, I could not inflict unbearable pain on two good people, my husband and Marjorie. As I walked the streets – strictly forbidden because of the whites' hysterical fear of natives and the constant imagined threat of Mau Mau warriors, which was incredibly low where we were in the city – carrying my secret inside me, I plotted and planned, thinking about damage limitation and a way forward that would do the least harm to those I loved the most. Finally I stopped putting my own needs first.

First I broke off my relationship with Harry. I can't write about that because it is too painful. I have never stopped loving him. Today, while I write this, understand that I love him still. For me it was the affair of my life.

Then came the lie. It was a bold lie planned in detail and acted out in public. Ann, I staged an event that never happened. I acted out a night-time break-in that never took place. Marjorie was with me very soon after the supposed Mau Mau attack, in which I had swung from a shutter to tear it off its hinges and had pushed my fist, wrapped in towels, through the window pane. Then, calmly, I had dialled her number in the middle of the night, feigning shock, and soon she was roaring up the path and running a hot bath. She was supportive, sympathetic and kind. I think, looking back, that Marjorie was a feminist before the word was invented.

Once he knew that I was pregnant, David turned away from me, physically revolted. He could not stomach the fact that I had been sullied and spoilt by a black man, even when I repeatedly told him that the man might not have been black. Nothing I said convinced him that the phantom intruder could have been a drunken subaltern or a soldier who had flipped his lid after looking for Mau Mau once too often in the dank and dripping forests of the night. For David, for a very long time, I was damaged goods and it was years before he touched me again, except in a vaguely affectionate or supportive way. Our marriage was over in everything but name and convenience. He wanted nothing to do with the unborn child, and he wanted me out of his sight and out of Africa as soon as possible.

My devious exit strategy from a situation that would otherwise have ended in divorce, or worse, a court-room drama for custody of my two girls, was possible and plausible only because of the terrorist regime we were living under. At any other time, in any other place, I would have dreamt up a different story.

The person who supported me most during the days and weeks that followed my staged attack was Marjorie. She stuck by me. Between us we kept Harry away, making excuse after excuse as to why I could not see him and somehow I got through the worst time with her help. I confess that until then I had not been especially fond of Marjorie, but as I got to know her, as she came more and more often, and as we talked and walked together, I began to see through the carapace she had grown around herself as a protection. Her outward persona – so independent and competent and unemotional – had always alarmed me because I thought that was her. Full stop. But Marjorie had a core that was quite different. While she was all the things I describe, she was also a warm-hearted, humane woman who did what I could never do – she found a way of keeping her true self private. And so finally I understood what Harry had seen in her and why she was indeed his match. One day, when we were walking together, she confessed how much she had wanted a child, and how much she envied me my two daughters. Telling me this, she wept.

I told her before anyone else that I was pregnant, as soon after the fake attack as was feasible. Then I told my husband. I remember his exact words because they left such scars even though I had predicted his response.

'It might be black,' he said.

So blunt. I recoiled from his disgust and his prejudice.

'Yes,' I replied with bitter sarcasm. 'The baby may be black. Or white. Or orange.'

'So. You will go away to give birth and you must have it adopted.' I noted the 'you' and swallowed my bile. 'No one need ever know.'

'But if the baby is not black…' I began. I had to know.

'The chances are it's not going to look like you or me,' he said.

'If he or she is white… since we don't know who the father is…'

'Father!' he spat. 'How can you say that word?'

'Would you consider keeping the baby?' I asked as directly and plainly as I could, to make absolutely sure.

'No,' he replied. 'Never.'

As I had predicted all along. I had gone through every possible alternative scenario long before I put that final question to him because I needed to know if there was any mileage in pleading and begging for clemency, but it was clearly futile. And so it was crystal clear that if I continued to confront him about keeping the baby, he would have turned on his heels and left me. I know that. If I had obeyed my instinct, which was a desperate longing to keep you, I would have lost Eve and Clara because he would have fought for custody in an army court and in that archaic masculine world of black and white mores, I was doomed before I began. And, as I have already said, the future for a single mother with an illegitimate baby was untenable. He would have cut me off financially. You and I would not have survived.

I hear your sharp intake of breath, Ann. Did you just re-read that last sentence and re-read it again?

Yes, Ann, I am your mother, in the sense that I gave birth to you. You were the baby that David refused to father. You were the invented baby of that fake attack, the outcome of a black man's rape of a white woman. You were the Mau Mau baby. In a climate of hatred and pillage and brutality, you were a convenient lie made up by your mother.

But you were not invented. You were real.

You were born in a nursing home in London where I went alone just as soon as David could arrange it. He did not want to see any evidence of you in my swelling belly. My husband stayed on in Nairobi with my two girls, and, a few months after your birth, he reluctantly applied for a posting on compassionate grounds, claiming that I was ill and unable to return to Nairobi. He was livid to be dragged away from the only place he had found a sense of purpose and fulfilment since the war. He was in his element playing hide-and-seek with the Mau Mau in the Aberdare Mountains. However, his anger and resentment was a small price to pay.

And your father? Of course you know now. You are Harry's daughter. I have seen photographs of you and you look like him. I imagine that you might have guessed.

All I need to do now is to tell you about the practicalities of how you came to be adopted by Marjorie and Harry. I will be brief because these details are not important and you have a lot already to think about. When I told Marjorie that I was pregnant and that David would not accept the child, she did not hesitate. She offered to adopt you – black, white or turquoise – and of course Harry agreed. After your birth, Marjorie flew back to London and took you from me. I will skip over this part because my anguish at that time is not your concern. Harry followed soon after, having found a post with MI5 in London. They have kept me posted so that I have been able to follow your life from a distance. I have photographs of you. I know the steps you have taken and know the milestones in your life.

The letters stopped when Marjorie died two years ago, and although Harry wrote to me a couple of times it was not long afterwards that he became ill himself. I heard about his death, of course. There was a full-page obituary in the *Guardian* and no doubt in every other paper as well. He was so respected and admired.

Very soon it will be my turn, and then only David will be left.

Ann, one thing I can tell you. You have been truly loved all your life, of that I am sure, and that gives me some peace. You had wonderful parents. I wonder now how much they told you about your past. I find it hard to believe that when you grew up to have Harry's blue eyes and his reddish-blonde hair the truth did not come out. I feel sure that Harry must have known that he was your father. Did they tell you what they almost certainly suspected? I like to imagine that this letter comes not as a complete shock but as an affirmation of a truth you already know.

And so, dearest Ann, I leave you with this story of the beginning of your life. I ask only that you try gradually to understand what happened in Nairobi all those years ago.

Your Mother,

Mary Dell